"Baiting an officer i͏ offense."

Tate laughed. He laughed so hard he knew he was on the verge of bellowing, but it was hard to care with Aida gazing up at him, laughing, too.

"Cookies!" Sylvie's voice called. "Cookie time in the courtyard."

Neither of them moved. Tate was disinclined to ever move, unless maybe he could move closer to Aida.

Where had that come from?

She was still the sheriff who had it in for him, even if she had just brought closure to painful past experiences.

"You guys coming?" Willa poked her head into the ballroom.

"Be right there," Tate said.

Aida stood. "I guess it's cookie time." She gave him a quick smile, then took several paces toward the door.

Tate reached out and caught her arm. "Thank you." He gestured to the soccer ball. "Really, thank you for all of this."

"I should have offered to help earlier. I didn't know the whole situation."

Tate gazed at her, acutely aware that he didn't know her whole situation, either.

Dear Reader,

Welcome back to Pronghorn, Oregon! Five young teachers are recruited to revive a high school in the tiny, contentious town of Pronghorn, and wind up ruffling more than a few feathers along the way.

PE teacher Tate Ryman can't stay out of trouble. The beautiful sheriff, Aida Weston, has cited him for everything from jaywalking to creating a public nuisance. When the volunteer principal recruits nine new exchange students, Tate is roped into coaching his least favorite sport, soccer. He needs help, and the only person in town with any soccer skills is the same woman who can hardly look at him without handing him a ticket. Can Tate and Aida work together to help Pronghorn revive its soccer tradition?

This book is for my husband, a great athlete coach, and teacher. I wish every student athlete had a champion like Jeff.

I'd love to hear what you think of Tate and Aida's story! You can find me on social media, and at my website, anna-grace-author.com.

Happy reading!

Anna

WINNING THE SHERIFF'S HEART

ANNA GRACE

Harlequin

HEARTWARMING

Harlequin®
HEARTWARMING™

Recycling programs for this product may not exist in your area.

ISBN-13: 978-1-335-05118-9

Winning the Sheriff's Heart

Harlequin Enterprises ULC
22 Adelaide St. West, 41st Floor
Toronto, Ontario M5H 4E3, Canada
www.Harlequin.com

Printed in Lithuania

MIX
Paper | Supporting responsible forestry
FSC® C021394

Award-winning author **Anna Grace** writes fun, heartfelt romance novels about complex characters finding their way with humor and heart. Anna's Oregon roots and love of family and community shine through in her Harlequin Heartwarming series, *Love, Oregon* and *The Teacher Project*.

Whether exploring the West in a remodeled Sprinter van or wandering new city streets in search of an art museum, Anna loves to travel and spend time with friends and family. You can find her on social media, where she's busy stamping likes on images of cappuccino, books and other people's dogs.

Twitter: @AnnaEmilyGrace
Instagram: @AnnaGraceAuthor
Facebook: Anna Grace Author
Website: Anna-Grace-Author.com

Books by Anna Grace

Harlequin Heartwarming

The Teacher Project
Lessons from the Rancher

Love, Oregon
A Rancher Worth Remembering
The Firefighter's Rescue
The Cowboy and the Coach
Her Hometown Christmas
Reunited with the Rancher

Visit the Author Profile page
at Harlequin.com for more titles.

To my husband, Jeff Hess. I love our life.

CHAPTER ONE

TATE RYMAN WAS SMART, charming and handsome. And he was breaking the law. Again.

How many tickets did one teacher need before he finally figured out how things went down in Pronghorn, Oregon? Yes, it was a small town. Yes, the five teachers they'd recruited to revive the high school were unfamiliar with rural customs. And sure, the newcomers had worked tirelessly through the end of August and into September to breathe new life into the failing high school.

But seriously?

Tate couldn't follow the most basic rules if they were tattooed on the back of his hand. Was he raised in a barn? Or a parking garage, or however you wound up with no manners in the big city?

Sheriff Aida Weston sighed and pulled the ticket booklet out of her back pocket. Her partner, Greg, perked up his ears. She rubbed the soft fur of the German shepherd's neck and together they approached the perpetrator.

"Mr. Ryman, are you aware that you're jaywalking?"

Tate stopped in the middle of the street.

"What?! Are you kidding me?"

Now he was jay-standing.

"Do you see a crosswalk under your feet?"

Tate looked down, as though the broad white stripes of Abbey Road might materialize under the soles of his shoes. The only thing on the street was a stubborn cat named Connie, who spent her days lounging in the middle of the pavement. Jay-lounging.

Tate gestured to the empty highway in both directions. "I don't see a crosswalk for a hundred miles."

"When there's no designated pedestrian crossing, you use the nearest intersection."

"How was I supposed to know that?" He ran a hand through his thick black hair, making it stand up even more than normal.

Also making him more attractive than normal; but Tate's looks were not germane to the present circumstances.

"Ignorance of the law excuses no one." Aida clicked the end of her pen and prepared to flip open to a fresh ticket.

"Come on! I'm walking from my home—" he gestured behind him to The City Hotel, the beautiful, if inappropriately named, building where the teachers all lived "—to my place of employment." He pointed to the two-story brick building across the street.

Pronghorn Public Day School, Proud Home Of The Pronghorn "Pronghorns" was scrawled in yellow paint over the main doors. Arguably, the lettering could also be considered a crime. But poor signage was out of her jurisdiction.

Ten years had passed since Aida had graduated from the same institution. At the time, she hadn't been aware that funds were dwindling, that the school and town were dying as families moved away one by one. Her only focus during those years was soccer. Had she learned math and language arts? She must have. She regularly called on information stored somewhere in her brain. Mrs. Moran had taught her Spanish, and she'd gone on to minor in that language in college.

But the visceral patchwork of memories that surfaced when she caught a glimpse of the school was all soccer.

Her lungs and legs burning as she charged the pitch. The wind, scented with a heady mix of sage and dry autumn prairies grass, steady on her face. Spectators crowding the sidelines. In those days, when the sidelines were too full, fans backed trucks up to the field and stood on their tailgates to watch. Aida could still hear the ref's whistle. Two arms up and the call of "Goal!" barely audible over the roar of the crowd.

Then a full ride to college. Then the heartbreak; the loss of her identity and chosen profession when she'd graduated with no prospects of ever playing professionally.

Ideally, she'd never have to walk past the soccer field again. But her grandmother lived here and someone had to care for Flora as she aged. Aida's job was here. Annoying at present, but overall, she enjoyed the challenges and rewards of being a sheriff in a rural area. She loved Pronghorn. The tiny town at the sparsely populated center of Warner Valley was her home. Rimrock rose on all sides, as though protecting the miles of prairie grasses and wetlands. Hart Mountain stood sentinel to the east and, in the distant west, the Coyote Hills caught the evening sun as it set each night.

Pronghorn was her home. She was invested in its success. And while the school, like Aida, was a little worse for wear, she was glad the community had rallied together to recruit the new teachers. She just wished Tate hadn't been among them. He was too charming, too gregarious, the constant epicenter of loud, cheerful groups of people. The moms of Pronghorn found excuses to meet with the handsome PE teacher to discuss their children's progress in his classes. The grandmas of Pronghorn swooned when he offered to carry their groceries from the market. Old men invited him to play checkers. Dads offered to teach him how to fish. Even her dog liked Tate.

And, yeah, that stung a little.

It wasn't that Aida didn't like charming people and the cheerful groups they inspired. She did. It was that Tate had supersized charisma and he used it to try to keep from getting in trouble with the law.

"Look, I was just running back to the hotel to grab something," he said, a soft note of contrition in his voice.

She glanced up at him. His gaze met hers. It was possible that a ticket, while totally within the law, was a little out of line.

But then his lips twisted in a smile that managed to both annoy and charm her and he added, "I'd apologize, *Officer*, but I'm not sorry about taking the quickest route from my job to my home."

"The attitude isn't helpful, Ryman."

"That cat lies in the middle of the road all day long!" He pointed to Connie. "Ticket her."

Greg swiveled his furry head toward Aida. He'd been advocating for an apprehension of the feline for as long as she could remember.

"Class starts in ten minutes," a voice intoned from the school. Aida recognized the speaker as Vander Tourn, the young science teacher. Because there was no bell, the town had grown used to his 7:50 a.m. call.

Tate put his hands on his hips. "School's starting. I need to get to work. Can you just give me a warning—?"

"Maybe next time you should plan better."

Tate held up a delicate, pale green cardigan sweater that might fit on his left arm. "I was doing Willa Marshall a favor." He tilted his head to one side and gave her a hard look, something he might throw out if one of his students was misbehaving. "If you want to give Willa a lesson on planning, be my guest."

Oh.

Willa was the lead teacher at the high school, far and away the most levelheaded of the newcomers. She'd negotiated with the board, and garnered community support to keep the school up and running. Willa, and her fiancé, Colter Wayne, were two of the most respected people in this town. If Aida were the sort of person who made new friends, Willa would be near the top of her list.

And the weather in Pronghorn did have a habit of dipping dramatically two weeks into September. It wasn't unreasonable that Willa Marshall would leave the hotel without a sweater. And it was kinda sweet that Tate would run back and grab it for her.

Aida flipped her ticket book shut. She risked another glance at Tate, intent on giving him a warning without appreciating his bright blue eyes.

But then he rolled those eyes and said, "You *do* know there are actual criminals in this world. While you're here, ticketing me for standing in the middle of a highway no one ever drives on, there are crimes being committed."

Aaaaaand here she was, opening the book again.

"Really?" She glanced casually toward the east, the sight of her latest arrest. "Is that what that man I pulled over, the one transporting marijuana laced with fentanyl, headed for the Idaho border, was committing? A crime? I guess it's a good thing I'd been tracking his movements for months and was able to catch him in the middle of a run."

Tate shifted uncomfortably. "You stopped a drug runner?"

"And the Hart Mountain squatters? That couple who were breaking into vacation homes, stealing valuables and leaving the homes trashed with angry graffiti messages? It's a good thing I got them to stop by arresting them and testifying at their trial so they're now in jail. Is that the kind of crime you were thinking of?"

"You apprehended the squatters?" His expression was somewhere between concern and respect.

It made her feel like she might want to blush. She didn't, but her nervous system was definitely interested in making her face bright red.

She shrugged. "Me and Greg."

"Okay." Tate held up his hands. It wasn't necessary, inasmuch as all he possessed was a nonthreatening sweater. "It just feels like… I don't know." His long lashes obscured his blue eyes for a moment. "What did I do wrong?"

Aida furrowed her brow. "Jaywalking." And they were still all standing in the middle of the road, two officers of the law, one perpetrator and a cat.

In Tate's defense, this highway really did *not* get a lot of traffic.

"No, I mean—" he ran a hand through his hair and gazed into her eyes "—did I offend you?"

A wisp of September breeze brushed against her cheek, his scent joining the sage and prairie grasses. He had a distinctive scent. Aida hadn't paid enough attention in those language arts classes of her youth to put it into words, but it was something along the lines of *athlete with good personal hygiene.*

"Jaywalking isn't offensive," she explained. "It's dangerous to you and potential drivers. I don't want you to get flattened by a car."

He grinned, his eyes lighting up in a way that felt exciting and dangerous, like a soccer match against a small, well-funded private school. "What about Connie?" He held his palm out to the feline. She lolled comfortably in the shade of his shadow, stretching out even farther.

Aida smiled back. "She's already pretty flat."

He threw his head back and let out something someone more versed with words might call a guffaw. When was the last time she'd made anyone laugh? Besides her grandma, of course. Flora had always gotten Aida's sense of humor, and seen Aida as more than a soccer player, more than a cop.

Tate's eyes were bright as he glanced at her. It felt like flirting.

"Seriously, why are you always picking on me?"

Greg gave a muted whine, asking the same question.

Was she picking on Tate? All of the new teachers could be a little clueless. They stumbled around breaking laws and local customs like a herd of newborn buffalo calves in an admittedly old and shabby china shop.

Aida straightened her shoulders. "You break the law, I deliver the consequences. That's not picking on you. Are you picking on your students when you give them lunch duty for misbehaving?"

He made a thoughtful expression, acknowledging her point. "Okay, but since I've been here, you've given me a ticket for reckless driving—"

How many times was he going to bring that up?

"You were driving an ATV on the sidewalk."

"I thought that's where they went."

"No one thinks that. No sentient human would think to drive an ATV on a sidewalk."

"An ATV has the same rules as a bike," he said with unwarranted confidence. Then he undermined his own bluster with, "I think."

"If that were true, which it isn't, a bike would go in a bike lane."

"Of which Pronghorn has zero! I don't see why you couldn't just give me a warning."

"I *did* give you a warning. Then you started arguing with me. Then you got a ticket. Can you see a pattern emerging here?"

"I was arguing because the night before you'd given me a ticket for an open container." He tugged at his hair and she was determined not to appreciate how cute that was.

"We don't drink beer on the streets in Pronghorn. I'm sorry if that's not the way you do it in Portland."

"I walked out of the restaurant for half a second with a beer in my hand. There were eighteen antelope walking down the highway and I thought it was amazing. Sorry, I forgot to hand off the beer."

"There's nothing amazing about eighteen antelope. Eighteen antelope on these streets is your average Tuesday morning."

"Well, Officer, I can't help it if I still feel wonder and joy at the sight of nature."

"You can feel wonder and joy inside The Restaurant."

The moment the words left her mouth, Aida recognized her mistake. Tate quirked an eyebrow, his blue eyes connecting with hers. Aida didn't manage to contain a smile. The Restaurant wasn't generally associated with pleasant emotions.

But whatever was passing between them at the moment felt uncomfortably pleasant. She needed to give this guy his ticket and get back to work.

Tate continued, "Since I've been in town, one month, mind you, I haven't seen you ticket anyone else, but you've given me four tickets and I don't know how many warnings." He held up his fingers, counting them off as though she were the one breaking laws. "Reckless driving, open container, public nuisance—"

"You are loud, Tate Ryman."

Surprisingly loud. Mind-scramblingly loud.

"I was enjoying the evening with my coworkers. Vander played the guitar. Luci and Mateo were arguing about acceptable times to eat a cookie. Yet I'm the one who gets a ticket."

"You were bellowing. Greg thought there was something wrong with you."

"Mrs. Moran and I had won a round of pinochle. I was celebrating."

Aida closed her eyes and let out a short breath. She didn't intend to single Tate out. He singled himself out. Every time he was within six hundred feet of her, he did *something*. It was like he was looking for trouble.

"The problem is that you flout the rules in this town. You think none of them apply to you."

"Really? Because it seems like I'm the only person the rules do apply to."

She put her hands on her hips and stepped right up to Tate. Unfortunately, that meant she was surrounded by his warm, clean scent. The police academy could have been clearer about the danger of nice-smelling repeat offenders.

"Welcome, Pronghorn Public Day School!" The words sounded like they were coming from a bullhorn inside the school. There was only one person around these parts who regularly used a bullhorn, and if "too much yellow" was against the law, Aida would have apprehended her a long time ago.

Tate swore under his breath.

"I have to go," he said, like he was inconveniencing her by ending this conversation. "Loretta Lazarus has some kind of all-school rally happening this morning. I'm not going to make the other teachers deal with it on their own."

Aida pulled the ticket from her booklet and handed it to him. He clenched his fingers, hesitant to take it. She really hoped he'd learned from prior experience that refusing to take a ticket was a good way to get a second one. He reached out and snatched it from her, maintaining eye contact for a moment. Aida wasn't sorry and she wasn't going to pretend she was.

Tate scoffed and shook his head. Then, in a flagrant act of defiance, he knelt and gave Greg scritches around his ears.

Greg, who knew better, leaned his chin on Tate's shoulder and soaked up the love.

"You do know it's illegal to pet a police dog without permission from the handler."

Greg gave her a baleful look, reminding her that she'd never once enforced that rule. Not in Pronghorn.

"If snuggling this dog is wrong, then I don't want to be right." He gave the dog one last pat then flashed his gorgeous, irritating smile and trotted into the school. "See you around, Officer."

THE TICKET CRUMPLED in his fist, Tate jogged up the front steps and yanked open the door to the school.

Aida Weston was the most frustrating, unforgiving, mean—

Tate scrambled for words to mentally hurl at the sheriff, well aware that his inner monologue was something you might find on a grade-school playground.

But seriously, jaywalking? In Pronghorn?

It was ridiculous. Even the dog agreed with him.

About the cat situation anyhow.

It wasn't helpful that Aida was also beautiful, intelligent and had a deadpan sense of humor that almost had him anticipating apprehension.

Almost but not quite.

Tate ran through the front entrance, past the empty main office and bright yellow lockers. The walls were awash with inspirational signs. They'd been purchased at a Goodwill, three hundred miles away in Pendleton, by the local real estate maven and volunteer "principal" of Pronghorn Public Day School, Loretta Lazarus.

Some of the decorative messages made sense for a school.

These Are Your Good Old Days.

It's Okay to Color Outside Of The Lines.

In a World Where You Can Choose to Be Anything, Be Kind.

Others felt a little out of place, like, What Happens At Grandma's Stays At Grandma's.

But Loretta loved a bargain as much as she loved pithy sayings written on plywood. If Tate was confused by the placement of a pastel-colored sign in the shape of a bunny with Hoppy Spring! written across its belly, it was the least of his worries.

Tate trotted past the cafeteria. Glossy wooden floors reflected light from the main entrance. He turned a corner into the long hallway where the main classrooms were located. Three doors down, the gym was situated across from the library. At the end of the hall, two double doors were open to the September sunshine.

Loretta's voice reverberated from the gym. Tate slowed his steps and took a moment to scan the hallway. Funny, how a place he'd only been in since August could feel so much like home. Within these walls, he'd made good friends, overcome challenges and become the teacher he'd always wanted to be. His old insecurities of not being enough still lingered, but only faintly. It was a lot easier to accept his parents' disappointment in him when he lived hundreds of miles away, with bad cell service. In high school, he'd put on the character of gregarious, fun-loving Tate to cover up a sensitive, emotional young man. In Pronghorn, as a teacher, he could be both. Here, he really was fun-loving, and found it easy to joke and enjoy life.

Unless someone was handing him a ticket.

"Coach Tate!"

He looked up to see one of his students, Mason, slipping in through the back door. For the first few weeks of school, Mason had been late on purpose, trying to avoid morning PE. Tate had worked tirelessly with the kid, helping him to feel more confident in gym class and inspiring him to step up as a leader at the school.

"I know what you're thinking, but it's not my fault," Mason said. "Besides, you can't get mad at me for being late since you're late too."

Tate chuckled. "I bet my excuse is better than yours."

Mason made a face. "My mom needed my help emptying the deep fryer at The Restaurant."

"That sounds disgusting. How often does she change out the oil in that thing?"

"I don't remember her ever changing it before."

"You win," Tate said. "Let's go see what Loretta's got for us today."

"Do you know what the big surprise is?" Mason asked.

Tate had an idea, but it still seemed so improbable.

"Let's go find out."

Loretta droned on in the gym. The great thing about having a scatterbrain for a principal was that she took forever to get to the point. Tate was confident that he and Mason had missed very little content so far.

Tate's friend and coworker, Mateo Lander, leaned out the gym door then headed over to Tate as Mason slipped into the gym. "Where have you been?"

Tate held up Willa's sweater and the crumpled ticket. "Jaywalking."

"Right. Sorry." Mateo dropped a hand on his shoulder. "We'll all pitch in and help you with the ticket."

"I got it," Tate grumbled. Getting a random ticket from a beautiful woman was one thing. Having his friends feel sorry for him and help him pay it was even worse.

"So, I think we have a situation on our hands," Mateo said.

Loretta's voice reverberated from the gymnasium. One month into his sojourn in Pronghorn and Tate was no longer surprised or even bothered when Loretta threw an impromptu school assembly.

"What else is new?"

"Yeah." Mateo waffled his hand back and forth. "I think this might be more impactful than normal. Before we go into the gym, the others and I wanted to make sure you're still okay running an after-school sports program, maybe even coaching."

Tate stopped walking. "Yeah. Of course. That's part of my position as a health and PE teacher." Tate ran his fingers through his hair. "There hasn't been a lot of interest yet, but I'm hopeful."

The kids of Pronghorn had endured online school for three years due to insufficient funding. The community had rallied to support in-person school, and the students had returned to the old brick building one month ago. Skill levels varied dramatically from student to student and socialization had been a huge challenge. And without the daily routines of school and sports programs, many kids were uncomfortable with any kind of organized physical activity.

It broke his heart. Not just in Pronghorn, but across the country, kids had fewer opportunities to run around and get exercise. Sports programs were becoming increasingly competitive. Steep fees and unreasonable time commitments turned after-school activities into elite pursuits, leaving the mass of kids with no vehicle for fun and exercise. At the same time, damaging messages from social media eroded kids' confidence in their bodies. The boys felt they had to be swol. Girls were pressured to be strong and curvy at the same time. Everyone was convinced they needed to lose weight.

While getting random tickets from the sheriff was annoying, a system that made kids feel uncomfortable in their own bodies infuriated him.

From the first day of school, Tate had worked to increase his students' activity levels and confidence. He'd encouraged kids to start the day by running a few laps around the track, and taught them fun movement games. Despite pressure from the community, he hadn't introduced competitive sports yet. Sports teams could be great places for kids to connect, and he appreciated the lessons learned on the field and court. But high school athletics didn't have to be the pressure-cooker experience of his own youth. Tate would chart a new path in Pronghorn. Every kid would be encouraged to view sports as a lifetime activity, not a do-or-die battle that left so many feeling unworthy.

"Okay." Mateo nodded. "I'm thinking it might be time."

"Great. I've been hoping we could get a cross-country team going. And the league is fine with us registering a team late because of the situation out here."

Mateo shrugged. His easygoing personality made him a favorite with the students. He taught math and managed to make that subject the least stressful class at Pronghorn. Whenever Tate walked past Mateo's class, he saw kids sitting around tables together, working on math concepts. Mateo had "borrowed" several lamps from the hotel they all lived in and lit the space like a living room in which people happened to be discussing algebra.

"This is the moment you've been waiting for!" Loretta's voice echoed out of the gym.

Mateo groaned. "We really should get in there."

"Let's do it," Tate said, clapping him on the shoulder then jumping ahead. Mateo tried to cut him off, but Tate made it into the gym first. He might not lean on competition as a teaching tool, but Tate loved challenging his coworkers to a race, or board game, or card came, or sandwich-eating contest.

Okay, he loved a challenge.

Tate jogged into the gym to see it was full-ish. Like, actually pretty full, which was unusual since the school only had thirty kids.

Luci Walker, the social studies teacher with more argyle in her closet than anyone he'd ever known, gestured them over to where the teachers stood together. Tate joined the group then scanned the room. Among the crowd, there were several new faces.

"I'm thrilled to introduce nine new exchange students!" Loretta cried.

Exchange students?

"I can't believe she managed it," Willa Marshall, the respected English teacher and de facto school leader, whispered.

Tate scanned the new students. They ranged in age and size, and appeared to be from all regions of the globe.

"We are soooooo lucky to welcome these kids who will call Pronghorn their home!"

The newcomers didn't appear to be feeling particularly lucky. Their expressions were sullen. In some cases, defiant. In others, just lost.

Loretta was chirping along, but something felt off. Why didn't the exchange students look happy?

Instinctively, Tate turned to Willa. She was the direction everyone turned in a crisis. "How did she get exchange students this late in the game?"

"And why?" Mateo asked.

Willa looked each of them in the eye and spoke clearly. "I do not know."

"But you're dating the board president," Tate reminded her.

"Engaged to," Luci corrected him.

A quick smile flickered across Willa's face then she rolled her eyes. "Are you suggesting Loretta would think to discuss a major decision with the board president?"

Vander Tourn, the contemplative, empathetic science teacher, studied the new students. "They don't look nearly as happy about this as Loretta does."

Tate's stomach twisted. He understood enough about human anatomy to know it was physically impossible for his stomach to do a full one-eighty flip, but it sure felt like it was trying to.

Loretta's chirping finally wound down. She beamed at the exchange students. "Any questions?"

The new students stared back at her. Unspoken questions of *What is this place?* and *Who is this lady?* and *What's the Wi-Fi?* seemed to radiate from the kids.

Finally, a young man with bright eyes raised a long, lanky arm. He spoke with a lilting accent, his words clipped. "When does the football club meet?"

Tate took a closer look at the student. He was wearing a Senegalese soccer jersey and had the easy movement of a natural athlete.

"Football?" Loretta batted her long tangly eyelashes. "Well, welcome to America, young man!

We can certainly play a few games of football with our international guests—"

Tate stepped forward, to keep Loretta from stepping in it any further, but the student was quicker. "You call it soccer, no? When is the club to meet?"

"Soccer?" Loretta asked.

"Soccer," another one of the students said. The girl was scrappy and about half the size of the boy who had spoken. "You said there was a good team here."

It was then that Tate picked up on clues he should have seen immediately. Soccer jerseys, soccer shorts, an actual soccer ball tucked under the arm of a student who wore a shirt repping Brazil.

What had Loretta told these kids?

He looked back at his coworkers. They knew how he felt about soccer, and smiled hopefully. The exchange students had somehow been roped into spending the school year in Pronghorn, and it was likely the tiny town was a major disappointment.

The one expectation they'd voiced was soccer. He was the only person on staff with any chance of making good on that promise.

Tate pulled in a deep breath then stepped forward. "Right after school."

And just like that, he'd committed to coaching his least favorite sport. With any luck, his impending failure as a coach would at least be less dramatic than his failure as a player.

CHAPTER TWO

"Psst! Tate! In here."

Willa stuck her head out of the library door and motioned him in. On most days at 3:05 p.m., the teachers would be in their classrooms helping kids, or facilitating a meeting of one of the few clubs that had popped up so far. Willa had the writing club. Mrs. Moran, the one veteran teacher at Pronghorn, ran the pinochle club with Mateo's help. Vander, or Mr. V to the students, hosted a group of kids who were slowly painting a mural of sea life on his classroom walls. Last Tate checked, they were starting in on the octopi.

But given the influx of nearly thirty percent more students to their school, an emergency meeting was no surprise.

Tate followed Willa into the library to find his coworkers huddled next to an extensive collection of *Field & Stream* magazines—a generous, if less-than-practical, donation.

"How'd it go?" Luci asked the group.

"It was weird," Willa admitted. "I'm glad we have these new students. Individually, they're smart, interesting, and clearly brave if they're willing to spend a year abroad without their families. But…"

Willa drifted off, so Tate finished the sentence for her. "But they don't seem to want to be here."

"Yeah." Mateo nodded. "It's almost like an enthusiastic volunteer principal convinced them all to come to the middle of nowhere under false pretenses."

Vander cleared his throat. No one needed to mention that they, too, had been convinced to take these jobs by an energetic woman with a shaky relationship between her hopes and hard facts.

"My biggest problem this morning was Ilsa, the girl from the Netherlands," Luci said. "She refused to speak in class, and that doesn't fly in my classroom. At first, I thought maybe the language barrier was giving her trouble, but she snapped at that kid from Brazil in perfect English."

"They've all got to be a little homesick," Vander noted. "They've only been in the States for three weeks."

"But where in the States?" Luci asked. "And why are they here now? I can't imagine a single one of these kids got to their original placement then asked the program director if they could move somewhere with one paved road, herds of semidomesticated antelope, and a bad internet connection."

"Colter's already trying to get some answers," Willa said. As she brushed back her bangs, Tate caught a glimpse of the large gaudy ring on her finger.

Tate couldn't resist. "You think your engagement ring might be able to stand in for a cell tower?"

The others cracked up as Willa gave him a mock punch to the shoulder. "I told you guys, he bought it when he was nineteen and flush with rodeo prize money. How was he supposed to know we'd have both grown up before he got the chance to propose?"

"Awww!" Luci wrapped an arm around Willa's waist. "That's so sweet. Plus, your left hand's gonna get really strong."

"Colter's practical." Tate grinned at Willa. "Your ring is a reminder of his love, and an upper body workout."

Willa untangled herself from Luci's embrace. "I'm wearing this ring, and you all can deal with it."

"We're only teasing," Mateo reminded her.

"Because that ring is legitimately funny," Vander clarified.

"Enough!" Willa cried. "We have a serious issue here."

"The Pronghorn kids did a great job of greeting the newcomers," Tate said, returning to the subject at hand. "That was cool."

"Did you see Sylvie and Antithesis teaching the girls from Korea and Armenia to play pinochle?" Luci asked.

Willa smiled at the mention of Sylvie, her soon-to-be stepdaughter. "That was really sweet."

"A lot of the kids from the commune stepped it up today," Vander said.

"I noticed that too," Luci confirmed.

The Open Hearts Intentional Community sent several of their "emerging adults" to the high school.

After a rocky start, the kids from the ranching families and the kids from the commune were finally getting along. It was nice to see the lessons of the first month of school informing the action of the second month.

Tate grew more serious. "The new students seem like great people. Our Pronghorn kids are welcoming. The only problem is, these exchange students don't seem to want to engage, you know? They weren't excited about anything."

"Oh, that's not true," Vander said. "They're excited about soccer."

Everyone turned to Tate. It was no secret that he hated soccer.

"What?"

Mateo cleared his throat.

"I mean they weren't *just* excited about soccer." Vander tried to backtrack. "They were also excited about…lunch?"

"It's no big deal," Tate lied. "I'll run a few soccer drills with the kids after school."

His friends exchanged glances again. Tate wasn't fooling anyone.

"What is it you dislike about soccer?" Luci asked.

Tate shrugged. "I just don't like it."

"Yeah, but I want to know *why.* You like all the sports. You're annoyingly knowledgeable about everything from tetherball to ice yachting." Luci pierced him with a sharp look. "Yet you randomly hate this timeless, lovely game. I want to know why."

If the teachers had become like the close, fun-loving siblings Tate had always wanted growing up, Luci fit the bill of a bossy younger sister.

"I just don't like it." He gestured to Mateo. "Mateo loves food, but he doesn't like the vegetable soup Angie serves at The Restaurant. I don't see you all questioning him."

"No one likes Angie's vegetable soup," Luci said. "It's a biohazard. Soccer, on the other hand—"

"Is the most popular sport in the world," Vander finished for her.

Tate folded his arms over his chest. The mere mention of soccer made his heart rate increase. He didn't need to get into the reasons why.

"Hello?" The word was accompanied with a knock on the frame of the door. They all turned in unison.

Suleiman, a seventeen-year-old from Senegal, stood in the doorframe. Behind him were several other exchange students.

"Can you tell me, where do we meet our coach?"

Mav, a lanky, curious student from Open Hearts who had a track record of appearing anywhere and everywhere when least expected, joined the group. "Since when do we have a soccer team?"

"Since right now." Tate pulled in a breath and headed to the door. "Let's get out there."

"Good luck!" Willa called.

"I don't need it," he lied.

Tate was pretty sure he was about to lose what little lunch he'd eaten as he led the group of students out back toward the sports field. Not only did he abhor soccer, he didn't fully remember the rules.

No, *not remember* wasn't entirely accurate. It was more like he'd blocked them out.

He tried to steady his heart rate. This would be fine. Today he'd introduce a few movement games and they'd get to know each other. If any of the students balked, he could chalk it up to American coaching practices.

Tate glanced behind him. Five of the exchange students followed, along with a sizable contingent of kids from Pronghorn. Kids who, a month ago, had been trying to sneak out of PE were coming to play soccer?

Okay then.

Tate breathed deeply in through the nose, out through the mouth. *Smell the soup, cool the soup.* The exchange students were there to have a new experience. No one expected a small town in Southeastern Oregon to have a premier soccer program. Tate took a surreptitious peek at the student walking next to him. Antonio was a strong, compact kid from Brazil. Okay, that guy seemed to have some expectations.

"Who is that?" Antonio asked, pointing ahead to a small figure with white hair, loaded down with a ball bag, teetering toward the field.

"Mrs. Moran!" Tate called out then trotted to overtake her. "What are you doing? The students and I can carry the equipment."

Mrs. Moran, who had taught in Pronghorn for half a century, smiled. "Oh, I thought I'd help out for the first practice."

She had purchased the balls weeks ago, with some

money secured through a science grant. Tate hadn't questioned her at the time, since he'd started out the school year with a less than stellar equipment list: one hockey stick, six child-size jump ropes, and a deflated football.

Now Tate was wondering whether the elderly woman was thinking of coaching. Surely not?

"I'll watch from the sidelines," she said, setting the bag down. "You know, it's been about ten years since we've had a soccer game on this field." Her gaze drifted past him to the sheriff's office, as though waiting for something.

Ilsa, as quiet and grumpy as Luci had described her being in class, grabbed the drawstrings of the bag.

"Let's wait to—" Tate started to say, but Ilsa was already opening the bag. Antonio reached in and withdrew a soccer ball "—start with the balls."

Too late.

Within seconds, twenty soccer balls were scattered across the grassy field. Kids grabbed balls and dribbled, kicked and passed. Suleiman began a complicated juggling sequence using his knees, chest, shoulders and head to keep the ball moving and off the ground. Ilsa saw this and began an even more complicated sequence.

Mav observed them with interest then bounced the ball off one gangly knee, sending it straight into Ilsa's ball and knocking her off balance. Ilsa snapped at Mav. Mav jumped into an argument, questioning her assumptions about the need to keep a ball in the air in the first place.

Each time Tate heard a ball make contact with a foot or knee, or anything human, it felt like a slap.

"You're not good enough."

"You need to work a lot harder."

"You might as well just quit."

Tate shook off the voice. He'd grown adept at blocking out his father's words over the years. If he hadn't, there was no way he'd be in Pronghorn right now, doing important work that he loved. There was no way he'd have learned to champion a student's confidence in their body and an appreciation for movement over winning.

Tate blew his whistle. All eyes on the field turned to him. Tate had always enjoyed being the center of attention, but the center of attention of a soccer field was not a favorite memory.

As a teacher, though, he'd learned that sometimes you just had to buck up and do hard things.

This was one of those times.

"Circle up," he called.

DWAP.

Aida looked up sharply from her paperwork and Greg perked up his ears.

Dwap.

Aida frowned and tapped her pen on the desk. Tate Ryman was probably leading the kids through one of his new-age movement activities. He was always getting the students involved in some rowdy activity on the old soccer field. As much as his disregard for the law annoyed her, she could respect him as a teacher.

He was actually…

Well…

Okay, fine. From all she'd observed, and every-thing she'd heard around town, Tate was a brilliant teacher.

His morning PE class took place on the soccer field, so she couldn't *not* see him teaching when she arrived at work. His class wasn't a *Lord of the Flies* situation. There was no stereotypical guy in polyes-ter shorts egging on a group of bullies in dodgeball and threatening to call the "whaaamulance" when a less-athletic student inevitably got hurt. Instead, "Coach Tate" encouraged all the students, spending the most time with the least athletically confident. Kids like Mason and Cece, who'd tried every which way to get out of PE, now called it their favorite class.

Dwap.

No, if Tate had soccer balls on the field, it was probably some ball-handling skills drill he'd break down for the kids. Soccer was far too mainstream for Tate.

Greg trotted over to the window. Aida's tiny of-fice was on one side of the brick building she shared with the post office, sandwiched between the school and The Restaurant. Her windows looked out on The City Hotel, the school and the playing fields. Her view was half the reason Tate had gotten so many tickets. Every time he broke a law, he was in her field of vision.

Dwap.

Greg gave a cautious whine.

"What's he up to this time?" Aida asked.

Greg sat down and gave her a serious look, something along the lines of *You're not going to like this*.

"What else is new?"

Aida stood, stretched, then walked over to the window.

Her initial reactive thought was that she was late for practice. Aida turned sharply and ran out the door. She'd sprinted ten steps, her heartbeat pounding in her ears, before she remembered.

She wasn't dressed for practice.

She wasn't a student.

This wasn't her team.

Aida blew out a breath. The moment felt eerily like her recurring dream of playing again. Dreams of power and joy as she flew across the field, connected with the ball, connected with her team and community, only to wake up in this life, deprived of the right to play.

Aida stood in the September sunshine, waiting for her heart rate to come down.

Tate was coaching soccer. That was fully legal in the State of Oregon.

She shrugged her shoulders, like she could fool her dog, and turned to reenter her office.

"That's not how you do a drill," a student snapped. The voice was annoyed, and had a heavy accent Aida didn't recognize.

"It's how we're going to do this drill," Tate responded.

Despite every instinct telling her this was a terrible idea, Aida turned back around.

A lanky young man, clearly one of the exchange students the town was buzzing about, stepped up to his coach. "But this way, it does not make sense."

And Tate, rather than smile, cajole or deliver that head-tilt glare that always got kids in line, seemed nervous. That was a surprise. He was normally so confident, which was part of what made him so annoying. He was always calm with the kids, no matter how poorly behaved they were. And in this town, that was saying a lot.

Greg, already sensing trouble, trotted toward the field. Aida followed.

Tate's argument with the student intensified. He ran his fingers through his hair, making it stick straight up like a caricature of a stressed-out teacher. Greg began to run to him, but Aida called the dog back to her side.

"I hate this town!" the student exclaimed. "No one here even knows how to play football."

Oh, that's not gonna slide.

Folks could say what they wanted to about Pronghorn, and they did. But a decade ago, the Pronghorn Pronghorns had won four state championships. It'd been a few years, but this was a soccer town.

Aida took decisive steps in the direction of the field, ready to set the kid straight, but she stopped midcharge.

What was the plan here? There was no way she'd get involved with soccer again. Ever.

And while Tate was annoying, and gorgeous, and a public nuisance, he did know how to handle a group of teenagers. What could she add to the situation?

Nothing.

Aida crossed her arms and looked over her shoulder at her office.

Dwap. Dwap.

She glanced back at the field. Kids scattered as the argument continued, passing the balls to one another. A girl with light brown hair picked up a ball and started in on a skillful juggle.

Tate was now talking calmly to the unhappy exchange student. The kid was scowling but no longer arguing. The professional teacher had the situation under control. And even if he didn't, it wasn't any of her business.

Tate blew his whistle. The kids returned to their original formation and the drill recommenced.

Good lord. No wonder the kid was upset.

Tate had spaced the players at regular intervals for the drill, standing still as they passed the balls in an overly complex sequence, like a pinball machine designed by Rube Goldberg. But once the kids understood the sequence, they knew exactly where their next ball was coming from. They responded by rote rather than by developing the reactive skills they'd need in a real game.

So, the drill was both overly complex and too basic at the same time. The kids with soccer skills knew enough to understand they weren't getting much out of it, and those without experience were befuddled by the complexity.

It was an impressively bad soccer drill.

Tate jogged backward, encouraging kids, but with a tightness to his voice she hadn't heard before. Or rather, she *had* heard it, but only when he was talking to her, not his students.

Aida refocused on the field. Several of the new exchange students were quite good. The girl with light brown hair kept up a steady stream of smack talk to a boy wearing a Brazil shirt. The lanky student who'd been arguing with Tate wore a jersey from the Senegal national team. He didn't like this drill, but his movements were precise and powerful.

Mav was all gangly arms and legs, but he was smiling and having fun. Antithesis seemed baffled. Cece was terrible, missing nearly every ball, but she was out on the field, trying. For Cece, attempting a physical activity in the presence of others was World Cup–level success.

Mav whacked a ball with the toe of his sneaker, sending it flying toward the sidelines. Aida reacted, stopping the ball with her foot and sending it back to Mav with a satisfying kick.

Okaaaay. Time to head back to the office.

Another ball sped across the field, straight at her. Aida made eye contact with the kid repping Brazil, and before fully thinking it through, sent the ball back in a controlled, high-powered drive. He tracked the ball, stopped it easily with his left foot, then folded his arms and stared at her.

She'd been found out.

A complex mix of joy and heartbreak washed through her. Handling the ball felt right. The kid's acknowledgment of her skills brought back the heady pride of leading a team to victory. Love of the game came flowing back to her.

That love made her furious as she recalled the shame of failing her dreams and the town's dreams for her.

As Aida swiveled toward her office, she heard an accented voice calling, "Hello! Lady with the dog!"

She sped up. A hearty *dwap* alerted her to another kick. She didn't want to look, but it was impossible not to track the lofted kick heading her way.

Keep walking.

An unplanned flicker of her gaze alerted her to the arc of the ball. Instinctively, she projected the point of contact.

And while her head was fully on board with a beeline to the office, her body turned. She met the ball, trapping it with her chest and then dropping it to her foot. She dribbled four paces then launched it back to the kicker, the young man who'd been arguing with Tate.

"Hello, *madame*!" he called to her. "Come. *Venez*."

Venez sounded like French to Aida, as did the next string of words he launched at her. In his excitement, the kid seemed to be throwing out words in every language he knew. A few of the other kids joined him.

Tate, who had been working patiently with Cece,

was watching her now. She saw his curiosity quickly give way to annoyance. He shot Aida the head-tilt/glare combo.

"Can I help you, Officer?"

Aida took a step backward. "Nope, Greg and I were just finishing up the day." She waved and turned to leave. Greg's big brown eyes asked if he could run over and get some more of Tate's ear scritches.

Absolutely not.

Tate tucked a soccer ball under one arm. A breeze flattened his T-shirt against his chest, sparking a number of questions about how he found the time to work out and what he was doing to get those results. "We're not breaking any laws?"

"No." She let out a chuckle so fake it probably sounded like she was coughing up a small mammal. She waved then shook her head. "No, of course not. Bye!"

I mean. That drill...

"She knows football," the young woman who'd been slaying the juggling said.

"Thanks, Ilsa," Tate said to her. "Let's get back to work."

"But the lady with the dog knows how to play—"

"Suleiman, my job here is to teach the *students* to play. Sheriff Weston has work to do." He turned to her. "There might be someone trying to cross the street five feet from an intersection. And that's *not* how they do things in Pronghorn."

CHAPTER THREE

"OF ALL THE bad days, this takes top honors." Tate pulled at the roots of his hair with both hands. "This is the worst."

"Hey!" Angie barked from behind the counter. "I heard that."

"Not the food," he called over his shoulder to where Angie was entrenched in the kitchen.

"This food is bad," Mateo muttered.

"Yeah, but no worse than normal." Tate spun back around and scooped up a forkful of potatoes. "This day, on the other hand? Worst."

The teachers generally ate at The Restaurant on Thursday nights, but Tate's terrible, horrible, no-good, very-bad day had inspired a Monday-night visit to the one eatery in town.

"No," Luci disagreed. "The day Loretta tried to shut down the school was the worst."

Tate shook his head. "I considered that. But when you think about it, the day was great up until then. We'd finally hit our stride in the classrooms. Also, that was the day Mrs. Moran taught the whole school how to play pinochle, which I think we can all agree was a win."

"Okay, what about our first day here?" Willa asked. "We get on a bus at 5:00 a.m., drive for seven hours, arrive in a desolate town and learn that absolutely no preparations had been made for the school year. *That* was a rough day."

"Then Tate nearly got arrested for creating a public nuisance!" Luci added, setting the whole table laughing. Except for Tate.

"That wasn't funny."

"No, it was funny," Vander said.

Sure. If you found beautiful women handing out arbitrary tickets humorous. Tate would never forget the day he'd met Aida. The school was in disarray, the principal was stunningly incompetent and none of the new teachers was prepared for the year ahead. He and the others had gone to the one restaurant in town, where Tate had gotten into deep trouble with the proprietor for asking to substitute corn for peas.

At that moment, he'd been on the verge of quitting.

Then a woman had come running into the restaurant. Tate hadn't noticed her uniform, he'd been too busy staring at her pretty face. Sun-streaked hair, hazel eyes, the easy movement of someone who loved to run. Pronghorn was looking a whole lot better. It was a perfect moment: a beautiful woman with a well-behaved German shepherd heading straight for him. What more could a guy hope for?

That was when she'd pulled out her ticket book and nearly fined him for arguing with Angie about corn.

"Yeah, that wasn't my favorite day. But this one tops everything. I start with a ticket. I end with a painful soccer practice where I've got players who range in competence from Lionel Messi to a disinterested three-year-old."

Then Aida shows up to witness my incompetence as a coach.

"I don't want to argue your point, but the day's not over yet," Vander reminded him.

Tate groaned.

"What are you complaining about?" Angie snapped, appearing at the table. Tate set his fingers on the rim of his plate. Angie was an aggressive dish-clearer. If you put your fork down for any length of time, she swept in like a hawk with a penchant for lukewarm leftovers.

But she didn't reach for his plate. Instead, she unceremoniously plunked a basket of rolls in front of him.

Tentatively, Tate lifted one from the basket. "What's this?"

"It's a roll."

The teachers exchanged glances. Tate twisted in his seat to get another look at the menu.

No, *menu* was too generous. It was a barely legible sandwich board that listed the offerings for the day. Presently, diners had a choice of chicken-fried steak, baked potato and corn, with vanilla ice cream for dessert, *or* chicken-baked steak with mashed potatoes and gravy, peas, and chocolate ice cream for dessert.

Don't even think about asking for a substitution.

"They're not on the menu," she snapped. "I baked them this morning. For my kids. They're home-made."

Homemade was a funny term in this establishment, since the home Angie lived in with her three teenagers was attached to the restaurant. Did she fix better food for her family? Could it be any worse?

But none of that mattered because what she was really saying was that she counted the young teachers as her kids.

Vander flashed a smile of gratitude. Luci blinked back tears as Willa cleared her throat.

"Thank you, Angie," Mateo said.

Angie harrumphed like it was their fault she was giving them special treatment.

Tate stood up and enfolded the grumpy mediocre chef in a hug.

"Oh, stop it," she said, patting him on the back. "It's just a roll."

Tate squeezed harder.

"Eat your meal," Angie commanded then stomped back into the kitchen.

Tate, feeling better for the first time since seven forty-five that morning, took a big bite of his roll. It was *not* bad.

Willa smiled at him. "Tell us about soccer practice."

All the better feelings vanished.

"Practice was a disaster."

"I don't know that it was a disaster," Luci said.

"You weren't there. It was awful. The exchange students are demanding soccer practice, but they didn't want to do what I asked. Meanwhile, I'm trying to teach kids who have never played before, along with getting Mav to accept that there are actual rules in this game—"

"Cece showed up, didn't she?" Mateo asked. "That's incredible, man. One month ago, she was refusing to walk laps around the track. And now she's going out for a sport?"

Tate nodded. It had been pretty cool to see Cece on the field.

"And the exchange students are going to settle in," Luci predicted.

"Absolutely," Willa agreed. "You're able to provide something a few of them feel passionately about. That's going to be key in helping them adjust to Pronghorn."

That was true.

And to their credit, none of the exchange students, or anyone in Pronghorn, knew what a sore point soccer was for him. It wasn't Suleiman's fault that Tate felt incompetent, *was* incompetent. The kid just wanted to play.

Tate had signed on to be a teacher, knowing it wouldn't be easy. He valued doing hard things. Coaching soccer was an emotional challenge, and he could take it on with the correct attitude and preparation. He'd watch some coaching videos on

YouTube, find a coach's guide somewhere on the internet.

Continuing with that strategy depended on getting a good Wi-Fi signal, which could be tricky in Pronghorn, but not impossible.

Tate stared at the front door as though he could see through it to the school and soccer field at the edge of town. He would do this.

The door opened, interrupting his positive self-talk.

Not interrupting his staring, though. Not for a second. Tate's jaw dropped as a stunning woman entered The Restaurant, her dog at her side. Aida was always gorgeous, even in her brown polyester uniform. But in jeans and white tank top, with her hair falling down around her shoulders?

Mercy.

She had the easy grace of an athlete, and after seeing her on the sidelines today, Tate had a pretty good idea what her sport of choice was.

Aida walked up to the counter. Tate tried to keep his eyes trained on Willa as she spoke, but it was hard, like trying to keep a Corvette's speedometer at sixty-five on an open stretch of road with no one around for a hundred miles.

He gave in and glanced again at Aida. Her gaze met his briefly before she refocused on the sandwich board. Her hair brushed her shoulder and she pulled it back.

Tate breathed in through his nose and out through his mouth. *Smell the soup, cool the soup.* It would be so much easier to deal with the sheriff if his heart didn't get all doe-eyed every time she was within fifty yards of him.

Greg glanced up at his handler then back at Tate.

It would also be easier if she didn't have such a good boy as her partner.

"You picking up for Flora?" Angie asked her.

"Yes, and I'm joining her tonight."

"What'll you have?"

Aida scanned the sandwich board. "Chicken-baked steak? I've never seen that before. How is it?"

"It's fine," Angie said.

Luci made eye contact with Aida and shook her head, making an urgent X motion with her hands.

Aida seemed surprised to get the intel, but went with it. "Hmm. Baked potato sounds really good, though."

"Flora likes my corn," Angie reminded her.

Tate was curious about this Flora. Who was she? And what was it about the corn she liked?

Aida lifted a small note card next to the sand-wich board then held it up to Angie. "Vegetarian option? That's new."

Tate had been wondering about that himself. Angie only ever had two options, and those always included meat.

"It's for the, uh, vegetarians." Angie pointed to a corner table where four members of the Open Hearts Intentional Community, dressed in orange, sat. The vegetarian option appeared to be baked po-tato, corn *and* peas.

"That looks good," Aida said. "I'll take two vegetarian plates."

"No."

"No?"

By now, all the teachers were watching the interaction, so Tate didn't feel so conspicuous.

"That's what I said. Do you want chicken-fried or chicken-baked steak?"

"Why can't I order the vegetarian option?"

"Because you're not a vegetarian," Angie said as though vegetarianism was a condition rather than a choice.

"But I want—"

"If you don't like the way I run things, you can take your business elsewhere," Angie snapped. It was a serious threat. The Restaurant was the only restaurant for fifty miles.

Tate couldn't contain himself, not after all the flack Aida had given him within the last twelve hours.

"Is that customer giving you trouble, Angie? Because I have it on good authority you can get a ticket for arguing in The Restaurant."

"I wasn't arguing," Aida grumbled.

Tate winked at the proprietor. "That attitude isn't going to get her any homemade rolls."

Aida turned to glare at him.

Tate pulled off a fluffy bite of roll and popped it in his mouth.

"Speaking of bad attitudes." Aida took a few

steps toward his table. "You seemed to be having a time of it at soccer practice today."

"I gave it my best," he said as the last drops of his good humor vanished. "That's what we ask of our students and ourselves."

"That was your best? That weird, static, overly complex drill was your *best*?"

"What's wrong with my drill?" He knew the drill was bad. The kids had participated out of a sense of obligation, but they hadn't had fun or even learned anything about soccer from it. But he was not in the mood to be called out by the sheriff.

"It was terrible. That may have been the worst coaching I've ever seen."

While he'd gotten in trouble for "bellowing" in the past, he couldn't keep his volume from rising as he said, "What makes you a soccer expert?"

Aida's eyes widened as the color drained from her face. Silence fell throughout the restaurant. People set aside their silverware, shocked by his words, which, while loud, weren't terribly offensive. Once again, the citizens of Pronghorn were staring at him.

Calling her expertise into question was clearly the wrong thing to say, let alone bellow.

Great. What law had he broken this time?

GREG STEPPED CLOSER, pressing himself against Aida's leg. She rested a hand on his head, not needing to look at her dog to confirm that she'd absolutely set herself up for that one.

It's hard to enforce personal boundaries around a

sport when you allow yourself to watch a practice then make your opinions known about that practice. She'd just forgotten how much the right drills mattered.

She'd forgotten how much anything mattered.

In truth, she hadn't really cared about much since the abrupt, unexpected end to her soccer career. The pain and disappointment served as a buffer between her and anything else she might feel passionately about.

But there was no denying that she cared about that soccer drill and was attached to the idea that it should never be repeated within the city limits of Pronghorn. Her mistake had been bringing it up in front of people who knew about her past failures. The people who were now staring at her and Tate in shocked silence.

Aida gave the room a quick, authoritative glare.

Everyone bent their heads back to their meals. The noise of humans consuming mediocre food resumed.

"I don't claim to be an expert."

He met her eye. Something seemed to click through his mind. "Really? Because I saw you handling the ball on the sidelines." He leaned back and crossed his ankle over his knee. "You play soccer."

She shrugged and gave the room a second cautionary glare. No one had better be thinking about enlightening the teaching staff of Pronghorn Public Day School about her past.

"Played."

"Okay. Great." He refocused on his meal. "You know how to play soccer. Good for you."

Tate picked up a butter knife and began sawing at his chicken-fried steak. The muscles in his forearm engaged as he tried to get through the meat.

This would be a good time to return to the counter and finish placing her order.

Tate sawed away on the beef.

Aida crossed her arms. "You might want to tweak that drill."

Tate dropped his silverware with a clatter. "Is there any part of my life you're not gonna criticize?"

"It's not criticism, it's just an idea. A good Speed of Play drill would be a much better warm-up."

"Fine, I'll google it tonight." Tate picked up his silverware.

Aida nodded. She leaned against the counter then turned back at Tate.

"What?!" he snapped.

"A World Cup drill could follow." She spoke quickly, as though the faster the words came out, the less of a bad idea talking to him was. "In a World Cup, you could separate your advanced players from those needing more help."

"How long is this going to go on?" he asked his coworkers.

Luci patted Tate's shoulder. "She's only trying to help."

Tate speared a piece of steak with his fork, but sadly it was still attached to the main. He waved the steak at her. "She hates me!"

"I don't hate you," Aida said. She needed to leave it at that, but the words came tumbling out again. "I just think some overlapping runs would make more sense than that static thing you were doing."

Tate took a deep breath in through his nose and blew it out through his mouth.

"Look, it's been a day. Soccer is my least favorite sport, and I would rather train rodents to tango than coach it. If you want to write down the names of those drills, I'll research them tonight."

Greg tilted his head to the side in a question. Aida voiced it for him. "How can soccer be your least favorite sport?"

"I don't like it."

"What's not to like?" For the first time, Aida felt genuinely sorry for Tate. What kind of sad and empty person didn't appreciate soccer?

"Seems as though you like it enough for the both of us." Tate gave up on the steak and turned to his corn.

"It's the beautiful game," she reminded him. "A perfect sport that anyone can play. All you need is a ball."

"If you like soccer so much, why don't *you* coach?"

The Restaurant went silent again. This wasn't the first time that suggestion had been made.

Tate glanced around and back up at Aida. His expression shifted, despair morphed into curiosity then hope. That smile, the one that felt like flirting, spread across his face.

"No," Aida said.

"You'd be a great coach."

"I'm not certified to work with kids."

"You could run your own background check."

"I don't play soccer anymore," she said.

Tate scoffed. "I saw you handle the ball."

"I wasn't handling it."

"Footling, whatever."

"*Footling* is not a word."

"It could be a word?" Tate looked to big-sister Willa for support. She shook her head.

Undeterred, Tate leaned toward Aida, eyes bright. His Tate scent managed to block out the smell of canned peas. "You were really good with the ball today."

"No, I wasn't."

He tilted his head and eyed her. She shrugged.

"Okay. Let's put it this way, you're better than me." Tate's sly smile shone up at her. "You know the names of soccer drills. You care about the efficacy of these drills you're capable of naming. Presumably, you even know the rules of soccer."

Aida threw her arms up. "Everyone knows the rules of soccer."

"That is a gross overstatement," Luci interjected. "I'd estimate only about three-quarters of the world's population know the rules of soccer."

It took Aida a moment to realize Luci was teasing her. It had been so long since Aida had hung out with a friend group her own age, she forgot what it was like. She felt shy suddenly, like her inner middle schooler wanted to grab Luci's hand and ask her to be best friends.

Not that such a thing was ever going to happen. Aida shook her head.

Mateo leaned forward and spoke to Tate. "How can you *not* know the rules of soccer? You know the rules to every game. Even pickleball."

"Pickleball is pretty simple."

"So is soccer," Mateo said.

Tate shifted uncomfortably. Aida caught his eye. Something else was going on here. She'd interrogated enough people to know Tate wasn't spilling the whole truth.

Of course, neither was she, so perhaps it was best to let this slide.

"Here's what I see." He held eye contact, as though they were negotiating a business deal. "You know enough about soccer to handle the ball, and you have opinions on the drills I run. We got an influx of soccer-loving students who expected to be anywhere in America except here. Pronghorn has got to be a pretty big shock to a kid expecting something more like LA or New York."

"He's right," Vander said. "Modern geographers put Pronghorn at about twenty miles from the middle of nowhere."

"Five of our new students want to play soccer. As their teachers, offering a fun activity where they can connect with others is near the top of our list. But as you so eloquently put it, I'm the worst soccer coach you've ever seen."

"Those weren't my exact words."

"Um?" Mateo rocked his hand back and forth. "Pretty close."

Aida turned to Luci, the nearest thing she had to an ally at the table, for support.

"I hate to agree with Mateo, but he's right," Luci said.

"There are worse coaches," Aida said.

"Theoretically." Tate was grinning now, his freckles shifting across his handsome face. "For all we know, Angie might be worse."

"I heard that!"

He pointed to Aida. "But *you* would be better than *me*."

Aida felt the words fall between them, weighty and full of hope, but ultimately untrue. There was no way she could coach. She could barely look at the soccer pitch without bursting into tears of sadness or rage. She was too competitive; she cared too much. Her soccer ego had never been under control. Competing with teammates was one thing, competing with a homesick kid from Senegal wouldn't be good for anyone.

But Tate needed help. As annoying and frustrating as he could be, he and the other teachers were doing a tremendous amount of good for the town she loved.

She gazed into his blue eyes. A spark of attraction raced between them, launching Tate's smile. She closed her eyes briefly, gave herself one last inhalation of Tate's scent, then shook her head.

"I'm sorry. I'm unable to help out at this time."

Tate started bellowing, something about civic duty and the youth of America.

Aida returned to the counter to find Angie had already bagged up the order she'd never made. It was clearly not the vegetarian option.

"Thank you, Angie." There was nothing else she could say. Aida picked up the bags.

"Whoa, whoa, whoa." Tate stood and gestured to the to-go order. "No one gets takeout from The Restaurant. It's against the rules."

"Flora does," Angie said, handing Aida a package wrapped in tinfoil. "Take these rolls to your grandmother too. And think about Tate's offer."

Greg thumped his tail against the floor in agreement. Aida gave Tate's offer one half of a millisecond, then shook her head.

She turned to Tate. "I'm happy to write out a few drills for you, but I will not get involved with the soccer team. I shouldn't have interfered."

She brushed past him and opened the door, despite Greg's low whine. Turning back for a brief moment, she saw Tate looking about as defeated as she felt. She never should have gotten his hopes up about her coaching. But that was just what soccer did: got everyone's hopes up, then destroyed them.

CHAPTER FOUR

"LORETTA, I THINK that had to be illegal," Willa said.

Tate was impressed as the lead teacher took a step toward the volunteer principal. It had been a long day and he still had a soccer practice to run, but there was no way he'd have missed this meeting. Watching Willa call out Loretta was well worth his time.

Loretta just batted her long eyelashes. "It wasn't illegal. The kids were unhappy with their original placements."

"So the program sent them here?" Tate asked.

Her eyes flashed. "What's wrong with here?"

Tate looked at Vander, who gave his head a slight shake. Getting Loretta riled up never led anywhere productive.

Willa folded her arms. "Loretta, let's back up a minute. The exchange students are here and we can't do anything about that now. Understanding how you got them here will clarify the students' expectations."

"I don't see the problem. It's marvelous having international students in town."

"Marvelous for who? Us or the students?" Luci asked.

"Why do you all insist on insulting our town?"

Tate couldn't hold his frustration any longer. "We're not insulting it, Loretta. We're telling you the kids are unhappy with the placement, and we want to know what you told them to get them here in the first place."

Loretta gave a pouty shrug. "Well, none of them liked their original placements either. Maybe they just don't like America. Have you considered that?"

Several teachers sighed. Luci pinched the bridge of her nose.

"Walk us through this, Loretta," Mateo suggested. "Where did you find nine exchange students weeks into the school year?"

"Well, after the year started, I thought, 'Now, wouldn't it be fun to have a few international students?'"

Tate groaned.

"So I looked into it. I'm sorry if I have more initiative than other people around here, but I found out that sometimes, if a student isn't happy with a placement, they're given the option to switch."

The teachers silently communicated the one obvious question to each other. *What placement could be so bad that students wanted to come here?*

"I met with each of the kids on Zoom. I answered a few questions, and they all chose to come here. If they're not happy, that's on them."

The teachers knew Loretta far too well not to be able to fill in the rest. She'd described the town as up-and-coming, selling the school like a two-bedroom fixer-upper in a trendy subdivision.

"What did you tell them about soccer?" Tate asked.

"The truth," she said, her voice rising in a way that belied the statement.

"The truth is we don't have a soccer program," Tate said. "I cannot believe that Suleiman, or Ilsa, or any of the other kids interested in soccer, would have chosen to come here if they knew we don't have a team."

"The truth," Loretta repeated, all five feet of her stepping up to Tate, "is that Pronghorn dominated the league for years and won four state championships in a row."

"When? The nineteen seventies?"

"No." She scrunched up her nose as though *everyone* knew the team was no good in the seventies. "Ten years ago. When Aida Weston played. That was before she went off to UCLA, of course. We all thought she'd go pro, but in the end, she came home." Loretta sighed. "But we have a rich history of soccer in this town and you're going to revive it."

The words filtered into Tate's understanding of Pronghorn, of Aida, illuminating everything like floodlights on a field at twilight.

The conversation around him continued, but he had all the information he needed.

Aida had been a big star in a tiny town. Going from a Single A soccer team to a huge program like UCLA suggested extraordinary talent, passion and grit, the magical combination that made people truly great at anything.

Loretta, in another one of her half-baked schemes, had said anything she could think of to bring international students to Pronghorn. She'd promised them a top-notch soccer program that he was completely unqualified to lead.

Mateo was clarifying a point about how she found homes for the exchange students, but Tate interrupted him. "Why doesn't Aida coach soccer?"

"Oh, honey, she can't. Not after the disappointment."

"The disappointment of…" Tate gestured for her to finish the sentence.

"Soccer, I guess. She just came home and has been disappointed ever since."

"And no one's tried to help her resolve this?"

Loretta snorted. "Well, I, for one, don't want to get a ticket."

"If we could get back to the subject for a moment," Willa said. "Today we had three significant rule infractions, all by exchange students. I suspect they are breaking rules in an attempt to be removed from this placement."

"That's nonsense." Loretta waved her hand. "The kids are going to love it here. They just need to get adjusted."

"We can all agree they need to adjust," Willa said. "It would be helpful, though, if you could explain why you thought exchange students were a good idea in the first place."

"I felt—" Loretta cleared her throat, pouted, then cleared her throat again. "I felt that I may have been a bit harsh on you in the first few weeks of school. We all were."

A bit harsh was an understatement. Loretta and the other board members had threatened to close the school down and cancel the teachers' contracts if they didn't meet a long list of unreasonable demands. In the end, the teachers had managed to convince the community to accept them, but it hadn't been easy.

"School has been going well," Loretta said. "I thought we should celebrate."

"We're celebrating with nine international students who don't want to be here?" Luci asked.

Loretta turned on Luci, far and away the most well-traveled and knowledgeable about other cultures, and asked her, "Why are you so afraid of people from other places?"

Mateo dropped a hand on Luci's shoulder before she was able to launch herself at the volunteer principal.

"And there's the stipend," Loretta said, picking up her large purse.

"Stipend?" Willa asked.

She leaned toward the teachers. "You didn't think we were teaching all these new kids for free?"

Before Tate could even start to ask questions, a heavy tap sounded on the doorframe.

"Coach Tate?"

Tate spun around to see Ilsa and Suleiman in the

doorway. They'd already grabbed the balls and orange cones.

Time to get to it.

"You all can head out and get warmed up. I'll be there in a minute."

Suleiman nodded. Ilsa rolled her eyes and marched toward the exit.

Tate excused himself from the meeting. He'd heard enough. Loretta had found some way to finagle these exchange students into coming here, and there was money at stake, which meant she wouldn't back down. The kids were stuck here, and he was the only person who could give them what they wanted: a great soccer team.

Tate swung by his classroom and picked up the notes he'd written out last night. Warm-ups, drills, scrimmage plans, encouraging comments he could make to students with no skills in any of the previous areas. Plans for what to do when someone challenged him.

He was overprepared in the extreme.

His stomach once again tried to do a full flip despite not being designed for such activity.

It reminded him of his student-teaching experience where he'd been working with a less-than-motivated educator at one of the wealthiest schools in Portland. She hadn't loved her job teaching health and PE and used student teachers to take over her workload. For the first few weeks, Tate had made daily mistakes. This had led the students to constantly challenge him while his "cooperating teacher" sat on her computer bidding on eBay items.

Tate had been determined to rise from the ashes he was reduced to on a daily basis. Every night he'd sifted through his mistakes, turned momentary failures into lessons to inform his teaching. It was trial by fire, and he'd let the experience strengthen him. Three weeks in, he'd had his classes under control. A week after that, kids were engaged and having fun. Halfway through his practicum experience, he'd begun to receive emails from parents saying his class was the best PE experience their kids had ever had. The principal had offered him a job before he'd even received his teaching license.

That was what he needed to do here—learn from his mistakes and let the experience strengthen him.

He loved teaching general-ed PE classes. It was a lot easier to prepare lessons for something you loved and believed in. But soccer was nothing but a reminder of what a disappointment he'd been to his dad.

Tate approached the back door, heading out to the field. Light shone through the opening, along with the ugly sound of feet hitting soccer balls.

"Coach Tate!"

The voice came directly from his right, and Tate swiveled to find himself nose to nose with Mav.

That kid.

"Your face looks distorted."

"It's nice to see you, too, Mav."

Mav wasn't being contrary. Nine times out of ten, the kid was argumentative, but in this case, he seemed honestly concerned. That, in and of itself, was annoying.

"Are your emotions running high?" he asked.

"No," Tate snapped.

"It's important to talk about your feelings."

Tate drew in a deep breath. Things were done differently at the Open Hearts Intentional Community, and Mav was only trying to be helpful. But discussing his feelings with a sixteen-year-old who argued about everything, including societal constructs like grades, or the concept of the sixty-minute hour, was not what Tate needed.

Tate dug deep and found a smile. "Word." He offered Mav a fist bump. Mav, who hadn't quite gotten the hang of the conventional gesture, slapped the fist with a high five.

They could work on that skill another day.

The two emerged into the sunlight. In addition to the kids already on the field, several community members were set up on the sideline to watch.

Perfect.

He had an audience to witness his attempted coaching. Tate scanned the crowd a second time.

One particularly beautiful community member was notably not there. Just as well. If Aida wasn't going to help him, he didn't want her distracting him. Or ticketing him.

On the field, Suleiman and Antonio were playing an intense game of one-on-one, nearly trampling Cece in the process. Mav headed to the field and immediately started an argument with Ilsa; his way of trying to connect with her. She engaged, but nothing about her body language suggested there was a friendship in the making. Meanwhile Mason, who'd gone out for soccer in a moment of bravery, was now slinking toward the edge of the field with the expression of someone about to fake an injury to get out of practice.

Tate pulled a deep breath in through his nose and let it out through the mouth.

This mattered. He could do it.

He blew his whistle. "Gather up!"

Imitating the stance of a capable coach, and speaking clearly, Tate managed to fake confidence long enough to get the warm-ups going.

It wasn't perfect. Mav argued. Cece got a side ache. Ilsa finished every sprint long before her teammates then asked, "What's next?" But it was a good set of warm-ups and everyone participated.

One small win for Tate Ryman!

The drills were a little trickier. To explain the drills, he had to handle the ball, which wasn't always successful. Or ever successful.

In his defense, soccer balls were the worst. A basketball had a secure texture covering it that gave the hand traction. A baseball was small and easy to handle. Soccer balls were just slippery.

Plus feet? Who came up with the idea of maneuvering a ball with the clumsiest part of the human anatomy?

The ball skittered away every time Tate tried to demonstrate a drill.

He tried to ignore the smirk rising off Antonio and the impatient sigh from Ilsa.

Once he got the drill underway and everyone was moving, he finally had time for his actual skill set, encouraging kids and helping them get better.

"Nice speed, Suleiman! Can you pass off the ball before you hit the cones?"

"No one is open," he called back.

"Cece's open."

Suleiman ignored the words, and Cece. Instead, he waited for Antonio to break free. Tate was about to stop the drill with a sharp blow of his whistle, but he paused. What was he going to do? Point out to the entire community that Suleiman disdained Cece's attempt at playing soccer? That would bring focus to Suleiman's bad behavior and Cece's lack of skills.

No, that was better suited to private conversation. But the list of topics for a private conversation with Suleiman was growing longer by the minute.

Over the last two days, Suleiman had broken several rules, flagrantly disregarding direct instruction. While Tate certainly knew what it was like to break a law without meaning to, Suleiman made a point of drawing attention to his misdoings. It was almost like he wanted to get caught. His actions weren't mean or harmful, but they sure were deliberate.

Tate blew his whistle. "Nice hustle everyone. Mason, you were exactly where you were supposed to be. Let's run it again."

The players re-formed and started the drill a second time. But, once again, Suleiman easily commandeered the ball and kept possession until Antonio or Ilsa was in a position to receive.

Tate raised his whistle. Before he could stop the drill, a tall woman in flowing orange robes left the sidelines, heading straight for him.

Not now, he begged whatever deity they worshipped at the Open Hearts Intentional Community.

No response.

"Tate." Today's Moment stopped right in front of him. There were fifteen kids, running in all directions, and she was right up in his face. "Let me say how much I value your commitment to the health of our emerging adults."

He gave her a quick nod. "Yeah, thanks. Can you—?"

"Our community has raised our hands in gratitude to you frequently."

He blinked. That was a surprise.

"And while I know you would never encourage a child in destructive competitivism—"

Tate raised a hand, but more in a *shush, you* movement than gratitude that he was being interrupted. Around them, the drill began to break down.

"Mrs.…Ms.…Moment."

"Today's Moment," she corrected patiently.

"I'd love to discuss soccer with you—" She started to interrupt him but he spoke over her as he took a step toward the players. "Later. Right now I need to focus on this drill."

"It's the drill that prompted me to rise and share my truth." Today's Moment moved to block his path.

Suleiman kicked the ball to Antonio and Mav flopped over it with his entire body. When Ilsa called that move for what it was, illegal, Mav started arguing that rules should be flexible and change with the times.

Today's Moment smiled and persisted. "You are setting the young people against one another in conflict."

"It's soccer."

"But does it *have to* be soccer?"

His question exactly.

Tate turned away, breathing in sharply. Deep inhale, exhale.

Don't get angry. Don't lose your cool.

Today's Moment was still talking. Out on the field, he was losing what little cohesion he'd managed to build that day. The drill derailed into a free-for-all. Cece slunk over to the sidelines. Suleiman and Antonio opted out of the exercise entirely, grumbling to one another and looking disapprovingly at Tate.

The exchange students were just kids. Disappointed kids. If he'd moved halfway around the world on his own at seventeen and found himself in Pronghorn, he wouldn't have handled it any better.

The muttering on the field amplified. Exclamations of surprise in several languages erupted. Tate turned to see five curious Pronghorn antelope approaching the field.

He took several long steps toward the animals. "Get out of here!"

A female focused her large, almond eyes on him then bent her head to nibble the field. The exchange students were baffled and a little frightened by the antelope. The kids from the Open Hearts community seemed to be calling them by specific names.

And no one was practicing soccer.

Tate scanned the field, taking in the players, spectators and invading antelope. What did he need to make this situation work? Not only for himself, but for these talented, determined exchange students, and for the kids in Pronghorn who hadn't had the chance to play sports for the last three years, let alone find out if they had any interest or skill in soccer.

The Pronghorn kids were on the field because he'd managed to spark an interest in organized physical activity over the last month.

The exchange students were there because this was the only activity the town had to offer that felt remotely familiar, and they loved the game.

The spectators were there because they valued the connection high school sports brought to a community.

It was unfortunate for all of them that he was the one in charge.

Tate scanned the field, letting the solution come to him. He needed two things to make this situation tenable.

One. Soccer couldn't be the only good thing in Pronghorn for the exchange students. The community needed to rally and show these kids there was more to this tiny little town than mediocre food and a bad internet connection.

Two. He needed help coaching this team.

And there was only one person in town who had the skills to make this work.

AIDA PULLED UP in front of the 1920s farmhouse she shared with her grandmother. The engine settled. The rumble of her vehicle gave way to the whisper of wind through sagebrush and the slow creaking movements of the aspen grove. Aida let out a sigh. Greg, sitting in the passenger seat, sighed too.

Home.

Finally home after a long, exhausting day of self-regulation for the both of them.

Aida leaned over and planted a kiss on Greg's brow then opened the car door. She was ready to roll into the house, be engulfed by some age-softened sweatpants and watch old episodes of *Murder, She Wrote* with her grandmother. The exciting life of a twentysomething in Pronghorn, Oregon.

But as her boots hit the dirt drive, the hairs on Aida's arm rose in warning. Greg's ears pricked up, sensing it as well.

Something was amiss. Aida turned slowly, scanning the property. Greg jumped out of the car, a flow of brown-and-black fur, nose to the ground as he searched for the clues she wasn't privy to.

Aida followed her partner, circling around to the back of the house, ready for anything.

An old ATV painted in a camouflage pattern of

fall leaves was parked next to the open back door. From inside, a charming voice wove with her grandmother's sweet laughter. Aida closed her eyes in disbelief.

A bellowing laugh snapped her eyes right back open.

Greg, off-duty pup that he was, took off up the stairs.

Aida was tempted to hop back in the vehicle and go find someone easier to deal with than Tate. Like a hardened criminal. Or Angie.

A lilt of interest in Tate's voice caught her ear, followed by the easy flow of her grandmother's chatter when she was talking about her favorite subject: Aida.

She sprinted up the steps into the house. God only knew how much Flora had already given away.

She flew through the mudroom, past the old-fashioned kitchen and the tidy dining nook and straight into the living room.

"Who's a good boy?" Tate had his nose to Greg's. "Who's the best guy named Greg?" Tate rubbed Greg's ears, making one stand up straight then the other. Greg soaked up the love like he'd never been given so much as a pat on the head.

"Stop questioning my dog," Aida snapped.

Tate looked up, a wry smile spread across his face.

"I'm not questioning your dog. We're communicating."

"You're literally asking him, 'Who's a good boy?'" She turned to Greg. "You don't need to engage. You *are* a good boy, don't let him question that fact."

Greg's soulful gaze connected with hers, reminding her that he knew exactly what kind of boy he was and Tate's phrasing was nothing more than an affectionate figure of speech.

Aida ignored the canine.

"Seriously." She waved her hand at Tate's head. "What if your students started the day by rubbing your ears and asking, 'Who's a good teacher?'"

"That would be weird."

"Exactly."

"Hello, Aida," her grandmother said.

"Hi, Grammy." Aida kissed Flora's cheek, even if she had committed treason by letting Tate into the house. "Goodbye, Tate."

"Aida Weston," Flora admonished her.

"Oooh! Called out with the last name." Tate widened his eyes at Aida.

"Why are you in my home?"

"Aida, that's no way to treat a guest." Flora turned to Tate and said, "She was raised better than this."

"Grammy! Why are you taking his side?"

"There are no sides," Flora said. "This nice young man came to see you. The least you can do is sit down and listen to what he has to say."

Aida exhaled loudly. Then she sat down heavily on the sofa and crossed her arms.

"It's nice to see you too," Tate said.

"Is this about soccer?" Aida asked.

Tate, still smiling like he knew something she didn't, nodded.

Okay she'd rehearsed this conversation in her head. She was prepared, ready to be kind but firm.

Or rather, she was prepared to speak. She wasn't entirely prepared to handle his bright smile and blue eyes while she let him down.

"Look, I am truly sorry you're stuck coaching a sport you don't like, even though it's weird you don't like soccer."

Tate didn't stop smiling. Greg jumped up next to him on the sofa, turned once, then laid down with his head in Tate's lap. She tried to give the dog a warning look but he closed his eyes in relaxation as Tate rubbed his furry neck.

"I appreciate everything you and your coworkers have done for the school," Aida continued. "You're all working so hard, and the town is grateful. But I can't help you. I don't have your skills with kids."

"You don't need my skills. I need *your* skills. You run the drills and call the plays, I'll encourage, cajole and organize."

Aida furrowed her brow. "You don't call plays in soccer."

"You don't?"

"No—" She stopped herself. He needed to figure this out on his own. "I'm sorry, Tate. I'm the only law enforcement for miles and my schedule is too chaotic to make a commitment to the team."

"Flora tells me you're only working three-quarters time, due to budget restrictions."

Aida turned to her grammy, who feigned innocence at the comment. To Tate, she said, "Yes, true, but I can't just turn my job off."

"I'm not asking you to. Help out when you can."

"I don't have anything to offer."

Tate exchanged a glance with Flora, a world of information passing between them.

"What did you tell him?" Aida asked.

Flora shrugged.

"Let me rephrase; was there anything you *didn't* tell him?"

Flora patted Aida's leg. "It won't make much sense to pretend at this point, my dear."

Great. Now Tate knew about her failure too. He'd tell the other teachers, and they'd all watch her with a combination of pity and disappointment like the rest of the town did.

Shame and regret rushed through her, fresh and cold. Did other athletes feel this? The enduring heartbreak of no longer being able to compete? Knowing she was a disappointment to everyone while simultaneously losing the opportunity to do the one thing she loved? A onetime, small-town soccer phenomenon who didn't have the chops to play beyond college.

On a regular day, Aida would have turned to her dog for comfort. But Greg was now sprawled across Tate's lap, and that could get awkward.

"You were the best 1A player in the state for all four years of high school," Tate said. "You played for UCLA, and nearly went professional. You have everything to offer."

Aida glared at him. She wasn't going to get mad at Flora. It wasn't her fault Tate had showed up and started asking questions. This was all on Tate.

"My past is none of your business."

"Your past can help me, five unhappy exchange students and a bunch of Pronghorn kids who've never had the chance to play a sport before. My business is teaching students and building their confidence. Your past couldn't be more a part of my business."

Was there anything more frustrating than a gorgeous man poking holes in your admittedly shaky logic?

"This isn't fair. You can't come into my house, pet my dog and charm my grandma!"

Tate scoffed. "I'm not charming your grandmother."

"Oh, I'm completely charmed," Flora said.

"See!" Aida gestured to her. "You're too charming."

"Too charming?" Tate furrowed his brow.

"You're way too charming. Beyond Prince Charming. You're like, emperor-level charming. Charismatic-autocrat charming."

A slow, easy and, yes, charming, smile spread across Tate's face. "Is that what's wrong with me? I'm too charming?"

Oh. Okay. Wow.

She'd painted herself into that corner.

"It's one of your issues."

"But I'm not charming to you, right?"

"No." She crossed her arms very tightly, like a suspect when they had everything to hide. "No," she repeated. Because that's a surefire way to make something true, just keep saying it over and over. "Intellectually I understand that you're charming."

He raised his eyebrows, daring her to continue.

"I'm saying this is my home. I had a long day. I don't need you coming in here and using your charming-ness to ferret information out of my grandmother."

"He didn't need to ferret anything." Flora waved her hand in dismissal.

That was the truth. Flora had a hard time not telling anyone and everyone about Aida's glory days on the soccer field. Gas station attendants, receptionists, medical specialists, no one was safe.

Flora's hand shook as she reached out and patted Aida's knee. It was easy to forget that Flora had been an athlete too. In a time when there was no girls' soccer team and they'd played basketball with girls' rules for a three-game season.

And now the Parkinson's ate away at her physical control, but you didn't see her pitching a fit about helping her community. Aida's parents had left Pronghorn years ago, repeatedly offering to put Flora up in a retirement community on the outskirts of Phoenix where they lived. But Flora belonged here. The one, tiny silver lining Aida could cling to was that she could be there to care for her grammy who did so much for others. Aida placed her hand over Flora's.

Tate watched the interaction with interest.

"I'm sorry for barging in before you got home." He sounded sincere. "I don't want to bug you. You probably don't believe me, but I've never wanted to bother you." He leaned forward, resting his elbows on his knees, which was a feat considering there was a large German shepherd draped across his lap. "But I'm uncomfortable with soccer. It's never been intuitive to me."

Aida glanced over at the first-team all-state trophy on the mantel. Nothing could be more intuitive.

Tate went on, "I don't know how to coach the exchange students. Their skills and understanding of the game surpass mine. We need leadership if we're going to make a team out of inexperienced Pronghorn students and hotshot international players. I need your help."

She swallowed then nodded, acknowledging this. "I hear you. I see you, too, while you're coaching. You *do* need help."

He grinned again, the borderline flirtatious smile. "It's nice to hear you admit that I need help."

She smiled back, hopefully with borderline kindness rather than attraction. "But I need to *not* help you. As you've gathered from Grammy, I have a pretty complicated relationship with soccer. I don't play anymore."

"I'm not asking you to play."

"Tate, you don't know what it is you *are* asking of me. I think, if you understood, you wouldn't be here right now."

He leaned even farther toward her. Greg re-adjusted himself, opening his eyes to give Aida a baleful glance.

"Do you want to talk about it?" Tate offered.

"Absolutely not."

"Aida," her grandmother cut in. "This young man needs you. He has students who have come from around the globe. These kids need to feel better, less homesick. The least you can do is offer a little help."

Tate gazed at her soulfully, which was somehow even worse than being called out by her grandma. "Please, Aida."

The air in the room seemed to still.

"Okay. Fine. I'll help you."

"Yes!" He leapt up in victory, leaving her dog scrambling to make sense of what had happened to the lap.

"Not the team," Aida clarified, remaining seated. "I'm not coming to practice. But I will help you help those kids."

His brow creased.

Aida continued, "I'll teach you what you need to know to coach. I'll help you plan practice, explain what to look for, suggest drills." She paused, unable to quite repress a smile. "We can work on your basic ball handling to give you a little more cred with the players."

Tate nodded. "That's a start."

"That's the final offer."

He widened his eyes at her hopefully. She shook her head. His smile broadened.

Time to take control of the situation. Aida stood and offered a hand to Tate. "I will stop by the hotel after work tomorrow and we can get started."

He clasped her hand in his, warm and easy. She had a better sense of why her dog was so willing to snuggle up with this guy.

Aida pulled her hand back then gestured to the door. "I'll see you tomorrow."

"Friday nights can get pretty wild around the hotel."

"I'll be sure to bring my ticket book."

His expression darkened briefly. "Are you serious?"

She shrugged.

"She's joking," Flora said. She didn't stand. The brief encounter with Tate had exhausted her. Aida needed to shut this party down.

"I'm joking," she confirmed.

Tate's grin sprang back into place then he knelt beside Flora and took one of her shaking hands in his. "Thank you for your hospitality. It was lovely to meet you."

Flora turned her cheek to Tate and tapped it. He delivered a peck as Flora said, "This has been charming."

Aida rolled her eyes. "Go home."

"I'm going!" Tate straightened, gave Greg and Flora a final goodbye, then bounded down the back steps and hopped on the ATV.

Aida followed him outside. "Six thirty?" she asked.

"That sounds like a perfect Friday night to me." As the words left his mouth, he seemed to realize that sounded a lot like a date, which it wasn't. He breathed in through his nose, then out through his mouth as he fussed with the ignition. But before he started the ATV, he glanced at her again.

"Thank you, Aida." She waved his thanks away, but he stressed, "I mean it. Thank you."

She crossed her arms and nodded. "It's the right thing to do."

Mostly right anyway. The right thing to do would be to help him on the field with the kids, but that hurt too much to think about.

He gazed at her then added, "If it's helpful, I have a pretty complicated relationship with soccer myself. I don't want to be out on the field any more than you do."

Vulnerability shone from his eyes as he made his confession. Here was this strong, happy, capable man admitting a weakness.

But he was only sharing this to get her to take over a job he didn't want to do. He was smiling at her now, and there had been more than enough charm this evening.

"Go home," she told him.

Still grinning, he fired up the engine and started to back up.

"Keep it on the streets and dirt roads this time!" Aida yelled after him.

He gave her a thumbs-up and drove away.

Aida watched as he and his cloud of dust left the property. The roar of the engine faded, leaving the breeze and the creaking of the aspen once more.

How was it that her home felt too quiet, her longed-for solitude too lonely, in his absence?

CHAPTER FIVE

Six fifteen, Friday night.

Aida stood from her desk and pushed in the chair. She changed out of her uniform into athletic clothes and walked across the street to the old City Hotel, like she'd said she would. She didn't want to, but she did.

It was only after she'd crossed the street and was standing at the archway opening of the hotel's courtyard that she realized she'd jaywalked to get there.

Whatever. Greg wasn't going to say anything.

Her dog nosed his way into the courtyard, where he immediately began quivering in excitement. She understood the feeling. The old courtyard was still glamorous, even a hundred years after the hotel's heyday and thirty years after it had shut down for lack of visitors. The property was owned by the town, and a unanimous decision to fix it up for the new teachers was possibly the only thing the citizens of Pronghorn had ever fully agreed upon. It was part of the deal Loretta had brokered to revive the school. The teachers had accepted lower salaries and uprooted their lives to move out here. The town had provided lodging at the hotel and vehicles to drive.

It had come as a bit of a shock to the young teachers when those vehicles had turned out to be an ATV and a snowmobile. But they were getting the hang of things.

Aida remembered walking by the old hotel as a child, feeling sorry for the beautiful, lonely relic of better days. But now the place was hopping.

In one corner of the courtyard, Vander Tourn strummed his guitar. No citizen of Pronghorn would say it out loud, but the slow, moving melodies he played to unwind each evening were an unexpected pleasure for the whole town. Everyone looked forward to the moment when Vander finished his supper and picked up the guitar. Most evenings, he played for an hour or more to unwind from what had to be a hectic day of teaching everything from introductory physics to chemistry to advanced biology. The music rose from the courtyard, floating over the little town, a signal to all that it was time to let go of the cares of the day and relax.

Luci knelt by one of the old rosebushes that still flourished, although the last blooms were fading with the end of summer. One might think she was tending the plants, but Aida, and now Greg, knew better.

Luci poked her head up and waved. "Hey. Welcome. Is he safe around the hedgehogs?"

"He won't harm them." Aida said. "He'd love to befriend them, though."

"What do you think?" Luci asked the four roly-poly little critters. They continued to scavenge for food.

"But if any of them are packing illegal substances, Greg'll shake 'em down pretty quickly," Aida added.

Luci laughed then gave Greg an affectionate pat. "A friend of Aida's is a friend of mine, and my hedgehogs."

That meant Luci might think of her as a friend? Again, Aida fought the urge to squeal and exchange matching bracelets to confirm this point.

"Tate's inside," Luci said. "Pacing, pulling his hair out, waiting for you."

"It's just soccer." *And just me.*

"That's what I told him."

Greg sat down next to Luci and politely asked to stay and befriend hedgehogs. "You okay if this guy hangs out with you?" Aida asked.

"Always." Luci turned to the dog. "You can help me grade papers when the hedgehogs finish their ramble."

Aida crossed the courtyard, her hand flinching awkwardly to give Vander a wave. He offered a welcoming nod. Aida stepped inside. The old foyer, with cream-colored molding and gold trim, was as magnificent as it had been when she'd snuck into the building as a kid. Antique furniture, upholstered in spring green and pale pink, remained in good shape. But rather than resonating with a stern, empty formality, the room felt lived in, a pleasant mess. A mishmash of coats hung on the tree rack. Student papers and lesson plans were spread out on the reception desk. One of Tate's sweatshirts hung off the back of a chair, spilling onto the trendy sneakers he wore to teach in.

Mateo popped up from behind the reception desk and caught sight of her. "Oh, hello! I didn't hear you come in."

Aida waved then dropped her hand. "Hi."

"Tate's in the kitchen." Mateo said, his eyes crinkling with mischief. "Go easy on him."

"What do you think I'm gonna do, cite him for mishandling the ball?"

Mateo's gaze connected with hers.

Okay, there was potential there.

"I told him I'd help, so that's my plan."

Mateo glanced over his shoulder, then leaned across the reception desk, toward her. "See if you can figure out what his problem with soccer is."

"You think he's gonna tell *me*?"

"Aren't police supposed to be good at that type of thing? You play good cop, bad cop, make him talk, right?"

Aida laughed. "The good cop is back in the courtyard, trying to connect with the hedgehogs, but I'll do my best."

Mateo gave her a salute then gestured in the direction of the kitchen where Tate's voice could be heard above the others. It was like the whole world had an agreed-upon volume, and Tate didn't come equipped with the ability to dial his voice down to that level.

Aida swallowed her nervousness and headed in. The industrial kitchen was overkill for five teachers and a family of hedgehogs: massive stoves, walk-in refrigerators and freezers, farm-table-size griddles, acres of steel-covered island and countertop.

"Aida, great to see you!" Willa called. Local rancher, Colter Wayne, stood on one side of her, his thirteen-year-old daughter, Sylvie, was on the other. The three were busy with a mass of cookie dough, baking sheets and cooling racks.

"Welcome." Colter nodded at Aida. The big smile he hadn't been able to shake since Willa had agreed to marry him brightened the room. "You hungry?"

"I, uh—" She'd planned on grabbing dinner at The Restaurant before coming over, but a combination of nerves, and wariness that Angie might be serving fish, had kept her at her desk. "Yeah, I am. Famished."

"We're making cookies," Sylvie said. "They'll be ready soon. Coach Tate?" she called over her shoulder. "Sheriff Aida is here. Can you make her a sandwich too?"

Aida started to protest but Tate emerged from a walk-in fridge, a large sandwich in each hand. He stopped short, staring at her. His eyes traveled slowly down her outfit, his expression one of shock.

What?

She was wearing athletic shorts, running shoes and an old T-shirt. They were here to play soccer and work on Tate's skills. It didn't seem like the outfit should be that much of a surprise.

Wordlessly, he held out a sandwich.

"Hello, Aida, welcome to our home." Willa spoke for him. "Would you like a sandwich?"

Tate recovered himself and smiled. "Sorry. Hi, thanks for coming." He jogged over to a cabinet and grabbed a plate. "I was going to eat both of these, but since you're here, I'll just have one for now and you can have the other." He was definitely nervous. "Or I can make you your own sandwich."

"Thank you?" Aida didn't know how to react here. She'd said she was hungry, which meant she couldn't back out now. But do you just take a guy's sandwich?

"Um. What's on it?" she asked. Tate handed her the plate and she lifted a slice of bread. Ingredients were piled haphazardly: meats, cheeses, spreads, vegetables, two kinds of potato chips. "Or rather, what's not on it?"

He laughed, releasing some tension. "Sorry. We finally made it to Lakeview to get some groceries, thanks to Colter here."

"They'd been surviving on Angie's food, supplemented with canned soup and saltine crackers from the store," Colter said.

"I'm so sorry." That could not have been kind on anyone's digestive system.

"We're good now." Tate's flirtatious smile crept out.

Aida looked into the sandwich. "I don't want to steal your dinner."

"No, it's okay. This is my second dinner. You eat one sandwich, I'll have the other, then I'll make us more after we practice," he said as though one regularly ate four or five sandwiches after dinner.

Aida picked it up. Like Tate, it was over-the-top yet strangely appealing. She took a bite.

Okay, very appealing.

"Plus cookies," Sylvie said.

"Always cookies," Tate confirmed. He took a bite of his own sandwich then picked up a soccer ball with his free hand. "Ballroom?"

Aida nearly choked on a corn chip. She swallowed carefully before managing to ask, "We're gonna work on soccer skills in the old ballroom?"

He cocked his head to one side. "You have a better idea?"

The soccer field came to mind. Or the gymnasium, or the courtyard, or any place *without* parquet flooring.

But Tate had a defiant set to his jaw, like he was waiting for her to challenge him. He wanted to practice drills in the ballroom, not outside, not around his friends.

Or anywhere others could see him.

Aida snuck a peek at Willa, who was watching the exchange with concern, confirming Aida's suspicion. This confident—no, this *cocky* man was afraid to be seen with a soccer ball.

"Great. Ballroom. Let's do it."

A relieved smile spread across Tate's face. "Cool."

Aida grabbed her plate and followed Tate out of the kitchen. "Come to think of it, there should be more chandeliers in competitive sports."

"That's what I say."

They exited the kitchen into the elegant dining

room. Aside from several tables that Luci had commandeered for what was probably a social studies simulation, the room was largely untouched.

"How do you like living at the hotel?" she asked.

"I love it. It's not what I expected, but I can't complain." He slowed his pace to walk next to her. "I mean none of this was what we expected. But five teachers running loose in an old hotel is a good time."

Aida had a feeling Tate was responsible for at least two-thirds of the fun they had together. "I'm glad to see the old building back in use. It's a special place."

"Yeah." He glanced at her. "Your home is cool too. I love the old farmhouses around here."

"There is nothing cool about living with my grandmother."

Tate laughed. "I disagree. Flora's awesome."

Aida smiled in acknowledgment. "I have a good Grammy."

Tate's gaze connected with hers and then his expression shifted. "Does she have Parkinson's?"

Aida nodded. "It's pretty frustrating for her. That's another reason I can't coach. I need to be on hand to help out."

Tate shook his head. "I don't think that excuse is gonna fly with Flora."

"Flora would probably come coach the team herself if you asked."

He held up both hands. "I don't want to be accused of charming anybody into helping kids."

Too late for that.

He reached out in front of her and opened up the door to the ballroom. Aida stepped inside, feeling more like Cinderella than Mia Hamm. They were seriously going to work in here?

The ceiling rose two stories high, with a balcony that ran around the second story. A ring of old sky-lights, some of which had been boarded up, let in the evening light. The walls were covered in shimmering silk and gilt-painted chairs were stacked in one corner. Aida could imagine the weddings and parties and formal occasions that had once taken place in this town. She could almost hear the big bands that used to play.

Or maybe medium-size bands. It *was* Pronghorn, after all. Even in its glory days, the town was never exactly bustling.

But rather than music, the sound of a beleaguered sigh filled the room. Aida spun around to see Tate, defeated before they even started. It didn't help that she wasn't sure where to start. She'd never taught anyone anything, except for maybe their Miranda Rights. She thought back to all the times she'd seen Tate working with kids in the field next to her office. How did he start his lessons?

She studied him thoughtfully then gave him the best smile she could dredge up.

"Okay, are you ready to have some fun?"

TATE TRIED TO stop the ball with his foot, but it slipped. He tried with his other foot and it went flying across the ballroom. Because it was *slippery*, unlike every other ball used in athletic competition. Tate ran after the ball then broke down and grabbed it with both hands.

Humiliating himself in front of his coworkers and students was bad, but doing so in front of this beautiful woman was almost worse. He was terrible at soccer.

"Tate Ryman, that is no way to stop a ball." Aida was clearly losing what little patience she had.

"It's the *natural* way to stop a ball."

"I don't think that's true."

He ran his free hand through his hair. It was probably sticking straight up by now, but who cared? "Who came up with a sport then was, like, 'Oh, and don't use your hands.'"

"The people who didn't want their hands to get kicked really hard?" Aida guessed.

Tate grumbled as he set the ball down at his feet.

"Let's try again," Aida said.

"I'd prefer to complain."

She laughed, the soft, cheerful sound filling the room echoing back to him. She was so pretty when she was happy. She was pretty when she was mad, too, of course. But right now, he could imagine for a moment that they were there for the room's intended purpose: a party. He could be using that charm she'd accuse him of to ask her to dance, to monopolize her attention.

To let her know he was more than a terrible soccer player who inadvertently broke laws and had no restraint when it came to sandwich construction.

Aida noticed him staring and clammed up like she regretted allowing herself to find him funny. *Right*. She was there to teach him some basic skills so he'd get buy-in from the kids, not stand around while he tried unsuccessfully to flirt with her.

"Focus on a light touch to stop the motion of the ball." Aida demonstrated, skillfully setting her toe on the ball. "The gravity of your foot will do the rest."

She gave the ball a soft kick. He tried to stop it with a light touch but his foot slipped. Reactively, he stomped down, sending the soccer ball skittering across the smooth parquet floor.

"This would be a lot easier out on the field," she said, again.

"We don't need to be on the field." Other people did not need to see this. "We agreed, today is basic ball skills."

Aida turned away, but not before he saw how frustrated she was.

"I'm sorry," he said, again.

She stared up at the painted ceiling. Tate followed her gaze. Within the ring of skylights, there was a wholly Pronghorn version of a rococo mural; rather than cherubs and angels, there were leaping pronghorn antelope and stylized sagebrush.

Finally, Aida turned to him, expression serious. "Is this what teaching feels like?" she asked.

He wrinkled his brow, not understanding.

"Like, I'm trying really hard. And I want you to learn this skill. I just can't seem to…help you."

Take chuckled. "Right. You're patiently feeding

someone information and not snapping their head off when they don't follow the simplest directions? Yes. That's a lot of teaching. Multiply me by thirty and you'll get a sense of my job."

Aida's eyes widened, she looked horrified. Then the woman who spent her days pulling over drug runners and tracking down criminals said, "Why would *anyone* choose this career?"

He laughed.

"I'm serious," she said.

"Why would anyone choose to play this game?" he countered.

Her expression fell, a flicker of pain and longing giving her a momentary air of vulnerability. "I don't know that anyone chooses soccer. It's more that the game chose me."

He moved closer to Aida. "I think maybe the way you felt about soccer is similar to how I feel about teaching. Yes, it's hard, and it can be heartbreaking. But the profession makes sense to me."

She captured the ball with her toe, elegantly directing it inches to her other foot then back again across the slick parquet floor.

"Teaching chose me. It's the only career I've ever considered." Tate kept his eyes on the soccer ball as he admitted, "My parents wanted me to go into business." *After being a professional athlete.*

"What kind of business?" Aida asked.

Tate shrugged. "Business...business? Where you make the money while wearing the business suit." Aida laughed, encouraging him to keep going. "I don't even know what businesspeople do all day. Open and close their briefcases? Maybe point at charts while standing at the head of a conference table? I have no idea."

She laughed again. Tate realized they were now standing very close to each other, his chest rising and falling with laughter, his pulse elevated.

This was so much better than soccer.

"Welp. In order for you to do your job, I need to teach you how to play soccer." She stepped away. "Let's back up and start with a few toe taps."

Toe taps were the worst. They brought back memories of the app his dad had made him download to practice basic soccer skills when he was nine.

Watching Aida flash through an example set wasn't helping. After several bungled attempts, Aida seemed almost baffled by his ineptitude.

He really was that bad.

"Stop." Aida put a hand on his arm. It struck Tate that this whole situation would be a lot more fun if they were dancing. This *was* a ballroom, and ballroom dancing had been a requirement for his degree in physical education. "You're making this harder than it needs to be."

"No, I think it's exactly as hard as it is."

"Obviously, I just think we need to reel it in a little. Teaching is hard, we've established that. But helping you with a few soccer fundamentals shouldn't be *this* hard. You're athletic, with excellent coordination and instincts. There's something about soccer."

He kicked the ball, doing his best to imitate the angle of her kick.

Aida stopped the ball with her foot and gazed at him. "What is it?"

"What's what?"

"Why do you hate soccer?"

He shrugged.

"This makes no sense. You are absurdly social yet we're tucked away in the ballroom. It's like you don't want anyone to see you try to handle the ball."

"I don't," he admitted. "No one should have to witness this."

"Agreed. This is ugly."

Tate let out a breath. "I'm really bad at soccer."

"You are."

He gave a dry laugh.

"And I can't understand why," she added. "I've seen you move. You're good at every other physical activity. This makes no sense."

He puffed out a breath. He didn't relish her line of questioning. He did, however, appreciate the fact that she'd been watching him move.

"What happened?" she pressed.

Tate ran his fingers through his hair. From everything he'd learned from Flora, no one had had to pressure Aida to play. Or to practice. She was one of those rare athletes who had a special combination of talent, love of the game and drive. Those were the people who became truly great players.

Aida gave the ball a soft push with her toe and drifted toward him. She placed a hand on his arm.

The noise and confusion of the games came back to him. The anger in his coach's voice. The scent of over-watered lawns and Astroturf in the afternoon sun.

"My parents," he admitted. "My parents happened."

"They made you play soccer?" she guessed. "And you didn't want to."

"No, it's not that I didn't want to." Tate stalked away from Aida. "You wouldn't understand."

"I might if you explain it to me." Aida headed over to a stack of wooden, gilt-encrusted chairs and pulled two off the pile, gesturing for him to sit. "If you're going to get better, I need to understand what's going through your head that's making you so bad."

Tate dropped into the chair. A concerning creak of old wood made him readjust his position, but somehow the chair remained intact.

He ran his hands through his hair and glanced at Aida. Were they really gonna do this?

She was staring back at him, steady and concerned.

"Okay. There was a lot of pressure. Growing up."

She nodded, encouraging him to keep going.

"My parents were pretty athletic people. Wealthy, middle-aged athletes. You know the type?"

"Nope. That's not a big subgroup around here." Tate smiled.

Color crept into her cheeks, but she kept her eyes on him.

"Well, it is where I come from. *'We're an athletic family,'* my dad used to say whenever I balked at an added activity. They had me play soccer, run track and cross-country, play tennis, volleyball, basketball and water polo. I was supposed to play everything, like my siblings. Be *good* at everything."

"That's…a lot of sports."

"It is. And I did it. As a kid, I liked competing, winning, making my parents proud. I met most of their expectations. I was always big for my age, so I could run faster, swim faster. I was coordinated. I loved sports."

Aida smiled at him, the smile that felt like they could possibly be friends. That smile kept him talking.

"My parents got it in their heads that soccer was the key to a D1 college scholarship. They based this on what they projected my height would be, and the fact that I'd play defender. Dad decided soccer would be my primary sport."

"They picked your main sport?"

"Yep. I mean, I still had to play everything else, but Dad thought soccer was going to be the meal ticket."

"Seriously? Parents do that?"

"Parents do that all the time. I grew up in a wealthy suburb of Portland. Status was everything, and having a kid play on elite teams and in college is key."

She shook her head, the competitive parenting of suburbia clearly not sinking in. "Wait. They picked your sport based on the one they thought you had the best chance of playing in college?"

"Yes."

"And they picked soccer?"

"Right?" Tate shook his head. "Rowing would

have made sense, if we're talking purely physical build. Track and field, if the decision was based on something I was good at. Basketball, if it was about my personal passion. Male cheerleading, if we're thinking something without a lot of competition for college recruits. But soccer?"

"I'm trying not to judge your parents right now, but soccer scholarships are among the most competitive."

"Judge away. I've designed my adult life to undo the negative impact people like my parents have on kids."

Tate liked the way Aida folded her arms and arched her brow. It felt good to have her on his side. For this one issue, anyhow.

"They started putting the pressure on when I was nine. They signed me up for an elite club team."

"I knew a lot of women in college who played on seriously competitive club teams. Like Olympic Development stuff?"

"Kind of, but more expensive. So they signed me up. I didn't make the premier team. My dad—" Tate shook his head, remembering his dad's disappointment in him. "My dad was humiliated."

"Because you didn't make the very best team your first year in the competitive club?"

"Yep. I could feel his disappointment, game after game. It was a fast-moving downward spiral. He was embarrassed to be standing on the sidelines of anything less than the best team. I was self-conscious because of his disapproval. I played poorly, he was more embarrassed. It was my fault he was embarrassed, because I kept letting balls slip by."

"How long did this go on for?"

"Not long. Four months? I got worse, game by game. My coaches dropped me down another level. I messed up." Tate covered his face in his hands, remembering the ultimate, horrifying, humiliating moment of the soccer pitch. "I really messed up."

"Not…not a…" Aida was staring at him, pity spilling from her eyes. "You didn't make an own goal?"

"I did. The game wasn't going well and then a kid kicked the ball right between my feet. I looked down then turned around and got confused as we fought for the ball. I launched it away from him, straight into our goal. It was a total noob move."

Tate could still hear his teammates groaning, see the crack of a frown from his terse coach. Embarrassment and anger boiling through him in hot red waves.

Then a huge hand landing on his shoulder. His father marching him off the field.

"You're never going to be any good. You might as well quit now."

"Yeah, anyway, it didn't end well."

"Did your parents allow you to quit?"

He tilted his head, evading the question. "Well, that was my last soccer game."

"Wait, did your *parents* pull you from the team?" Aida was mad now, like she got when he tried to talk his way out of a ticket. "They pulled you from the team for one mistake?"

"They pulled me from the team because I was horrible," Tate clarified.

"They pulled you from the team because of their own egos," Aida countered. "Defenders make own goals, it happens all the time. Particularly when you're nine."

Tate turned to Aida, appreciative of how close she was. "Did you ever get confused and accidentally score for the other team?"

Aida scoffed. "No." Then she quickly realized her mistake. "But that's different. I don't play all sports well, I played one sport obsessively. And I never got the chance to—" Her words cut abruptly. Aida stared down at the floor.

The silence of the empty ballroom crowded in, stifling further conversation. Questions bubbled up in Tate's mind, but none of them felt right. He started to take her hand. *That* felt like the right fit. Fortunately, he managed to remember they didn't have that type of relationship before his fingers made contact.

Tate pulled in a deep breath then asked, "What did you never get the chance to do?"

She shook her head, lips pressed together.

Tate understood that no matter how unpleasant his soccer memories were, they didn't compare to her loss.

Aida gave him a grateful smile for not pushing it and sat back in her chair.

"Did your dad ever get over it?" she asked.

"Eh, yes and no. I redeemed myself over time in other sports. I was a star in high school track and basketball. But I betrayed his expectations by refusing to play sports in college. After my soccer experience, I knew I didn't want to play any sport at a high level. Not in college and certainly not professionally." He closed his eyes, trying to block out his father's voice, his disappointment that his only son was going into teaching. "I was supposed to be a great athlete."

Aida glanced up at him, concern and confusion on her face. "You *are* a great athlete. I mean you're a terrible soccer coach, and way too loud."

"Some people think I'm too charming."

She hit his arm.

"Ouch!" Tate rubbed at the spot she'd tapped him, really wishing she'd do it again.

"You're a great athlete. And a wonderful example to the kids of a lifetime of pleasure in physical activity. When you think about it, you *are* a professional athlete. One with job security, health insurance, federal holidays."

"And a camouflage all-terrain vehicle to drive."

"You *are* a great athlete," she repeated.

She was serious. She wasn't trying to be encouraging or to make him feel better. She was stating the truth as she saw it.

And just like that, her words became *his* truth. He was a great athlete.

He was a great athlete who hadn't done particularly well in soccer at the age of nine. As a man, he'd turned his father's harsh words into the foundation of his inclusive teaching practices.

He felt so much better.

Why had it taken him so long to tell anyone? And why had he told Aida?

He glanced at her again.

Right. Because she was so beautiful, he'd probably spill any and all state secrets. Or Tate secrets, as it were.

"Thank you," he said, not sure if he could ever get across what this meant to him. "You're right. I've been focusing on one negative experience rather than seeing the whole situation."

She made an overly casual shrug, as though she were trying to backpedal the connection she'd forged between them. "From my point of view, the whole situation is going pretty well."

"If only I can stop breaking laws."

"This is day four of a no-ticket streak."

Tate bent his head so he could look directly into her eyes. "Am I going to offend you by reminding you that you're a great athlete too?"

Something unreadable flickered crossing her face.

"Baiting an officer is a ticketable offense."

Tate laughed. He laughed so hard he knew he was on the verge of bellowing, but it was hard to care with Aida gazing up at him, laughing too.

"Cookies!" Sylvie's voice called. "Cookie time in the courtyard."

Neither of them moved. Tate was disinclined to ever move, unless maybe he could move closer to Aida.

A flush ran up her cheeks.

Would kissing be okay here?

No. No way. Where had that come from?

She was still the sheriff who had it out for him, even if she was wearing a tank top that showed off her shoulders, and had just brought closure to some of his painful past experiences.

Her eyes dropped to his lips.

"You guys coming?" Willa poked her head in the ballroom then spun around to examine the faded, elegant space. "Wow. This is beautiful."

"Be right there," Tate said.

Aida stood. "I guess it's cookie time."

"Cookie time isn't unusual around here. Luci is a big fan of cookies, and Sylvie is expressing her excitement over the upcoming wedding by creating hand-held desserts."

"Nothing wrong with that." Aid gave him a quick smile then took several paces toward the door.

Tate reached out and caught her arm. "Thank you." He gestured to the soccer ball. "Really, thank you for all of this."

"I should have offered to help earlier. I didn't know the whole situation."

Tate gazed at her, acutely aware that he didn't know her whole situation either.

AIDA WALKED QUICKLY back to the courtyard, intent on getting out of there.

Had she seriously thought about kissing Tate? *Tate?* Of all the men she'd met in her life, she was catching a crush on this loud, law-ignoring, soccer-disdaining recidivist?

Also a really handsome, thoughtful, funny recidivist.

Aida entered the courtyard a few steps ahead of Tate to find the whole crew of teachers, along with Colter and Sylvie, standing around a plate of cookies. Tate strode over and grabbed two cookies, popping one into his mouth after the other, and somehow making a joke at the same time.

Classic Tate.

He reached for another cookie then held it up for her. The warm, nutty scent wafted toward her.

Okay, maybe she'd grab one cookie before she left.

She would walk over and pick up her own cookie, not the one Tate was offering, because that felt weirdly romantic. She'd grab her own cookie, say goodbye and go.

Aida's feet refused to acknowledge their role in that scenario.

As sheriff, and one of the few unmarried people in town, Aida didn't socialize much. She had learned to be social on a soccer team. A team was an instant friend group, but also a place where egos and feelings needed to be negotiated and relationships maintained. She was good on a team and, over time, had developed a reputation as someone who could unite a group. She was a good friend, too, but she'd never had to actually make friends. She had no idea how it was done.

Greg trotted over and sat next to her, leaning his soft head against her thigh.

Okay, she'd made one friend in her life, and she couldn't ask for a kinder, fuzzier or more loyal one.

Luci turned around abruptly and gestured for Aida to join them. "Come on, cookies."

"Do you like pecans?" Sylvie asked, holding out the plate.

Aida couldn't tell a pecan from a pine nut if the final score of a game depended on it. Did she like pecans? Probably.

"Yes, thank you." Aida grabbed a cookie and bit into it. Soft, crumbly goodness spilled after the bite and Aida quickly caught the remains in her hands. She took a second bite of the buttery cookie.

The jury had returned. She loved pecans.

"This is fantastic, Sylvie. Thank you."

Sylvie beamed at the compliment then nibbled on one of the strings of her oversize hoodie.

"How'd he do in there?" Vander asked, gesturing at the ballroom.

Aida glanced at Tate. "We made some progress."

"Did we?" Tate asked, thirteen decibels above everyone else.

"Yeah," Aida said. "We established that this is possible for you."

His gaze connected with hers and he nodded. "That's a start."

Aida grabbed another cookie.

Conversation veered off in the direction of Loretta Lazarus, the teachers cracking jokes and stepping on one another's words to get the next witty comment in. Their conversation was like a complex game she was in no way prepared to play.

So she'd just have to stand around eating cookies. There were worse fates.

"Are you cold?" Luci asked her abruptly. "You look cold."

"I'm fine." Aida rubbed her arms. Temperatures dropped quickly in Pronghorn, and she should probably head home anyway.

"Come up to my room, we'll grab you a sweater."

Aida gestured to the door. "Well, I should—"

"If I don't loan you a sweater, you'll get cold and have to go home. Then who's gonna be here to help me make fun of Tate? Come on." Luci grabbed her arm.

"The striped one or the argyle one?" Mateo drawled as they walked away from the table.

"It's better than the choice of sweater we'd find in your room—the old one or the shabby one."

"My favorite sweater is always the clean one," he yelled after them.

"Slim pickings," Luci called back.

Aida followed Luci up the grand set of stairs in the foyer, fully prepared for Fred Astaire and Ginger Rogers to come waltzing down in the opposite direction at any moment.

Greg trailed after them, as though he understood that Luci was the path to hedgehogs.

"The elevator might work, but we always take

the stairs," Luci said. "We honestly don't know and none of us really wants to put it to the test."

Aida wanted to say something clever, or funny. Something a friend would say. All she could come up with was, "Good call."

"And besides, I kind of like taking the stairs," Luci continued. "It feels old school."

Given that Luci dressed in classic, preppy clothing and didn't step outside the hotel in anything that wasn't pressed and perfectly coordinated, old school seemed appropriate.

They emerged from the stairs into a bright hallway. Gold-framed pictures of flowers hung at regular intervals in between large mirrors and deep-set windows.

"I've never been up here before," Aida said.

"Never?"

"No. The hotel closed down before I was born."

"But you never snuck into the kitchen window through the shed roof?"

Aida laughed. "Yeah, actually. That's how everyone snuck in. I was just too chicken to go upstairs." This was fun; they were having a normal conversation like two people of the same age who might be friends. Aida continued, "How do you know about the kitchen window?"

Luci froze for a barely perceptible second.

The police officer in Aida cataloged everything about the moment. Luci's uncharacteristic stillness, the tilt of her chin, the evacuation of color from her face. The sense of being trapped.

Then Luci shook her head. "I must have heard one of the kids talking about it." She turned her bright smile on Aida. "I jammed that window closed with a two-by-four, by the way. So don't get any ideas of sneaking in to give Tate some clandestine soccer lessons."

Since understanding how young people used to sneak into the hotel wasn't a crime, or even a concern really, Aida rolled with the new circumstances while tucking away the reaction.

"I promise not to give Tate any unsanctioned time with the soccer ball."

"Good. I wouldn't put it past him to deflate every ball in a twenty-mile radius."

Luci pushed open the door to her room. The walls were painted pale pink, a soft complement to the gleaming oak floors. To the right was a small sitting area with polished antiques in the same pale green fabrics found in the rest of the hotel. To her left was an old-fashioned wrought-iron bed piled with crisp white bedding and an army of throw pillows. The room was neatly organized and free of clutter, with the exception of a cardboard box lined with a fuzzy blanket. Greg trotted over and curled up next to the box, even though it was empty of spiny nocturnal creatures.

"Are all the teacher's rooms this nice?" Aida asked.

"No," Luci said. "They all started out this nice, but *some* people keep their rooms clean and others... not so much."

Aida had a pretty good idea of who Luci was mess-shaming. Good thing Luci couldn't see Aida's room.

Luci walked decisively to her closet where color-coordinated blouses and sweaters hung on fancy padded hangers. Skirts, trousers and, yes, even jeans, hung neatly down the line. Luci pulled out one sweater, reconsidered and grabbed a second.

With her back to Aida, she said, "Technically, we are here to get you a sweater, but I also wanted to hear how things went with Tate. We're all worried about him."

"How so?" Aida asked.

"Because he's being so weird about soccer. Of all of us, he is the most enthusiastic, fun, confident—"

"Loud," Aida added.

"That too. He loves being the center of attention. He loves working with kids. But when you send him out to soccer practice, it's like he's heading into an abandoned junkyard full of feral dogs."

"That's quite an image." Aida could picture the fear and resignation on his face, soccer as the pile of old junk he didn't want to deal with, and unhappy students ready to snarl when he did the wrong thing. She could imagine nine-year-old Tate, humiliated and not wanting to let down his dad.

"You'd think he'd never played a sport or given a kid direction in his life. I want to know what's so terrible about soccer. And if he won't tell me, I'm hoping you can get it out of him, as a fellow athlete. It's worrisome."

It had been upsetting to see Tate so hesitant to play

soccer, even if Aida didn't entirely love his regular, everyday gregarious nature. It was also incredibly sweet that the teachers were looking out for one another.

Or rather, Luci was looking out for Tate, specifically.

Oh. Wait.

"Um, yeah…" Aida started to voice her concern. Or *not* concern. Comprehension. Luci, a beautiful woman with everything in common with Tate, was sharing *other* things with Tate.

She started to ask, various syllables stumbling out, but by the time she got the question formulated and she'd settled on a coherent sentence, Luci was raising her eyebrows, eyes bright and mischievous.

"What's up?"

"Oh, nothing. I just… So. You and Tate?"

Luci laughed out loud, a Tate-level guffaw.

"I was thinking, he's…and you…"

"Tate and I are good friends. We're like siblings," Luci said. "I'm not nearly athletic enough for him and he's way too tall for my taste."

Aida didn't take any time to process the fact that her breathing had regulated and her blood was once again pulsing through her veins at a reasonable pace, a reaction most would associate with relief. Instead, she asked, "You don't like tall men?"

"I need to be able to look someone in the eye when we're arguing."

Interesting. Also interesting? Luci and Mateo

were almost the exact same height, and they did argue an awful lot.

Luci, social scientist that she was, pinned Aida with a look. "Tate is very much single."

Aida redirected her gaze to a framed print of a day lily and said, "So that's not why you're worried about him."

"No. We've all been worried since we first learned these kids were soccer players. Any one of us would have taken this on for Tate, even though we're not coaches and I've literally never seen a soccer game."

Okay, so maybe it wasn't just Aida who needed Luci as a friend, maybe Luci needed Aida. Because how had she never seen a soccer game?

"It's not been going well for him, and we're all glad he reached out to you for help, and that you graciously agreed."

"Full disclosure, I wasn't super gracious."

"You're here. And given that Tate can't so much as walk out the door without breaking a law around here, it's generous of you. But it's a big step for him, then you show up and then…the ballroom? How weird is that?"

Arguably, on the Pronghorn scale of weird, it barely made the register. It was a bad idea, but in this town, you had to work a lot harder than soccer in a ballroom to be considered weird.

Luci held up a sweater to Aida then rejected it and returned to combing through her closet. "I mean, don't get me wrong, I love a good ballroom, but it's almost like he didn't want anyone to see him play."

Aida nodded noncommittally. That was exactly what he'd wanted, but he hadn't given Aida permission to share the reason.

He'd told her a secret he hadn't told his friends, somehow letting her into his most vulnerable spot. And, judging from his reaction, she'd done a pretty good job lifting a little of his pain.

Huh.

"So you'll tell me?" Luci asked somewhere between a question and a command. "When you find out why he hates soccer?"

"I promise to tell him to tell you, so you won't worry so much," Aida said. "But I think…or I hope, anyway, that he's going to be okay."

Luci crossed her arms, preparing to argue.

Aida braced herself.

Then Luci shook her head. "That's a really good answer."

"Thanks."

"I don't like it, but it's good. Here." Luci held up a cream-colored sweater with navy stripes running horizontally. "How do you feel about Breton stripes?"

"I feel like I'm going to look like you if I put on this sweater."

"What could be better?" Luci grinned, slipped the sweater off the hanger and handed it to Aida.

Aida battled her way into the garment. Her head popped out to meet Luci's evaluative gaze.

"You look great in stripes. We should be friends."

THE LIGHT WAS beginning to fade as they walked into the courtyard. Strings of twinkle lights glowed and hedgehogs rustled in the bushes. The teachers sat around the table, talking with one another.

At the center of it all was Tate, his head back and laughing. Letting out a bellow.

He leapt up when he saw her. "Hey! You're back."

"What did you think was going to happen to her?" Vander asked.

"I'm just saying." He turned to Aida. "You've returned."

"I have," Aida confirmed. She checked reactions from the others to see how this behavior struck them. Did he always celebrate people returning in sweaters?

Tate pulled out a wrought-iron chair, its legs scraping the flagstones. "Have a seat."

"Okay."

Mateo smirked at Tate. "You gonna take her order next?"

"I'm being polite," he snapped. He shook his head at Aida in disbelief. "Some people." His eyes dipped to the sweater then back to her face. "You look pretty...warmer. You look pretty warm."

Aida couldn't miss Mateo's eye roll or Colter trying to repress a laugh.

"That's a nice sweater. Luci has nice sweaters, and a lot of them."

He was rambling. Aida scooped up her soccer ball. She really needed to get out of there.

The rumble of an ATV caught her attention. A loud sound like a whoop or hoot came from the street outside.

Someone was having a rowdy Friday night. That might not raise any red flags in another town, but here? People didn't have rowdy Friday nights in Pronghorn, and anyone who might be inclined to such behavior was literally within five feet of Aida at this moment.

The whoop-hoot happened again and the motor cut out, setting the hairs on her arm to rise.

"Shhh!" she commanded.

"What, am I creating a public nuisance—?" Tate asked.

"Quiet." She grabbed his arm to silence him. That meant she was holding on to his arm. His very strong, athletic arm. A fabulous arm, really.

The hooting sound came again. She forced herself to drop her grip on Tate and advanced on the archway opening from the courtyard into the street.

It was a human noise, but a voice she wasn't familiar with.

"What is that?" she asked her dog.

Tate responded, "Teenagers."

CHAPTER SIX

AIDA AND GREG launched themselves toward the courtyard's entrance and ran out into the street. Tate grabbed a cookie and followed. He wouldn't have noticed the sounds if Aida hadn't pointed them out, but it was concerning. The whooping didn't just sound like teenagers, it sounded like teenagers about to do something unwise.

An ATV was parked haphazardly in front of the school and the telltale sounds of two kids getting into trouble echoed through the empty town.

It took less than a minute to find Antonio and Suleiman in the dirt parking lot next to the cafeteria. The two boys had a can of deck stain, a six-inch paintbrush and, bizarrely, a drop cloth spread out at their feet.

It had to be the worst attempt at vandalism he'd ever seen.

Aida advanced on the pair. "Hold it right there," she commanded.

Antonio lowered the brush then looked significantly at Suleiman.

"Whose ATV is that?" Aida barked.

Antonio stepped forward. "It belongs to Ms. Raquel. My host."

"Does she know you have it?" Aida asked.

"No."

"Does she know you're gone?"

"No."

Aida shook her head and let out a sigh. "Attempted vandalism, absconding with a vehicle, creating a public nuisance." Aida reached into her back pocket, like she did when pulling out her ticket book, then stopped. She glanced down as though just realizing she was wearing soccer shorts and one of Luci's striped Breton sweaters.

"Ugh! I forgot my ticket book."

"*You* forgot your ticket book?" Tate asked.

"Technically, I'm off duty."

"But you were coming to see me and you didn't bring the book?"

Aida rolled her eyes.

"I want you two to wait right here," she said to the exchange students. "And don't bother trying to run because I know where everyone lives."

The boys weren't trying to run. They also weren't trying to excuse their behavior. They were standing there, shoulders back, attempting to look guilty.

"Aida, stop," Tate called after her.

She spun around and gave him a curious look.

"Let me..." He paused, unsure of how to put this. *Let me teacher* was the phrase he was going for. But Willa was less than two hundred yards away in the hotel and could sense a noun being made into a verb. Her vengeance would be swift. "Let me handle this."

Tate studied Antonio's sullen expression then Suleiman's. "What are you two up to?"

Suleiman gestured to the deck stain and the school, as though it were obvious.

"Vandalism. Okay. What were you going to write?"

The boys glanced at one another, as though this detail hadn't been worked out.

"Pronghorn sucks?" Tate guessed.

"Maybe." Suleiman looked to Antonio for confirmation.

Tate pressed his lips together. Laughing would not help the situation. But he suspected their world language teachers hadn't covered the American slang for insulting a small town. Google Translate might have been involved if they hadn't caught the kids.

"Taking the ATV could be construed as stealing, and you two are trying to vandalize the school. Beyond getting a ticket, you know you could get kicked out of the program for this?"

The words seemed to land on the dirt at their feet, heavy and serious. They didn't so much as flinch.

Tate examined the boys thoughtfully. "Are you *trying* to get kicked out of the program?"

Suleiman shrugged. Antonio reddened but kept his focus on the ground.

"You're trying to get kicked out of the exchange program and sent home." He whistled. "Man. That's a big deal. You must be miserable here."

"This place is miserable," Suleiman muttered.

"This isn't where we're supposed to be," Antonio said.

Tate gazed out at the Warner Valley, dry prairie grasses and sagebrush undulating in all directions until it met the border of rimrock Hart Mountain, smoky-blue in the distance.

"Where were you supposed to be?" Tate asked.

"I thought…" Antonio trailed off.

"You thought, maybe, Los Angeles?" Tate asked.

"Yes," Suleiman said. "Or New York City. Or Miami."

"Okay. Makes sense." Tate raised his arms and gestured to their surroundings. "You thought you'd be in an awesome big city, but you wound up here."

Suleiman glanced around, suspicious, like the place might be getting more remote by the minute.

"What do you hate about Pronghorn?"

The boys looked at each other, unsure of where Tate was going with this.

"It's okay. Let it out. I arrived here a month ago, and I hated it too."

"Will she get mad at us?" Suleiman asked, nodding at Aida.

"She only gets mad at me."

Aida harrumphed. Greg took a few steps and sat between Suleiman and Antonio, suggesting that at least someone was on their side. Tate kept his focus on the boys. "I'll start. The town is too small."

"It's not even a town," Antonio said.

"And the people are weird," Suleiman added.

"Right?" Tate agreed. "I think every single person in this town is a little weird. But you'll probably find that to be true in LA, or Miami."

Antonio shrugged. "Rio too."

"I don't like the food," Suleiman added.

"My host mom serves zucchini and venison casserole on many nights," Antonio said. "It's hard to be polite."

"That's legit," Tate said. "The food is terrible here."

"The internet doesn't work at school," Suleiman said. "All my friends in Senegal want to see America and I can't post any pictures."

Antonio held up his phone. "I can't message anyone except when I'm with my host family."

"Is Raquel pretty strict about when you get to use your phone?"

Antonio rolled his eyes. They were starting to get somewhere.

"And then you have me. The worst soccer coach in America."

Suleiman nodded enthusiastically.

"Eh. You are getting a little better," Antonio offered.

"Thank you."

"It's nothing."

Aida looked both confused *and* like she was about to spit fire as he facilitated students complaining about her hometown. It was a lot cuter than she could possibly intend. He winked at her. This wasn't over yet.

"So, you two apply to an exchange program, and it's pretty competitive, am I right?"

"Very competitive, to come to America."

"And your friends and families back home think you're going to be hanging out with Taylor Swift and playing football with David Beckham."

"Tyler Adams," Suleiman corrected.

"Of course." Tate had to assume Tyler Adams was a major soccer star, but he had no idea. "Then you're stuck in Pronghorn." Tate let out a breath. "That's a bummer."

Aida was now following the conversation with curiosity. Finally, she got to witness something he was competent with: misbehaving teenagers.

"It's not just that we're—" Suleiman looked around, defeated "—here. I have to keep up with football, or I will lose my place on the team back home."

"Me too," Antonio said.

The two boys stared miserably at their attempted graffiti, beginning to comprehend that it wasn't getting them the ticket out of here that they wanted.

"Okay, so you're sent to Oregon, which wasn't your first choice. Then you are convinced to move to an even smaller town with a truly terrible soccer program. And, meanwhile, everyone back home thought you were going to someplace cool, but you can't take pictures of yourself doing something awesome, or American, let alone post them. And the food is bad. Do I have it all?"

Antonio shifted, not quite comfortable with the assessment. "The school *is* nice."

"Is it?" Tate asked.

"Very good. I like the teachers."

"I appreciate the students in orange," Suleiman added.

"That's great. I bet that's a new experience, going to school with kids from a—" Tate didn't finish the sentence. *Rural hippie commune* felt disrespectful, but also accurate.

"Intentional living community of shared values," Aida filled in.

"Right." He pointed to Aida. "What she said."

"Yes. They are kind. All the students are welcoming."

Tate bobbled his head, not committing to the positivity just yet. "It's possible you might make some friends?"

"I have friends," Suleiman asserted. He pointed to Antonio. "Antonio. Oliver, Antithesis, Mav."

"That's a good crew," Tate admitted. "Look, I'm not going to ask you to like Pronghorn. I'm not going to try to convince you to stay. In fact, if you need someone to kick you out of the program, I'm happy to do so if we can make a deal."

Antonio glanced from Tate to the sheriff, still suspicious. "What do we have to do?"

"Give it two weeks," Tate said simply.

"Just two weeks?"

"Two weeks. I am, as you kindly noted, getting better at coaching. Sheriff Weston here is seeing to that."

She nodded.

"And we have a field trip planned for you."

"What is a field trip?" Suleiman asked as Antonio said, "We're going to a field?"

"We're going to a ranch. Sylvie's dad has invited you out to see his horse rescue operation."

"Who is Sylvie?" Suleiman asked.

Antonio nodded his head toward the front of the school. "She is the cute girl who reads in the lobby and brings cookies."

"Ooooh, Sylvie."

Tate held out a hand. "Do yourselves a favor and don't think of her as the cute girl. She's young for her grade and her stepmom-to-be is your English teacher."

Antonio was dead serious as he told Tate, "There are many cute girls at this school."

"Well, that's another win for Pronghorn, I guess?" Tate glanced at Aida who was trying to keep from laughing. "Things are looking better. At the ranch, Colter is going to teach you all to ride horses, then we'll have a traditional American barbecue."

"Will we wear the hats?" Suleiman asked.

"The hats?"

"Like the cowboy wears." Suleiman used his hands to indicate something like a cowboy hat. Tate remembered the boxes of hats Colter had collected during his days as a rodeo star. He'd given one to Vander, and offered them to all the teachers. Tate didn't feel right in the hat, but Suleiman in a Stetson would make for a seriously Instagram-worthy picture.

"Absolutely." Tate promised. "Stetson hats for all."

Suleiman looked at Antonio and the boys nodded.

"Two weeks," Antonio confirmed.

TATE RYMAN WAS pure teacher magic.

Aida had been ready to throw the boys in the back of the Ford Interceptor, drive them all the way to Lakeview and drop them off at the station. Now Tate had them anticipating the most Pronghorn activity she could think of: horseback riding and a barbecue at C & S Ranch.

He'd gotten the kids excited about staying here, at least for two weeks. And, *man*, did he look good doing it. He wasn't angry, didn't yell. He listened, validated their feelings and then presented some alternate information.

No, it wasn't just that. He must have planned the trip to Colter's some time ago, already recognizing the kids needed more than soccer to connect them with Pronghorn. As a citizen of Pronghorn, Tate was annoying and unable to follow basic rules, but as a teacher, he was a magician.

What would he come up with next?

"Then the following weekend, the Open Hearts Intentional Community have invited you out to take part in their harvest celebration."

"Mav told us about that festival," Antonio said.

Suleiman nodded, a slow smile growing across his face. "I would like to see the harvest celebration."

Aida felt good, like it was cool to be part of making a kid smile. Or, maybe she didn't make him smile. But she kind of was a part of this, being the person who was helping Tate not be the worst coach ever.

Tate pulled out his phone and checked for an internet signal. "I'm going to text your host families and let them know what happened. That means you're going to get a lecture from Raquel when you get home." He pointed to Antonio, who sighed in acknowledgment of his fate. He turned to Suleiman. "And while Edie and Bryce are probably more worried than angry, you still need to apologize."

"I am sorry," Suleiman said. "You will tell them about our deal?"

"I will." Tate tapped on a contact in his phone and began typing.

Then Suleiman turned his big grin on Aida and called over his shoulder to Tate, "Tell them I'll give it two weeks, if *madame* agrees to coach soccer with you."

Wait, the kids were bringing her into this? Aida straightened. "This isn't a negotiation."

"Yes, it is," Antonio said.

"That's exactly what it is," Tate agreed and turned back to his phone.

All the warm and fuzzy feelings she'd been harboring for Tate washed away.

"Well, then, no. Sorry. I'm not coaching."

Suleiman shrugged theatrically and asked, "What's so bad about coaching? List the reasons."

"Well, it's a big commitment—" Aida stated then

shook her head. "Oh, no, I see what you're doing here."

"'Let it all out,'" he quoted Tate.

Despite herself Aida couldn't help but laugh. "You are too smart for your own good."

Suleiman made a circular gesture near his chest, encouraging her to speak.

"Fine. I don't have enough time to coach. I'm too competitive. I'm not going to deal well if the team loses, and no one needs to see that. Like, that's already a concern and I'm not even involved."

"Yes, I agree. I hate to lose."

"What else?" Antonio asked.

"Um, what else? I don't like teenagers. They're annoying."

Tate looked up sharply from his phone.

"Please don't tell kids they're annoying," he snapped at her, moving protectively in front of two people who were about to write *Pronghorn Sucks* in deck stain on the side of the school.

"But we are annoying," Antonio said. "We've been trying very hard."

"We stole a vehicle," Suleiman reminded him.

Aida laughed even harder. Tears sprung to her eyes as the boys backed up her assertion.

"Okay, I actually like you two, now that I've gotten to know you."

"We are very likable," Antonio said, "when we want to be."

"What else is there?" Suleiman asked.

Aida pulled in a deep breath. She looked at Suleiman then Antonio. She thought about Ilsa. "You guys are probably the good players back home, right? Like stars on your team?"

"We're the good players here too."

"Yeah, right. Of course. You know how good it feels to be the best? Everyone is cheering for you, they know you'll carry the game."

"Yes."

"That used to be me," she admitted. "And sometimes it's hard to remember those days."

The boys seemed confused. Tate moved toward her, like he was using all five senses to figure out what she meant by this.

She cleared her throat, trying to sound casual. "I miss it. I miss playing."

"Then be a coach," Antonio suggested.

Be a coach. Just coach. It was the final resting place of all great players, and some mediocre ones too. As though running drills and yelling from the sidelines could ever take the place of playing.

"It's not the same thing."

The boys nodded. She could tell they didn't get it, but they were kind enough to nod. Tate gazed at her, like he *did* get it. And she didn't like that one bit. She shook out her shoulders and adopted a cheerful tone. "I don't think I'd like coaching."

"I'm not asking you to like it," Suleiman said. "Just give it two weeks."

She let out a dry laugh. "I cannot argue with your logic, can I?"

"It worked on me," he admitted.

"So this is Coach Tate's fault, right?" She hiked a thumb at him. "If I'm stuck coaching, we can blame him?"

"I take all responsibility," Tate said, raising his hands.

Aida studied the boys. They were homesick and unsure of this place they'd landed in. She felt the same way sometimes, homesick for her youth and her days on the field, unsure of this adult life she found herself living.

Returning to the game as a coach was going to be painful, but in doing so she would lessen the pain these kids were feeling. There was only one thing to do.

"Okay."

"Okay?" Tate asked.

"Sure, whatever. It's not a big deal. I can stick it out for two weeks."

Tate gazed at her and the desire to kiss him returned. That had to stop. She tossed the ball she held under her arm in the air.

"Quick scrimmage? Me and Coach Tate against you two?"

The boys responded enthusiastically, calling boundaries, dragging their toes through the dirt to mark goal posts. Greg trotted alongside them, excited by the action.

Tate was hesitant but not unwilling. "You want me on your team?"

Aida gave him a smile. "Against teenagers? You're my first pick."

He held her eye for a moment. The Tate Magic was strong, inspiring her to consider several bad ideas.

Then, all in one moment, Aida dropped the ball and nudged it with her toe. She was playing again, for the first time in five years.

Suleiman tried to steal, as he'd been stealing literally every ball since he'd arrived in Pronghorn. She did a quick tap and spun the ball to her other side then charged past him. He stumbled over his feet as he raced to catch up. She passed the ball to Tate, who executed a respectful stop, dribbled a few feet and kept it away from Antonio long enough to pass it back to her.

Even the boys cheered.

As they played, two on two, everything she loved about the game flowed back to her. For those brief moments in the dirt parking lot of Pronghorn Public Day school, she was no longer lost and sad. She was fast again, and still the best player on the pitch. She lost all track of time, of herself, of everything but the score, which, at five to three, was a little close for her liking.

Aida threw a foot in front of Suleiman, quick enough to grab the ball and retreat before she could be accused of tripping him. But rather than get angry and try to retrieve his ball, Suleiman stopped in his charge.

"Look!" He pointed. "It's the deer."

On the edge of town, a herd of pronghorn watched with interest. Their golden-brown fur caught the light as the sun set. Long curving horns extended from their heads, as though the species was so majestic, they grew their own crowns.

"Those are pronghorn antelope," Tate said, coming to stand next to Suleiman as they stared in awe. Greg leaned up against Suleiman and the teenager absently petted him while watching the antelope.

The pronghorn stared back, wondering at this new human nonsense in their valley.

"You know they're the fastest land animals in the Americas?" Tate said. "They can run sixty miles an hour."

"Uau!" Antonio said.

"Does that mean 'wow'?" Aida asked.

Antonio kept his eyes on the herd, speaking softly. "It means...*uau.*"

The four of them, still catching their breath from the game, stood together watching the pronghorn as the sun slipped behind the Coyote Hills.

"It's getting late," Tate said. "Time to send you boys home."

Time to return to real life.

The boys cleaned up their vandalism supplies then got back on the ATV. Antonio expertly maneuvered into the street and around Connie, who sat alert and ready for cat action in the twilight.

Vander's music wafted into the street and, in the courtyard of the hotel, she could hear a spirited conversation between Mateo and Luci. Greg ran ahead of her, tongue lolled out in greeting as he entered the courtyard.

"That was quite the Friday night," Aida said.

Tate grinned at her. "It was fun."

"Yeah."

It *was* fun. The most fun she'd had in a very long time.

"And it's not even over, 'cause guess what we've got at the hotel?"

"Crisp table linens?"

"An internet signal!" he said, emphasizing the excitement of this development with two hands in the air.

"Dang. Wild night in Pronghorn."

"Wanna watch some cat videos?"

"Greg and I are always down for a cat video. And did you say something about another sandwich earlier?"

"I did. Let's get it."

Aida laughed as he dramatically headed to the intersection to cross the street back to the hotel. Hard to believe, but maybe Tate Ryman might have landed in the right place, after all.

CHAPTER SEVEN

THE LIGHT SHINING through the west window of Aida's office seemed brighter than normal. Greg paced by the door. Her heart paced in her chest, knocking against one side of her rib cage then the other. She glanced out the window. At least thirty people had chairs set up along the sidelines to watch practice.

That was a small town for you. Soccer practice was the most interesting thing going on in a hundred-mile radius.

She checked the time on her phone. Three fourteen.

Ugh. But also, *yay!*

Since *ugh-yay* wasn't a word, and shouldn't be a feeling, she'd have to go with something else. Maybe Antonio's *uau.*

Aida pulled on a sweatshirt and yanked the door open. The fresh fall air *seemed* like an innocent harbinger of winter. That was the type of thing "fresh fall air" was always getting up to. What it really meant was soccer season.

Aida took a step out of the door, then another, forcing herself toward the soccer field.

Greg trotted ahead, scanning the crowds for anything that might be amiss. Finding nothing but the citizens of Pronghorn sitting in lawn chairs, he turned back to her, clearly questioning her nerves.

"You wouldn't get it," she told him under her breath.

He stepped closer, pressing his soft, furry side into her leg, suggesting he was there for her anyway. On the sidelines, Tate was joking with Aida's grammy and Mrs. Moran, who both sat in lawn chairs. The two of them had been friends since JFK was in office and were always getting up to something.

Flora waved at her.

Awesome. Literally half the town was here, including her grandma.

Aida was intensely aware of people watching as she approached the field. Out of the corner of her eye, she saw Raquel Holmes turn to Melissa O'Conner and whisper something. The grizzled old rancher Pete Sorel stood as she passed by, like she was a coffin at her own funeral.

She kept her focus on the soccer pitch. Most of the kids were already juggling or passing balls back and forth to one another. Mav was doing some kind of wild stretching exercise, made all the more dramatic by his long, gangly limbs. Other students were coming out of the school to watch the practice as well.

She turned her attention back to Tate. He was

now having a serious conversation with Cece near the goal. She wasn't dressed for practice. He was patient with the girl, but Aida recognized his stance and expression. He was probably asking her to give it two weeks.

Aida came to a stop at the sidelines.

Was she really going to do this? Get involved and get her heart broken again?

A low whine drew her attention. Greg glanced up at her, communicating something along the lines of, *Go on, now.*

She ran a hand over his fuzzy head. "Fine."

Greg turned in the direction of Luci, suggesting he might like to sit with the neatly dressed blond woman, who may or may not have a few hedgehogs in the basket she was carrying.

Aida nodded and Greg trotted over, mouth open in a wide dog smile.

"*Madame!* Hello, welcome!" Suleiman's bright smile broke out as he launched a ball toward her. Aida reacted, stopping the ball, dribbling a few feet then launching it back to him.

Antonio raced over to her, talking a mile a minute about which international teams Aida supported. She was confidently able to say Brazil was on her list.

Ilsa looked up with interest then asked Suleiman, "Is she here for us?"

Aida responded, "I'm helping out for now."

Ilsa's eyes widened. For the first time since arriving in Pronghorn, this student from the Netherlands seemed hopeful. Aida didn't want to get anyone's hopes up unnecessarily, particularly on the soccer field.

"It's a trial, for a couple of weeks," Aida reiterated.

"For me too," Suleiman reminded her.

Ilsa got a sly smile on her face. "That makes six of us."

"Hey there, welcome!" Tate was heading toward her. His bright smile and easy saunter were a stark contrast to what she'd seen of him on the soccer field so far. The breeze pushed his dark hair up on his forehead, making him look like a model at an open call for Handsome Soccer Coach. He was his regular, joyful, law-breaking self.

Same guy she'd almost kissed in the ballroom Friday night.

Aida waved awkwardly.

Tate stopped right in front of her, his chest rising in deep breaths. "I didn't know if you were going to show up."

She wanted to glare at him, or to make some sharp comment, but inasmuch as she'd been sitting in her office ten minutes ago trying out every excuse she could think of to back out of this, it wasn't an unreasonable statement.

"Two weeks," she reminded him.

He grinned, like he knew something she didn't. "It's gonna have to be a really fun two weeks then."

"Don't think you can bribe me with barbecue like you did the kids."

"Have you had Colter's barbecue?"

Well, no. Maybe she could wrangle that as another perk in her two-week trial.

Aida plucked the clipboard from Tate's hand and went over the schedule. Then she whispered, "Are we really going to do this? Coach together?"

Tate backed away a few paces, still holding eye contact.

"We don't have much of a choice." Then he blew his whistle and yelled, "Gather up everyone!"

"Go, go, go, go, go!" Aida yelled. "That's it, step it up! Nice work." She clapped loudly.

Tate did his best not to grin like an idiot. But, dang, she was cute when she was coaching.

"Mav!" she snapped. "Focus."

Okay, cute, but also a little harsh.

Tate had expected his and Aida's talents would balance each other on the field, but this exceeded his expectations.

They'd met before school that morning, planning out practice over coffee in the hotel courtyard. Aida was cheerful, and a little goofy before 8:00 a.m. He hadn't expected that, and it was fun to plan with her. Also fun to get off topic occasionally. By the time he'd headed to the nearest intersection to cross the street for school, they had the next several practices planned out. She would introduce the drills, together they'd demo, then he would break the movement down further for kids who needed extra help.

They'd executed perfectly, but he'd forgotten to factor in community involvement.

Everyone had an opinion, so Tate was running interference with the spectators, which always took more time in Pronghorn than one would expect.

The blast of Aida's whistle cut the air. "Stop. Mav, you have got to keep your eyes on Ilsa for this drill."

"But what if—?"

"No buts," she told him. "You want to argue, go take a philosophy class."

Mav stalked away, mumbling his arguments to himself, but he returned to the line of kids running the drill. Aida's hair was starting to slip out of her ponytail, light brown wisps framing her face as she ran next to the players.

"Tate?" He spun around to see Raquel Holmes waving at him from the sidelines. He took one last look at Mav. He seemed fine. Aida's harsh correction hadn't hit a nerve. Tate could spare a moment for Pronghorn Public Day School's most vocal mom.

"What's up?" he asked, trotting over to the sidelines.

"Have you coordinated your volunteers for snacks? I'm asking because we're less than a week out and, as far as I can tell, no one has organized snacks for the first game."

Tate closed his eyes briefly. He'd barely finished the paperwork for the league. They needed uniforms and transportation. They hadn't come close to finalizing which position each student would play. Plus, he was still working a more-than-full-time job. And this woman was worried about snacks?

"We're all still getting the hang of practice," Tate said.

"Well, when I taught school——" Raquel started up her usual refrain. She'd taught part-time, for one year, fifteen years ago. That brief experience somehow emboldened her to speak on every issue from Willa's curriculum to Luci's choice of penny loafers.

Tate interrupted her, "The league has been very generous with us, given our late start. But I'm not sure we're going to be ready for the first game. We may just take a forfeit and——"

"Forfeit?!" Pete Sorel, the rancher who served as a highly invested member of the school board, rose from his lawn chair. "We're not going to forfeit. Pronghorn always shows up."

Tate didn't *want* to sigh in their faces. Raquel and Pete were good people. They cared about the school. But, as of now, the team had thirteen players, one coach who wasn't qualified to be there and one who might bail at any minute. Planning snacks for a game they might not even have enough kids to compete in didn't seem like the best use of his limited time.

"I want to see that hustle, Mason," Aida called. "Move it!"

Tate spun around and took a step toward the field at Aida's reproach. Surely, she could see that Mason wasn't as fit as some of the other kids. It was a tribute to his character that he'd taken the risk to show up and try in the first place.

"If we're not going to play the first game, you need to let people know," Raquel admonished. "Folks are planning their weekends around it."

"Sheriff Weston and I will make a decision about the game later this week," he said firmly.

"There's no decision to be made," Pete said. "We're playing."

Smell the soup, cool the soup.

"I know Antonio would be very disappointed if there was no game," Raquel said. "I'd hate to think he came all the way from Brazil to experience our country only to be deprived of a soccer game."

Raquel seemed happy to gloss over the fact that Antonio had tried to get himself kicked out of the program. Tate fought the urge to mention that he would also be very disappointed to learn that they were having zucchini and venison casserole for dinner again.

Aida's voice commandeered his attention. "Suleiman, you have got to step it up. If you're not giving your all during a drill, how do I know you're going to give your all on the field during a game?"

"I'm sorry, Coach."

"Don't be sorry, be better. This isn't good enough."

Tate sprung onto the field.

"Hey!" he yelled. Pete and Raquel could have gotten beamed up by the Starship Enterprise for all he noticed them at this point. "Don't talk that way to the students."

Aida and Suleiman turned to him, like two prong-horn standing in a vegetable garden, unclear on why you're yelling at them to leave.

"You *are* good enough," he told Suleiman. "You're the best player we have out here."

"I know," he said, baffled that anyone would think to remind him of the fact.

Tate put his hands on his hips and turned to Aida. "Don't talk to the kids that way," he said again.

"What way?" She looked truly confused.

It was likely she didn't realize what she was doing, but that didn't make it okay.

"You're being too harsh."

"I'm coaching them."

"You cannot tell a student they're not good enough."

Aida blinked once, then something seemed to land. She turned to the kids. "Am I being too harsh?"

The team members shook their heads, coming to Aida's defense. "She's a good coach," Ilsa said.

"They're not going to answer you honestly," Tate told Aida. "They like you too much."

"Why would they like me? You're not supposed to like your coaches."

Tate was acutely aware that this was not the time to be having this conversation. He tried to wrap it up quickly. "Nine times out of ten, it's fine to be hard on players, so long as they understand you're pushing them out of respect for their abilities. It's the tenth kid I'm worried about."

Aida's expression fell. "I thought you wanted my help."

Tate took a deep breath. *Great.* In trying to keep Aida from being too harsh with the kids, he was being too harsh with her, in front of the whole community.

"I'm sorry. I do want your help. I need your help."

She blinked and he got the sense he'd hurt her feelings. He placed a hand on her shoulder to console her. "You're doing an amazing job. I'm so grateful you're here. But when you're coaching—"

"You're much better than he is," Ilsa chimed in.

"Thank you, Ilsa," he said dryly before refocusing on Aida, pulling her a few paces away from their players. "When you're giving kids feedback, focus on the action, not the person. And try to start with a positive comment."

Aida crossed her arms and stared at the ground. "I'm not an expert magical teacher like you."

"You're doing great," he said. "And there's no magic in teaching."

"There's a little magic," she said. "In your teaching, there's magic."

Tate felt warmed by that comment even as he realized he'd done the exact thing to Aida he'd asked her not to do to the kids. He'd focused on her mistakes and called her out publicly. And of everyone on the field, she was far and away the most vulnerable.

He leaned toward her ear, giving them more privacy. "For example, I should have said, 'Aida, you're doing an incredible job of coaching, and I'm so glad you're here. We make a great team. Please don't ever tell a kid to *be* better.'"

She nodded but still seemed hurt. "I'm not being hard on the kids who aren't as good," she whispered. "I've been real encouraging to Cece."

"And can you see how that singles her out? When you're only hard on the skilled players, it makes the less skilled players feel like you're patronizing them."

She glanced up at him. "I hadn't thought of that."

"There's no reason you would. This is your first time working with kids. And if I tried to do your job, I'd…well, I'd probably get beat up by the first person I pulled over for a speeding ticket."

She gave him a brief laugh.

"Am I going to get a ticket now for correcting you?" he asked, hoping for another smile.

She shook her head. "I'm off duty. I left the booklet back in my office."

"In that case, may I take the opportunity to say you are an extraordinary athlete, the kids are responding well to you and I will do everything I can to keep you coaching with me the entire season?"

She swallowed then nodded. "Okay, what would you have said to Suleiman?"

Tate stepped back and addressed the player. "Suleiman, good try. I really liked what you did in the first two runs on this drill, but your focus seems to be slipping. Focus is a practice, like everything else in this game. Let's run it again."

Aida looked at Suleiman. "Good try."

"You are also trying very well," Suleiman said.

"Can we run the drill?" Ilsa asked.

"Yeah, let's get back to it," Tate said.

He started to back away but Aida reached out and grabbed his arm. "Thanks."

Tate paused, searching for the right words. "I reacted too strongly," he admitted.

"You did. And I think Suleiman can handle some attitude from his coach. But you're probably right about not knowing which kids might be hurt by my words and which won't."

"I am right. I have a master's degree in this."

"And a little magic."

"I shouldn't have snapped at you," he said. "It's just, that's one of the things my dad used to say to me. *Be better.*"

"Then we won't use that phrase, ever."

Practice rolled on. Aida's coaching still came out a little harsh, but she was working on it. Trouble continued to brew on the sidelines as Pete trolled the onlookers, asking people what they thought of a coach who would forfeit a game for no good reason. Raquel seemed to be spreading the news that no one was organizing snacks when she could have just as easily been, you know, *organizing snacks.*

"Tate?"

He turned around to see Today's Moment heading onto the field. He knew any sort of social conventions about parents in long orange robes walking onto the field were either unclear to her or she'd ignore them anyway. Tate made brief, meaningful eye contact with Aida, letting her know he had to deal with this.

"Hello," she greeted him with her hands in prayer, fingers pointing at his chest. "I am so pleased to witness—"

"How can I help you?"

"I appreciate your direct communication to the subject of my heart." She paused, gathering her words. Her robes shifted in the breeze. "You understand the significance of the color orange, don't you?"

It had something to do with the sun, although Tate hadn't been fully listening when it was explained to him. The folks at Open Hearts believed the center of the human heart was made of the same substance as the center of the sun, and that their souls would not be liberated at death unless they were wearing orange. Liberated to…what? Maybe join the center of the sun? He wasn't entirely sure. But they had to be wearing orange. Which was fine.

On the field, Aida yelled, "Good try!" followed by sharp comments about speed, focus and skills. Today's Moment kept talking in circles and Tate resisted the urge to yell, *Spit it out!*

Finally, after a long, long time, she said, "Our emerging adults have learned to embrace their differences and thrive in the community at school."

"They have," Tate acknowledged. "They've done a great job of making friends, and joining in school activities, while still maintaining their core beliefs. It's impressive."

Today's Moment nodded. "We have you teachers to thank, as well as the openness of the other students. We are grateful for your leadership and their accepting, generous hearts."

"But?" Tate asked.

"But elsewhere, people are not so welcoming."

Today's Moment was a powerful personality. She had a leadership position at Open Hearts and didn't hesitate to get into it with townsfolk or teachers. But right now, she looked nervous.

"Are you afraid that when we play away games, the kids from the Open Hearts community are going to get picked on? Because that's against league rules—"

"I speak from experience," she said. "I do not want Mav or Antithesis or Spring Rain to be ridiculed by spectators for their beliefs. I understand that in sports it is acceptable for people to call out insulting comments, and while I don't agree with the practice, it happens. As a community, we have chosen to support our emerging adults as they play on this team. I don't want these precious humans regretting their upbringing because the ignorant are yelling at them."

It finally started to make sense. Today's Moment was worried the kids would be taunted, or worse, when they played against other teams.

"How will anyone know they're from Open Hearts?"

Today's Moment gestured toward the field. "How do you know now?"

"Well, they're wearing orange. But in the game, they'll have on their…uniforms."

Today's Moment nodded. The uniforms.

All of the kids from Open Hearts would have to wear orange during the game. So, no matter what uniform he was able to wrangle in less than a week, the Open Hearts players would have orange on them somewhere.

To Do:

Prepare the team for a game.
Choose positions.
Find uniforms.
Deal with societal dysfunction, misinformation and prejudice.

There was no way they'd be ready for a game on Saturday. But a quick survey of the team and spectators suggested no one would agree to sitting it out.

This was going to take some serious teacher magic.

CHAPTER EIGHT

"NICE TRY AT TRYING!" Aida yelled. "But I need you to try more. Try better."

In response to her words, Suleiman screwed his face up in concentration, his foot connecting with the ball in a powerful kick. It was definitely better than last time. She was getting better, too, or at least more comfortable with the kids now that they were three days in. This practice was her best yet. Or she hoped it was anyway.

Feeling eyes on her, she turned to see Tate watching her, his arms crossed.

"How was that?" she asked.

He tilted his head to one side, indicating that her work, while not perfect, was improving.

"I'm trying," she reminded him.

"Very nice!" Suleiman called. "I don't feel insulted."

"Could you feel more motivated?"

So far, her coaching career wasn't awful. Occasionally, it was even fun.

Coaching had, however, sparked a host of vivid dreams. She'd had soccer dreams for years, the brilliant joy of finding herself back on the field, back in the game, only to wake up shackled to this life again. In the past, the dreams were brief moments of release in a depressing reality. Often she'd realize midway through that something was amiss. She might remember she wasn't a player, or realize she was the only one playing in a sheriff's uniform. She'd wake abruptly, cold confirmation settling around her: she wasn't a soccer player anymore.

But since starting to coach, Aida's dreams veered in a new direction. She'd be on the field, playing, engaged, winning, then remember she was the coach. Her players would tease her for letting her enthusiasm spill onto the field. In one dream, she got a yellow card for forgetting to remain on the sidelines. But in every dream, the game would continue until the narrative morphed into some other fantastical storyline, like Greg getting into an argument with Flora about whose job it was to keep the house free of mice.

Aida woke up confused rather than depressed.

That was admittedly better, if still uncomfortable.

Also uncomfortable was the growing crowd on the sidelines of practice. Some of the kids were really good, and then there was the novelty of Tate. But she could also see people pointing at her, whispering. Would she be as successful a coach as she was a player? Tate didn't seem to mind the public recognition. Aida gritted her teeth and got through it.

Practice wound to an end, segueing to post-practice

chatter. By the time students began to head out, it was well after six. Tate picked up the string bag full of balls then set it down.

"You want me to get that?" she asked.

"What? No." He shouldered the bag again but didn't move toward the school. Aida had been a cop long enough to know something was off.

"What's up?"

"Nothing. I'm just hungry. You know, ready for dinner."

"Me too." Luci had warned her that Tate burned through about three times as many calories as the average human and did not function well if he didn't keep himself properly fed.

"So, uh… Do you have plans for dinner?" Tate scratched the back of his head.

Technically, yes, but she didn't want to admit that the "plan" was a box of mac and cheese and *Murder, She Wrote*.

"Nothing special."

"I was thinking, if we're going to play the game on Saturday—"

"We *are* playing on Saturday!" Antonio yelled from where he stood on the sidelines with his host family. "We're still in the two-week trial."

"So, *if* we play, we need to figure out uniforms, talk about transportation for future competition and finalize who is playing what positions."

Aida glanced up to find his bright blue eyes trained on her. "We have a lot to talk about."

"Yeah." Tate started to put his hand in his back

pocket then seemed to remember he was wearing athletic shorts and didn't have back pockets. He morphed the move into an unconvincing triceps stretch. "Do you want to talk now?"

She did. That was the problem with Tate. He was like CrossFit, the more time you spent around him, the more time you wanted to spend around him.

"I should check with my... Flora."

Tate pointed to the sidelines where Flora was once again sitting with Mrs. Moran. "I think she's kickin' it with her crew tonight."

Flora waved back, clearly communicating that she wanted Aida to go get charmed by Tate.

"Oh. Okay. Let's go plan."

"And have dinner." he suggested. "At The Restaurant?"

Like a date?

"With, you know, everyone else. Half the town."

So not a date. Obviously.

"Sure."

They stood on the field, still staring at each other, as though making sure there was nothing left to be said. Given that the silence stretched on uncomfortably, she was pretty sure there wasn't.

Aida picked up her bag. Greg recognized the cue and trotted over. "Dinner at The Restaurant?" she asked her dog.

Greg brushed up against Aida's leg then Tate's leg, and trotted ahead. They followed her dog off the field, gathering cones and stray soccer balls as they went. Cool air began to settle, reminding everyone that summer was truly over. Ever since the end of her soccer career, the chill of September evenings had left Aida flattened and depressed. But this evening's descent in temperature sparked a long-forgotten anticipation.

"Bye, Coach Tate! Bye, Coach Sheriff Aida!" Antithesis called, approaching one of the bicycle/Segway things they traveled on at Open Hearts. "Have a pleasant sun-slumber!"

"You too!" Aida and Tate waved back and then waved to other students as they called their goodbyes. All around, families gathered their kids and belongings and headed home.

"This is cool," Aida said.

"You coming to dinner? Yeah. Super cool. We should do it—"

"No, I meant this." She gestured to all the people. "There hasn't been this much life in Pronghorn for ages. You five show up and the community is more connected than it's been in years."

He gave her a wry smile. "Now that we finally have a decent soccer coach."

"Hey, I'm still on my two-week trial."

He nudged her with his shoulder. She gave him a playful shove, but he was so solid, it didn't do much.

"Nice try," he teased her.

"Ha, ha."

"Bye, Coach Tate! See you tomorrow, Coach Aida. I mean, Sheriff Weston."

It was Cece, who had been at the entire practice, and hadn't faked a side ache once today. "Great job tonight!" Aida called back. "You were killing the drills. Nice tenacity through the scrimmage. Your focus was fierce."

Cece's face lit up. Her mom put an arm around her shoulder and reiterated the praise. Cece smiled shyly, blood rushing to her face at the unexpected compliment. Tate beamed down at Aida and she was pretty sure she'd killed it with the positive feedback.

Aida felt strangely, wildly, happy. It was an unfamiliar, fluttery feeling, like she had a passel of puppies romping in her chest. She glanced at Tate, suspicious. "Why do I feel so good right now?"

"Because through your patience and consistent feedback, you helped a kid do something difficult, something she wouldn't have done without your guidance."

Aida stared hard at the ground. This happiness felt like expressing itself in liquid form, through her tear ducts. She didn't want it to have a chance to manifest.

"Our patience," she said.

They dropped the equipment in the gym and set off for The Restaurant. Aida took a step into the street, following her dog, who trotted ahead, giving the cat a wide berth. Tate gently grabbed her arm and pointed. "If there's no crosswalk, you're supposed to use the nearest intersection."

Greg stopped and looked back. From the middle of the road, Connie, the school cat, eyed them critically.

It was probably time to apologize for the jaywalking ticket.

Tate raised his eyebrows, inviting the apology.

But expressing regret wasn't Aida's biggest strength.

As they approached The Restaurant, a shocking sight greeted them. The hairs on Aida's arms rose. Greg's ears pricked up.

"What is that?" Tate asked.

"That is…" Aida studied the scene before her carefully, making sure this really was what she thought it was. "That is outdoor seating."

Three tables were set up in front of The Restaurant. It was nothing fancy, no shade umbrellas, no cute wildflower bouquets, just a laminated note on each table that said, "Git your food inside."

Uau.

"This is wild," Tate said as he opened the door for her.

"I'm telling you—" Aida lowered her voice as she passed in front of him "—this is because of you guys. You're shaking things up around here."

People stared as Tate, Aida and Greg walked into the restaurant. It made Aida uncomfortable, but Tate seemed to expand with the attention.

"Sit over there," Angie barked, pointing to an intimate table by the window. If anything could be considered intimate with half the town staring at you.

Tate smiled at Angie, like he always did. He placed a hand on the small of Aida's back, guiding her to the table.

"You know you're her favorite?" Aida asked.

Tate said hello to Raquel and her family as they passed by. Antonio reached out a hand and gave Aida a high five.

"I'm not her favorite. She's appreciative of all the teachers. She's got three teenage boys. Angie's just grateful to get them out of the house."

Tate pulled out a chair for Aida, like he had at the hotel last Friday. It was sweet. It didn't mean anything. Or rather, it meant that Tate was uber-charming and had habits that made him everyone's favorite.

"Angie, can I grab a dog bowl and pour Greg some water? He had a big practice today."

Greg gazed at him in appreciation of a task Aida did five times a day, no puppy dog eyes necessary.

Literally, Tate was everyone's favorite.

"The bowls are outside," Angie snapped back.

"Cool! They do that in parts of Portland, leave out water for pups." Tate was standing in the middle of the crowded restaurant, gesturing broadly, comparing Angie's actions to those of hipsters living in a big city she didn't really consider to be part of Oregon.

And Aida didn't have her ticket book.

But Angie barely flinched at the insult. She just glared at Tate and headed back into the kitchen.

Tate stepped outside to grab a water dish for her dog. Greg sat down next to Aida and delivered a knowing look.

"It's not a date," she whispered.

Greg reminded her that Tate had pulled out her chair and was getting him water.

"That's just the way he is."

Greg's soulful gaze suggested that was a pretty good way to be.

"He's also very, very loud."

Greg sighed and curled up at her feet.

"Hi, Aida!"

Aida looked up to see Willa waving at her from the entrance. Colter stood behind her, hands at her waist, barely noticing anything beyond his fiancée.

Aida's hand flinched up, like she had to wave to get the attention of someone already waving at her. "Hi."

"We got kicked out of the hotel," Willa said. "Luci and Mateo told us they were 'Sylvie sitting' tonight, and we had to go on a date."

"Sounds fun."

Colter and Willa gazed at one another. It was enough to make a sheriff want someone to gaze at like that.

"You two gonna stand around talking, or are you here to eat?" Angie barked at them.

"We'll get dinner," Colter said calmly. He rescued wild Mustangs and had a good sense of how to work with troublesome critters.

"You two are outside," Angie informed them. "It's a nice evening."

Willa widened her eyes at Aida then placed her order and headed out, nearly crashing into Tate as he returned with a bowl of water for Greg.

Tate sat across from Aida, bright blue eyes shining as Greg slurped up water at her feet.

Time to get this dinner back on track. They were two coaches, planning for the season. Tate may still be on the fence about it, but Aida didn't want to forfeit Saturday's game. And she wasn't gonna lose.

Aida pulled a paper napkin out of the dispenser and placed it between them, quickly sketching out the eleven positions on the field.

Tate was smiling at her, the smile that felt flirtatious. She had a pretty good idea of how to knock the grin off his face.

"Okay, so I'm thinking Mav in the goal."

Yup, that did it.

"Seriously?"

"Well, think about it. Suleiman as striker."

"Right. Although he could play goalie too."

"But not at the same time."

Tate shrugged.

"Ilsa and Antonio will play midfield."

"Yes!" Antonio cried from where he was sitting nearby.

"Like he didn't see that coming," Aida muttered.

"My girls have volunteered to lead cheers," Raquel said from their table. "Right, girls?" Raquel's daughters, Taylor and Morgan, exchanged an unenthusiastic eye roll. "When I was in high school, I always led cheers in the stands."

Aida pressed her lips together, not wanting to get into any business with Raquel. She focused on Tate. "Here's what I like about goal for Mav. The rules are different for the goalkeeper. So rather than argue about why he doesn't want to do things like everyone else, he'll already be doing things differently, using his hands to stop the ball, directing people from the goal. Plus, the kid is all arms and legs. He's the largest person on the team. Some extremity will have to stop a ball eventually."

Tate gazed down at her. He didn't speak, he just smiled.

"What?"

"That's brilliant."

Aida pushed the tip of her forefinger against the plastic, red-checked tablecloth. "It's just logic."

"Yes, but logic based on an understanding of a pretty complex kid. I'd call that teacher magic."

Aida shook her head. "Up next, we've got defenders. Have you noticed that Mason has developed quite a kick?"

Together, they filled out the rest of the roster. With eleven positions on the field and only thirteen kids to fill them, they didn't have to make any big decisions about who started. Tate suggested a simple way of rotating kids in and out of the game, so everyone had playing time and no one got too exhausted on the field.

Aida was so deep in the conversation, she was surprised when a plate interrupted her view of Tate.

"You forgot to order," Angie told them.

This didn't seem to matter much. Angie had made the choice for her: a hamburger, Tater Tots and a small green salad.

Tate had been served a grilled chicken burger, french fries and coleslaw.

Angie plunked a PBR in front of Tate. She looked at Aida suspiciously. "You on duty?"

"No, I—"

Angie set a beer in front of her as well, then stalked back into the kitchen.

Tate lifted his bun to ascertain the contents of the burger. "Do you like tomatoes?" he asked Aida.

"Yeah."

He surreptitiously glanced over his shoulder then picked up his tomatoes with a fork and set them on Aida's plate. Aida leaned across the table and whispered, "How do you feel about Tater Tots?"

"I refer to them as Tate's-er-Tots."

Aida quickly slid her Tater Tots onto his plate. He reciprocated by sliding half his fries onto hers.

"Is this illegal?" he whispered.

"Inadvisable, but not strictly against the law."

They dug into their meals. Somehow, this was the best food she'd had at Angie's in a long, long time.

She glanced up at Tate.

It might just be the best food ever.

TATE WAS STILL laughing as he finished off his coconut cream pie. Aida had been all for sharing their meals until Angie had set a piece of chocolate cream pie in front of her. Then it became every coach for themselves.

"This was really..." Aida paused, as though searching for a word.

Tate leaned his chin on his palm as he mentally finished the sentence for her.

Sweet, fun, charming.

"Productive," she said.

That too.

He watched her savor her final bite of chocolate. Over the last week, he'd learned a lot about her and how she interacted with others. She was reluctant to share much about herself until she became comfortable. Once she felt safe, the humor he'd only had glimpses of came flowing out.

And she somehow managed to get prettier by the minute.

A tap on the window startled them. Tate looked up to see Willa gesturing at him. Then she held up her phone so he could read a text from Luci.

"There's internet?" he asked, raising his voice so he could be heard through the glass.

And apparently throughout the restaurant.

Willa rolled her eyes and gestured for them to join her.

"Has a scientist ever asked to study your vocal chords?" Aida asked.

"Want to head back to the hotel?" he asked, ignoring her question. "Because it looks like Willa wants us to, and she can get kinda bossy about these things."

"Sure."

Aida stood and called over to Angie, "Would you put this on my tab?"

"It's already paid for," Angie told her.

"By who?"

Tate closed his eyes, hoping Angie wouldn't embarrass him in front of the whole restaurant. Everyone said he was her favorite, and she did give him a lot of free beer. It wasn't inconceivable that she'd go easy on him.

"Your date," Angie snapped. "Who else?"

No such luck.

Aida eyed him. "Was this a date?"

Was it?

Her expression didn't suggest she was comfortable with that title for the evening.

Tate scoffed; a wholly unconvincing sound. So, he shook his head while shrugging his shoulders like a marionette in the hands of an enthusiastic first grader.

"Come on." Willa stuck her head through the doorway, saving him from further humiliation. "I think Sylvie, Luci and a couple of the exchange students have a surprise for you. She just texted to find out when you two are coming back."

"What kind of surprise?" Aida asked.

"Something fun," Colter said, grinning.

Tate opened the door, Greg trotted ahead and they followed the dog in the direction of the hotel.

"But what's going to happen?" Aida asked. "Did she make cookies, or does it have to do with the hedgehogs?"

"We'll find out soon enough." Colter looped an arm around Willa's shoulders.

Tate had to consciously stop himself from putting

his arm around Aida's shoulders. The appendage seemed to rise of its own accord and drift toward her. It was a situation in which some strategically applied duct tape would not be out of order.

"Can you just give me an idea of what they're up to?" Aida asked.

"You are *not* good with surprises," Willa noted.

"Hey," Tate snapped. "Can we try to avoid universal statements of deficit?"

"I'm *not* good with surprises," Aida confirmed. "No use trying to sugar coat it."

"I love surprises." Colter bounded a few steps ahead.

Since becoming engaged to Willa, Colter seemed to love everything: surprises, expectations, regular routines, momentary inconveniences.

They arrived at the arched entrance to the hotel courtyard. Cheerful voices and peals of laughter filled the space.

"You ready?" Willa asked.

Aida looked like she was about to implode. Or ticket Willa for unlawful delay of information.

"We're ready," Tate confirmed.

The first thing that registered as they stepped into the courtyard was yellow. Swaths of yellow fabric were spread out on every available table, chair and shrub with enough leaves to support them.

In the center of the courtyard were Luci, Sylvie, Antithesis, Oliver, Ilsa and Sofi, an exchange student from Armenia, standing around a homemade wooden frame of some sort.

Luci was wearing an old distressed, plaid shirt over a pair of shorts, which was so not-Luci that Tate wondered if something was wrong. Then he saw that the kids were also in older worn clothing.

Sylvie noticed them. A huge smile spread across her face. "Surprise!"

The other kids joined in the cheer as Sylvie lifted a piece of yellow fabric from the wooden frame.

It was a T-shirt with a freshly inked logo. Tate realized they'd put together a press and were making uniforms. A stylized Pronghorn was proudly emblazoned on the front of the shirt, along with the words "Pronghorn Pronghorns" in letters so bold no one would dare mock the name.

The logo was in bright orange.

She turned the shirt around and showed the back. It had large number 4, with Suleiman's name underneath.

Aida took the shirt in her hands. "You made uniforms?"

Sylvie bounced on her toes, biting her lower lip as she waited for the verdict.

Aida held up the garish, solar-flare-bright jersey and gazed at it. "It's beautiful."

The kids chattered over one another, explaining the process as Aida exclaimed in delight.

Tate scanned the courtyard. Sylvie and her friends had made uniforms. No one had asked them to— he'd never even mentioned how concerned he'd been about the issue. The kids in Pronghorn had just stepped up and created bright yellow-and-orange uniforms. They weren't the expensive, dry-fit polyester soccer jerseys of his youth. They were plain cotton T-shirts in two colors that, anywhere else, would only be used together in moderation.

"This is amazing!" Tate bellowed.

Aida was too entranced to even give him a side-eye for yelling. "These are fantastic," she confirmed at a reasonable volume. "Who designed the Pronghorn?" She pointed at the orange outline of the profile of a pronghorn, its horns curving back in a way that reminded Tate of something you would find as a decoration on an ancient vase.

Sofi raised her hand shyly.

"It's so cool!" Aida cried. "Wow, you guys. I mean. *Wow*."

"Sylvie came up with the plan and organized us," Luci said. "Oliver found the plain yellow T-shirts and orange dye, Antithesis researched how to build your own silk screen, and Sofi came up with that brilliant Pronghorn image."

"I'm only helping," Ilsa said. "Plus, I wanted to make sure I got my lucky number." She picked up a shirt and spun it around so they could see she had number 7.

"Who paid for all this?" Tate asked.

"Um…about that," Sylvie said. "Dad, don't get mad. We're going to sell merch to the fans to recoup the cost, but I might have used that emergency credit card to get us started."

Colter didn't seem to mind that his daughter considered soccer uniforms an emergency—which they kind of were. He was staring in pride.

"You organized this?" Colter asked. "You got everyone together to make the uniforms?"

"Yep." Sylvie stood tall, her shoulders straight like they were when she rode a horse.

"This is my daughter!" Colter proclaimed. He turned to Willa. "Would you look at this? My daughter did this."

"Daaaad!" She dragged the word out in mortification. "We all did this."

"Sorry, right." Colter shook his head. "Good work, everyone." Then he lowered his voice, but Tate could still hear him as he said to Willa, "Can we get Raquel and the other Pronghorn moms in here to witness this? Betcha can't find a shirt like that at N'Style in Klamath Falls."

Tate picked up a shirt then turned it around to see the number 11 and Antithesis's name on the back.

"Antithesis, was it your idea to do the lettering in orange?"

"No, that was Ms. Walker's idea." She pointed to Luci.

Luci readjusted the tortoise-rimmed glasses on her nose with two fingers. "I thought it would be best if everyone wore some orange."

And, that way, the Open Hearts players wouldn't be singled out. Tate took a long look at Luci, once again wondering how it was she understood the kids from the commune so well, and felt compelled to care for them as she did.

"You want to see yours?" Sylvie asked.

She picked up a shirt and handed it to him. "Coach Tate" was written in large letters on the back.

"Here's yours, Coach." Ilsa walked a T-shirt over to Aida. On the back was written "Coach Sheriff Aida."

Aida's hands trembled as she took the shirt. She swallowed hard and blinked. "Th-thank you."

"And we have this one too." Ilsa held up another shirt. "This was my idea." She turned the little shirt around so everyone could see "Coach Greg" written on the back.

Aida reached out and pulled Ilsa into a hug. Over Ilsa's shoulder, Aida's gaze connected with Tate's. He grinned at her.

There were a hundred moments when working with kids was hard. The work could be grueling. Hours of creativity and patience could be derailed by one person's bad attitude. You had to dig into reserves of confidence and patience most people never took the time to develop. But those difficult moments were like the frustration an artist endured while creating something beautiful. At times like these, when kids who had been encouraged to think creatively, work together and solve problems came together to do just that, every painful step was worth it.

Aida, struggling to hold back tears, held up Greg's jersey. "How amazing are our kids?"

"The amazingest," he confirmed.

"Not a word," Willa warned sharply.

"Gonna become one if they keep this up," Colter teased her.

"So that's all we need, right?" Sylvie asked. "The uniforms? Now we're all ready for the first game?"

Were they ready? Tate didn't want to walk into the first game unprepared. He didn't want to risk failing in front of the community. But they had thirteen kids who wanted to play, two coaches willing to see them through, and clothing that identified them as a team. That would have to be enough.

"Yep." He nodded, confirming this with Aida. "We're good to play on Saturday."

CHAPTER NINE

THE FIRST TRUCKFUL of spectators arrived in Pronghorn at 11:00 a.m., two full hours before kickoff. People had been steadily arriving ever since, both from the surrounding areas and from Adeline, home of the Bobcats. Folks set up lawn chairs and picnic blankets on the sidelines. Once that space was taken, people backed their trucks up and pulled down the tailgates for a second row of seating.

Aida shivered. It all felt too familiar. The excitement, the pressure, the relief of getting onto the field and doing the one thing she was truly good at.

It would all be a wonderful memory if she hadn't ultimately failed.

Aida gritted her teeth. She had a job to do. She couldn't undo her past, but she could help these kids develop a healthier relationship with the sport than she had.

It didn't help that by the time Tate and Aida led the team to the sidelines, there had to be two hundred people there to watch a coed, Single A soccer game.

There really was not enough to do in Southeastern Oregon.

"How you feeling?" Tate asked.

Aida scowled at him in response.

"It's gonna be okay," he said. "I'm here if you need anything."

She took a few steps in the direction of her office. "Maybe I should grab my radio, in case anything comes up."

"You hoping for a crime to get you out of this?"

"Is that what you think of me? That I've been sitting around all morning hoping for a five-car pileup to excuse me from the game?"

Tate raised his eyebrows.

Okay, maybe she wasn't hoping for *five* cars, and certainly she didn't want anyone to get hurt.

"I'm nervous too," he said. "Remember, I can't stand this sport."

"I thought you were starting to like it." Concern rattled her. Had he just been pretending to enjoy himself?

"I am, or rather, I like coaching this particular group of kids, with you." He held eye contact for a few seconds longer than he needed to, making her heart both warmer and fuzzier.

The reaction dissipated as Pete Sorel moseyed up to them. "Well, it's not football, but I guess it'll do—"

Before Suleiman or one of the others could remind him that in the rest of the world, it *was* football, Tate cut him off. "Glad you could make it." He gave the grizzled rancher his charming smile. "The students are excited and it's nice to have—"

he glanced behind him at the mass of humanity filling the sidelines "—so many fans here."

Pete placed one heavy hand on Tate's shoulder. "We all want to see what you can do." He dropped the other hand on Aida's shoulder. "We already know what the sheriff can achieve on the field. Question is, can her coaching live up to it?"

"It can't," Aida told him. "And I'd advise you against further baiting of coaches before a game."

"I wasn't baiting." His bushy eyebrows folded in on themselves. "I'm trying to be helpful, get everyone fired up."

Aida's hand reflexively moved to her back pocket. Tate moved to shield Aida from Pete. Or maybe it was the other way around?

"It would be helpful if you'd fire up the crowd." Tate gestured toward the fans, who were already so fired up, they were in danger of scorching a good portion of Harney County. "Fans these days? Do these millennials even know how to cheer?"

"Good point," Pete said, heading off in his distinctive bow-legged walk toward the crowd.

"That was well done," Aida muttered.

"His heart is in the right place," Tate reminded her. "His mouth on the other hand…"

She widened her eyes and flexed her brow.

Tate looked behind them again then leaned in toward Aida and asked quietly, "Is this normal to have so many people here?"

"For Pronghorn? Absolutely."

"Sorry, I keep forgetting we're on a different normality scale out here."

"Did you know that in Adeline," she said, gesturing across the field to the competition, "they only have *one* business? It's a restaurant and market combined. Inside, they have three framed, autographed pictures of Geraldine Ferraro."

"That's...a lot of pictures of the former representative from New York."

"They're big fans."

"Ooookay."

In addition to the ranchers, a good showing of folks from Open Hearts were there, too, decked out in orange, some wearing garlands of the expensive flowers they grew in their greenhouses. Supporters of the other team watched them with curiosity, pointing to the Lyfcycles they rode in on and muttering about their unorthodox clothing. Because the game was on Pronghorn's home turf, Aida didn't expect any issues. The reopening of the school had helped to heal the breach between the commune and the ranching community. And even if some misunderstanding lingered, together they were Pronghorn: a civilized town with a store *and* a restaurant.

Still, as sheriff, Aida would keep an eye out for any trouble.

Greg planted himself on the sidelines, his dark eyes asking again why he had to wear a shirt that covered up his handsome brown-and-black fur. She ran a hand over the top of his head, thanking him for rolling with it.

Next to him, the players fidgeted uneasily. Aida's own fidgeting probably wasn't helping their nerves. Throughout her soccer career, Aida's teams had always depended on her. She was used to keeping her head up and being a leader, but this was different. Back then, she'd been looking out for her peers. These were kids, and she was legitimately responsible for them.

And so nervous she could barely breathe.

Down the line, Antonio shook out his arms and bounced on his toes, focused and excited. Suleiman wore sunglasses, putting on the persona of an internationally recognizable soccer star, but he was focused on the opposing team, sizing them up. Ilsa stared out at the pitch, as though visualizing herself scoring.

Mason appeared at Tate's side about once every nanosecond, asking questions, confirming theories and generally trying to soak up his favorite teacher/coach's confidence in him. Tate's patience with the kid was astounding as he offered the exact right words every time. Mav was picking a philosophical argument with Angie, who stood behind him on the sidelines. This, while generally inadvisable, was at least keeping him busy until the game started. The rest of the players were similarly trying to distract themselves from the fact that every soul within driving distance had come to watch them try to play a game they'd only just begun to learn.

Why couldn't the town have gone easy on them for the first match?

Because it's Pronghorn.

At the end of the line, Cece stood a few feet off to the side, pulling at her shirt. She looked as nervous as Aida felt. The two of them were coming to this game with vastly different experiences, but the end point was the same. They'd do just about anything to get out of it.

Aida left Tate's side and jogged to stand next to the girl.

When she got there, she still had no idea what to say. She folded her arms.

Cece did the same, then surprised Aida by starting the conversation. "How are you feeling?"

"A little nervous. You?"

A sheen of sweat broke out across Cece's forehead as she stared at the field. "Hard same."

Greg, alert to a possible situation, squeezed his furry self in between Aida and Cece. The girl dropped a hand to Greg's ears as she said, "My mom said you might be nervous."

Aida whipped her head around to place Cece's mom and possibly ticket her for hitting the nail on the head. Unfortunately, Cece's mom was giving Aida the most grateful look for comforting her daughter.

Ugh. Was there anything worse than not being able to get mad at someone who pitied you?

"I'm only out here because Coach Tate convinced me to give it a try," Cece continued. "I didn't want to let him down. But now there's so few players, I can't quit, or I'd be letting *everyone* down."

"Exact same!" Aida said. "I'm only here because Coach Tate talked me into it too."

"And you can't quit now."

"Yeah." Aida made a show of shaking her head at Tate. "Without him, we'd both be happily at home right now. This is *so* his fault."

Cece laughed then knelt beside Greg and gave his neck a scratch. "He's so handsome in his uniform."

Okay? Sure, Tate looked amazing. But was that really the sort of thing a student was supposed to say?

"Don't you look good?" Cece cooed, scratching Greg's ears. "You are very handsome in your uniform."

Oh. She was talking about the dog. Greg gave her a kiss.

"You look great too," Aida said. "Aggressive yellow and orange suits you."

Cece glanced down at her shirt. "Maybe the opponents will be distracted by our uniforms?"

Across the field, the other team wore simple blue-and-white jerseys and matching shorts. *They* looked like a small-town soccer team.

Pronghorn, on the other hand, did not. In their homemade T-shirts, mismatched shorts, every version of footwear and varying levels of enthusiasm, they looked like the cast of an off-Broadway musical about soccer.

A musical written and performed by people who'd never seen an actual soccer game.

Aida blew out a breath. Cece stood and did the same.

"We can do this," Aida told her. "Our opponents

will take the field. They might be good, they might not."

"Our team is both good—" Cece pointed to the exchange students "—and not good." She pointed to herself.

"That's not true," Aida said. "The team is experienced and inexperienced. You're about to get more experienced."

Aida just prayed that her players remembered all the rules and put this thing together. But they might not, and Aida didn't know what would happen if they lost. She didn't lose well. There was nothing pretty about Aida's reaction to second place. But that concern would have to wait. Right now, her job was to help Cece feel better.

"You know what? This whole thing won't take more than two hours. All we need to do is roll our shoulders back and get through it. You think we can do it?"

Cece gave her head an exaggerated tilt. "I guess I can exist in the world, in this shirt, for two hours."

Aida laughed, raising a hand for a high five. Cece didn't respond.

"High five?" Aida asked.

"That's way too enthusiastic for how I'm feeling."

Aida folded in her thumb and pinkie finger. "High three?"

Cece laughed and pressed three fingers against Aida's. "High three."

Feeling eyes on her, Aida glanced down the line of players to see Tate watching the exchange. He nodded to her.

Does this pep talk fall under the label of "good job" or "nice try"?

The ref blew his whistle and waved the coaches over. Aida jogged onto the field. Tate ran next to her.

"Are you and Cece okay?" he asked.

Was he actually admitting their misery was his fault? Was Tate Ryman taking responsibility for his actions?

"Because no matter what you're feeling right now, I know this experience is going to be really good for both of you."

Nope, he wasn't.

"We're fine. Two women, existing in the world, wearing yellow shirts for the next two hours."

Tate grinned. "You're both going to do great."

They arrived at the center of the field. Reflexively, her body remembering what to do from another lifetime, Aida reached out and shook the ref's hand, then that of the opposing team's coach. Tate followed suit.

"Welcome," the Bobcat's coach said, even though the game was on their turf.

The young ref smiled at her then Tate. "I'm glad we could make this game work."

"So are two hundred other people," Tate joked, circling his finger to indicate the onlookers.

The opposing coach gave a silent open-mouthed laugh. Like, he just bared his teeth and tonsils in what appeared to be a laugh but made no actual sound.

What even was that?

Aida did *not* have to like a guy who welcomed her to her own field and couldn't muster up the air for a real laugh.

"We're ready to go," Aida said, taking a step back.

"Yeah, just a few details," the ref said. "I know you guys are new to the league. You've had…what, two weeks of practice?"

"Yep," Aida snapped before Tate could jump in. "Two *good* weeks."

One good week, but who's counting?

"Right. So, before we start, I wanted to let you know that we play to an inequality of ten. So, since you guys are new, if—"

Aida moved into the ref's personal space. "What are you suggesting?"

Color drained from his face, but he valiantly endured. "If Adeline gets up by ten points, I'll call the game."

Tate was now physically inserting himself between her and the ref just as he had with Pete. Aida was on to him. She feinted to one side then stepped around him. Tate might be big, but she was fast.

"And if Pronghorn is up by ten?"

The ref looked a little shocked. "Then I'd call the game?"

"Good to know."

Aida spun on her heel and headed back to the team.

"I have a few more points to cover," the ref called after her.

Aida held up a hand. "Talk to Tate."

Her vision blurred with anger. Who were these guys? Sure, they might have come into the season late, and have a spare-parts team, and be wearing shirts that could double as tarmac lighting. But they were *Pronghorn.*

Aida charged the sidelines, her vision clearing, bringing her players into focus. They were all staring at her.

She held her hands up and flickered her fingers, indicating the team should circle up.

The kids gathered around. She opened her mouth to speak. No, that wasn't a good idea right now. Spewing her frustration about a misinformed ref and soundless-laugh man wouldn't be helpful. Or mature. She breathed in through her nose, like she'd seen Tate do. What did these kids need to hear to understand the gravity of the situation?

"You need to *win* this game," she said.

The kids stared back at her. Then Cece nodded.

"We will win," Suleiman said, pulling off his sunglasses and handing them to Aida. "What else would we do?"

The ref blew his whistle again. He seemed real attached to that thing. Aida signaled the team captains, and Mav and Suleiman stalked to the center of the field. She focused as the ref pulled out a coin.

"You know you can't determine the outcome of a coin toss by glaring at the quarter?" Tate asked.

"You clearly haven't glared at that many quarters." Aida kept her eye on the coin as it was caught and revealed, leading to a swift and positive reaction from the Pronghorn team captain.

"Yes!" Aida shouted, raising her arms at the first triumph of the season.

Behind her, a few spectators chuckled. Aida dropped her arms. The citizens of Pronghorn still remembered her as a plucky, competitive player: her easy and frequent goals, cheers of joy and a well-choreographed victory dance. She couldn't let them think they'd be seeing the old Aida today. She was just a coach, and a reluctant one at that.

Aida relaxed her shoulders, determined to keep cool. It was only a game.

The opposing team's coach just smiled as he took the news of the coin flip. Who did he think he was, being all calm and easy about losing a coin toss? This day was stressful enough without Mr. Tooth and Tonsil thinking for one second that his appropriately dressed team was going to beat them by ten, or any points.

Aida's heart beat hard as their kids moved into formation. Ilsa tensed, ready to spring into action. Suleiman made eye contact with each of the opposing team members.

Mav took the goal box, waving his arms randomly, as though someone might try to score before the official start of the game.

Aida wanted to cry, or sprint into her office and lock the door.

Or run out and join the kids on the field.

Tate leaned down and whispered in her ear, "How

are you doing?" His breath shifted the strands of hair that had fallen out of her ponytail, and she shivered.

"I'm scared," she admitted.

"Are you afraid we'll lose?" he asked. "Because that's where I am. I don't *want* to want to win, but I do."

Aida scoffed. "We're not losing to—" she gestured dismissively "—that guy."

Tate's gaze connected with hers. "Then what are you afraid of?"

Of caring again. Of caring too much.

Of finding something worth fighting for, only to have it slip away again, no matter how hard I fight.

Tate nodded, like he'd heard her thoughts. He might not understand her, but he was there for her anyway.

Silently, Tate placed an arm around her shoulders. There were two hundred people, one dog and who knew how many actual Pronghorn antelope watching. His arm was warm and comforting, and somehow it became important.

Aida didn't question it. She didn't move away or shrug his arm off. She just leaned into her large, solid ally on the sidelines.

The ref blew his whistle.

In a rush of noise and color, the game began.

WAS THIS REALLY their creation? It didn't seem possible that the mishmash of humanity in orange and yellow were their players.

Because they were dominating this game.

The drills Aida had painstakingly, and somewhat rudely, trained the kids in were apparent on the field. All the strategies and positioning she'd hammered on about came alive. They controlled the ball, passed to one another, communicated in a variety of languages that somehow worked.

The fans were stunned and nearly silent for the first quarter, muttering in surprise as Suleiman made a goal, then Ilsa made another. Hesitant cheers began as the spectators allowed their hopes to rise. Even better, every time Pronghorn scored, or turned the ball, Aida would make some kind of celebratory dance move. The movement was subtle and varied, a roll of her shoulders, a slight sway of the hips.

It was cute, and pretty darn distracting.

Mason blocked a shot on goal and launched it down the pitch without inadvertently breaking any rules. Aida's feet shuffled.

"What is that?" Tate finally asked.

"What's what?"

"That…joyful flinch you're doing."

Aida sputtered out a disbelieving laugh, not taking her eyes from the game. "I'm not joyfully flinching."

"I don't know what else to call it."

She issued a dismissive smirk and kept watching. Sure enough, Ilsa got a good pass to Suleiman for an attempt on goal and Aida rolled her fists one over the other, like she was getting ready to audition for *Saturday Night Fever*.

She really didn't seem to know she was dancing this game out.

As the minutes ticked by, she wasn't the only one expressing happiness. Behind them, the crowd started to break its silence. Applause, then encouraging comments. He was pretty sure he heard Today's Moment yell, *"Huzzah!"* but didn't want to take his eyes off the game to check.

It wasn't until Mav managed to stave off a goal that things got loud. It was probably his skill, or maybe the ball just didn't have the energy for the argumentative teen, Tate was unsure. That was when the citizens of Pronghorn realized they might actually win this thing.

"Everyone! On your feet!" Pete Sorel commanded. "We're all gonna yell, 'Go Pronghorns' on three."

Before they could get the cheer out, Ilsa got possession of the ball. The fans stared in silence as she blew past several players twice her size. Within sight of the opposing goal, the defenders closed in on her. She couldn't shoot and instead skillfully passed to Antonio, who easily commandeered the ball and scored.

The crowd leapt to their feet, cheering the ordered "Go Pronghorns!" but Antonio, fresh off his victory, marched over, waving his arms to stop them. "In Brazil, when there is a goal, you say, 'Olé! Olé! Olé!'"

The crowd of Pronghorn natives silenced again and stared at him.

"Try it," Antonio commanded. He raised his arms. "Olé! Olé! Olé!"

Raquel's daughters, Morgan and Taylor, looked at each other, then back at the handsome boy from Brazil who had scored.

"Olé! Olé! Olé!"

Antonio raised his arms higher, shouting the cheer again. Ranchers, townsfolk and members of the Open Hearts Intentional Community all cheered back. "Olé! Olé! Olé!" rang out across the valley, connecting Pronghorn to a country six thousand miles and worlds away.

Tate glanced down at Aida to see how she was taking this. Her eyes shone up at him.

"This might be awesome," she admitted.

"It might be."

Antonio, confident in the crowd's cheering abilities, sauntered back to the sidelines.

"Antonio, you've earned a break," Tate said, checking his roster. "Cece, you're in."

The color drained from Cece's face. She glared at Tate, silent but clearly questioning why he'd gotten her into this in the first place. He was ready to make an encouraging statement about trying hard things but Aida stepped in front of him and held up three fingers.

"High three."

Cece responded by pressing the tips of three fingers against Aida's. Then she heaved a sigh and went in.

It wasn't horrible.

Cece tracked the play, ran to where she was supposed to be and didn't look miserable the entire time. She didn't get anywhere near the ball, but she didn't actively run away from it either.

Thirty minutes in, they were up five to zero.

The whistle blew, signifying the half. Tate and Aida gathered the kids in an excited knot.

"Great focus!" Aida said to Suleiman. "Mav, you are killing it out there. And, Cece! Your excellent positioning kept the other team funneled off to the sides, exactly where we wanted them."

The players stared at her silently. Suleiman cleared his throat.

"What?" She looked up at Tate. "What am I doing wrong?"

"You're being so…positive," Ilsa said.

"We're winning."

"I'm not sure how to respond," Suleiman said. "She has not yet condemned with *good try*."

The team cracked up.

Aida laughed with them. "Good try," she told him. "I want you to try exactly the same way in the second half of this game."

Her pep talk worked, and the Pronghorns came back even stronger in the second half.

Suleiman, after making his fifth goal, seemed to understand that he needed to share the joy of scoring. When he turned the ball again, he fed it to Ilsa.

There was something decidedly squirrel-like about Ilsa. She could race through the traffic without so much as a bump from another player. When she made it through safely, she would chitter at the opponents like a squirrel taunting an uncoordinated human.

While Ilsa ran with the ball, Suleiman charged ahead of the defenders, positioning himself to score.

"He's offside, isn't he?" Tate asked. He still didn't fully understand the rule about when there needed to be a defender between a striker and the goal, but Aida hollered about it pretty frequently.

She placed a hand on his arm, communicating that he should wait and watch.

But, dang, it was hard to watch the game with Aida so close. And if something good was about to happen, he didn't want to miss another one of her grooving dance moves.

The attention of all three of the opposing team's defenders and the goalie went straight to Suleiman. Ilsa enjoyed the lack of limelight with a satisfied smirk as she launched the ball with her left foot into the upper corner of the goal box.

The citizens of Pronghorn were on their feet. "Olé! Olé! Olé!"

"No!" Ilsa turned sharply to the spectators. "When I score, you yell, 'Hup! Hup! Holland!' Try it."

"Hup! Hup! Holland!" the crowd, led by Pete Sorel, responded.

"That's good!" Ilsa pointed at them. *"Oranjegekte!"*

"What is *Oranjegekte*?" Tate asked Aida.

"I'm gonna have to google that one."

Tate checked the clock on his phone. "Okay, we

have ten minutes left. We're up nine to zero. It's time to give the other team a break."

Aida crossed her arms, as unhappy as he'd ever seen her.

"You know it's the right thing to do."

"The right thing would be for the other team to work a little harder."

"Aida."

She sighed. "Fine."

Aida signaled for a time-out. At the ref's whistle Tate picked up his clipboard and gestured for the team to circle up. "Suleiman and Ilsa, you get a break."

"I don't want a break," Suleiman said. Ilsa just glared her response.

"Too bad. Antonio, you're in, but your directive for the last ten minutes is to work on passing the ball so others can score."

"What if there's an opening for me to score?"

"Pass the ball," Tate said with the head tilt and accompanying tone that signified this conversation wasn't going any further.

Antonio looked to Aida to see if she'd fight this for him.

She held her hands up. "It's not my fault he's all sportsmanlike."

Tate turned to Aida, ready to remind her they were there to support kids, not pummel the other team into oblivion, when he caught her smile.

She was teasing him, and she was beyond gorgeous with her hair falling out of her ponytail.

Tate's heart started doing something that could be defined as joyful flinching.

The ref blew his whistle, signaling the end of the time-out. The Pronghorns took the field.

The team adhered to the letter of the law but not the spirit of it. Antonio showboated his way down the field then waited patiently for teammates to arrive so he could pass off the ball. This would be a topic of conversation at Monday's practice. Winning was fine, teasing another team was not.

As agreed, they kept the score nine to zero, but made it perfectly clear they could shut this thing down at ten points anytime. By the way the opposing coach kept checking the time, he seemed to be finishing this game with the same sense of trepidation Aida and Tate had started it.

With two minutes left, the Pronghorns let the Adeline Bobcats take the ball. One of their forwards made a good run but was intercepted by Mason, who managed to turn the ball. Unable to locate anyone open for a pass, he took off for the goal. He was slower than his teammates, particularly after nearly a full hour on the field, but he kept running.

"Dig deep," Aida called after him. "You've got this."

Mason's face contorted in concentration. He seemed to find another gear, dribbling the ball past the other team's defenders.

Then Mason, who only showed up at practice because Tate was his favorite teacher; Mason, who'd spent the first three weeks of school so uncomfortable in his body that he tried everything to get out of PE; Mason scored.

The crowd, and very specifically his mother, Angie, went nuts. A mixed chorus of "Olés" and "Hups" and "Pronghorns" rang out.

The ref's whistle split the air—the end of the game as one team was ten points up.

Aida pointed to the goal and made a funky little move with her shoulders as she took a step to one side. She jumped then shuffled to the other side, rolling her fists over one another, and swayed her hips. Then she did the whole thing all over again, completely oblivious that Tate and the rest of Pronghorn were watching. Not just watching, smiling with their whole hearts and applauding, as though they knew the dance well and had wondered if they'd ever see it again.

"Is that our victory dance?" he asked.

Aida, too happy to even put her guard up, started from the top. But she didn't get too far as she and Tate were swarmed with players. The kids were pinging from one coach to the other like someone had dropped a case of bouncy balls. Then they were rushed by parents and Pronghornians.

"How's that two-week trial going?" he heard Aida ask Suleiman.

He gave a theatrical shrug. "I don't know. There is still an American barbecue coming up. I'll wait and see."

"Nice try." She called out his bluster.

He laughed. "You will come to the barbecue and to see the horses too."

Aida shook her head. "Oh, no. The barbecue is for teenagers, for you exchange students specifically."

Antonio rested his elbow on Suleiman's shoulder. "We have to have chaperones, because we're so annoying."

Aida shook her head.

"You have to come," Tate said. "What if a soccer emergency breaks out?"

She gave him a sharp look. Aida's idea of a soccer emergency was his running drills.

Pete Sorel arrived at Tate's side. "That's how we do it in Pronghorn, eh?"

Since the vast majority of points scored had been from people not from Pronghorn, nor even the North American continent, Tate wasn't sure what to say.

Pete continued, "I knew Aida would step up."

Aida's head jerked up at the sound of her name, the color fading from her cheeks.

"Yeah. Uh. Thanks," Tate said to Pete, even though Pete hadn't actually said anything complimentary. He untangled himself from the conversation then battled through the throngs until he came to Aida. "How are you doing?"

Aida swallowed hard. She was exhausted. As much as Tate wanted to soak up the praise, public adulation was wearing on Aida. She held his gaze for a moment. Then, as though privy to his innermost wishes, she reached her arms out, sliding them around his waist, letting her cheek fall against his chest like he was a comforting pillow. She closed her eyes, her sigh soft against him.

Slowly he lifted his arms and wrapped them around her.

"We did it," he reminded her. "We won."

She nodded but didn't say anything. It was almost as though the landslide win had brought back more powerful memories. He wrapped his arms extra tightly around her, unable to solve the complicated emotions but able to shelter her from the crowd that inspired them.

CHAPTER TEN

COLTER'S PROPERTY LOOKED like the aftermath of a head-on collision between a rodeo and a skate park. Teenagers were everywhere: riding horses, eating barbecue, jumping off the boulders that lined a creek.

At the center of this melee were Tate and Colter. The two of them seemed to be having a great time, like a bunch of teenagers running amok on the property wasn't an issue.

Aida hesitated to put her car in Park. Why had she agreed to this?

Right, because a gorgeous, unlawfully charming man had asked her to come. By the end of that hug after the game, she'd have agreed to just about anything. Winning felt as good as it ever had. But even better was sharing that victory with the town and a group of kids who needed a win. Best was sharing the victory with Tate. When he'd wrapped his arms around her, she'd felt like she could fly.

And that feeling had landed her here, with wild horses and wilder teenagers, with a thud.

Aida took another peek out the car window.

"What do you think?" she asked Greg, who sat alert in the passenger seat next to her.

He pawed at his door, politely suggesting he thought he'd like to get out and join the mayhem.

Aida wasn't so sure.

Technically, she was off duty, but cruising the lonely highways on the lookout for lost tourists or potential criminals seemed a lot more inviting than trying to blend in with a billion humans under the age of nineteen. And one human over the age of nineteen who was beginning to make her very nervous.

The driver's-side door opened abruptly. Aida found herself staring at Luci.

"Thank God you're here. I'm desperate for your help with Ilsa."

"Hi," Aida responded.

"She's refusing to get on a horse. But if you do it, she'll do it." Luci, in an equestrian outfit she could have borrowed from Katherine Hepburn, was already stalking away.

Greg flowed out the door, following Luci like a baby duckling.

Aida sighed and pulled herself out of the vehicle, determined not to follow Tate around in the same manner.

"Does Ilsa have to ride?" she asked. "If she doesn't want to, why would we pressure her?"

"Well, she hasn't left the barn." Luci gave her a dry look. "She's a teenager, standing in a barn, loudly proclaiming she's not going to ride. If she really didn't want to get on a horse, she'd be somewhere else, and a whole lot quieter about it."

"Got it."

"Aida!" The world's loudest voice stopped her. She closed her eyes but could hear Tate's sneakers crunching across the gravel toward her. She looked up in time to see Tate's arms sweep around her.

"You're late," he said, pulling her into his hug.

This was unequivocally her fault. She'd initiated hugs into their relationship, and if she was now tucked up in his arms, she had no one to blame but herself.

It was legitimately a fabulous place to be.

"I was on duty."

"I worried something happened to you."

She pulled back and furrowed her brow. "Why?"

"Because drug runners. Angry criminals."

"I've had one speeding ticket this week. That's it." No need to mention the tip she'd received on a methamphetamine operation out past the O'Shay wetlands.

Tate studied her face, as though weighing the truth of her statement while simultaneously suggesting that even minor traffic stops could go awry. Then his sly smile appeared. "No jaywalking?"

"Not today. Our newcomers are finally learning the rules."

He winked at her, and Aida had the feeling that if Tate put his mind to it, he could find rules to break all day, every day.

And hearts.

"I'm supposed to help get Ilsa on a horse," she said.

"Yeah, that's been an issue. Follow me." Tate took

several long steps in the direction of Colter's riding arena.

"I thought I was supposed to be following Luci?"

"Greg's got that covered."

Aida made her way through the throng of kids, following Tate in the exact manner she'd planned not to.

"Isn't this place cool?" he asked, gesturing to the land around them. Aida hadn't been out to C & S Ranch since Colter had taken it over thirteen years ago. In that time, he'd built the pristine pine stables and riding arena, not to mention the house. The same creek that cut through her property flowed through Colter's, providing irrigation for his pastures.

"It is. I'm glad Colter and Sylvie found a home here. They add a lot to the community."

"And what about the other newcomers?" He grinned at her as they entered the riding arena. "What are we adding to the community?"

Noise?

"Coach Aida!"

It took Aida a moment to wrap her brain around what she was seeing. Suleiman rode toward her on a mustang. He had on blue jeans and a snap-button shirt that she guessed wasn't part of the wardrobe he'd brought from Senegal. He wore a helmet, but waved a Stetson in his free hand.

"We're riding!" he yelled somewhat unnecessarily.

"You are," she confirmed.

"Do you like my shirt?"

"Where's you get it?"

"Mr. Wayne, Sylvie's dad. He gave us shirts and hats, and he said we could ride anytime."

Tate leaned down and said in a low voice, "Colter has all this stuff he won on the rodeo circuit years ago. He's passing it out to the kids."

Tate was in his standard teacher outfit of jeans and a nice T-shirt. "What about you?" she asked. "You getting in on the new duds?"

"I don't think I can pull it off like these guys do."

Aida scanned the property. All nine of the exchange students had at least a Stetson if not full cowboy regalia. "How many pictures do you think they've posted this afternoon?"

"If Instagram shuts down from overuse, we'll know why."

Antonio came cantering up behind Suleiman, also with a helmet and a Stetson. "You will ride with us?"

"Is that a question?" Aida asked.

"Eh?" He shrugged.

Aida laughed. "We'll see."

"We'll see *you on a horse*," Suleiman clarified, using the same tone she did when redirecting her players during a drill.

Off to one side, Mav's voice caught her attention. "Life is short," she heard him saying. "Like a grasshopper. You should take the opportunity to ride."

"What's a grasshopper?" Ilsa asked. "And what does it matter if a grasshopper is short? I'm not riding a horse and why does anyone care if I do?"

Tate nodded in their direction. "You want to take this one?"

"I'm on it." Aida backed away. "But if she doesn't want to ride, she doesn't have to."

Aida trotted over to Ilsa. Vander was nearby, talking softly to a mustang. Mav and Ilsa carried on with their argument, using some complex metaphor about grasshoppers that neither of them seemed to fully understand but were deeply invested in.

She recognized the issue immediately. This wasn't about horses. Ilsa, their most argumentative exchange student, was enjoying a lively conversation with Mav, the most argumentative native of Pronghorn. They were having a grand old time. If the purpose of this field trip was to help the exchange students enjoy Pronghorn, this was all Ilsa needed.

Aida backed away and bumped into Vander.

"Oof! Sorry!"

He smiled, calm and easy. He'd arrived from the city but blended in so seamlessly, she often forgot he was one of the newcomers.

"No worries. Have you met Stet?" He gestured to the mustang. The horse hung his head, as though he'd had a rough go of it before coming to C & S Ranch.

"Hello." Aida rubbed his forehead. The horse leaned toward her. "Is this one of Colter's rescues?"

Vander, in his typically understated way, said, "I helped this guy out." He rested a hand Stet's nose. "Nearly skin and bones when we met, weren't you?"

Stet closed his eyes, as though wary of the rest of the world but feeling safe with Vander.

"You've found a friend," Aida said. "You're gonna need to spend half your time-out here with him."

"I'm working out at Jameson Ranch on the weekends. Colter suggested I keep Stet there, if it's okay with the foreman."

A second job? From what she could tell, the teachers were already working ten-hour days and weekends getting the school up and running.

"Have you met the owner, Harlow Jameson?" Aida had been trying to get a hold of Harlow for months. The wealthy, intellectual property lawyer rarely stepped foot in Oregon, while her cattle stepped hoof all over Warner Valley. She had more fines for illegal grazing piled up than Tate had citations, which was impressive.

"Nah. The foreman made it pretty clear she's not around. I work for him."

"That's fair."

Tate glanced over from where he was talking with Mason. His eyes darted from Aida to Vander and back again. Almost like he was…jealous?

Tate laughed at something Mason said then legitimately turned around and glared at Vander.

What???

Vander just smiled. "You want to ride? Stet here's not quite ready for the saddle, but we've got one last horse saddled up and ready to go."

"I…uh…"

Tate was now moving toward them. What was

happening here? She had constructed a quiet but well-ordered, post-soccer life. As sheriff, she kept people, and emotions, at arm's length. Yet here she was, surrounded by teenagers she liked, wondering if a man she liked significantly more was jealous.

"Coach wants to ride," Antonio confirmed, pulling to a stop next to them.

"Do I?" she asked.

"You should be our example," Suleiman said, "since we're still on our two-week trial."

Aida rolled her eyes. "Nice try."

Vander was already leading a horse over, but Tate intercepted him and took the reins. He brought the sleek gelding the last few feet to Aida.

"Here you go. This is Rocky." He handed Aida the reins as though he were somehow in charge here, which he definitely wasn't. "You need help up?"

Aida would bet good money Tate had never helped anyone onto a horse in his life. If she needed tips on playing foosball or throwing a discus, he'd be her first choice. But horseback riding?

Tate held out his hand, as though mounting a horse was similar to getting into a car. She eyed his fingers. That hand was not going to be of any use getting on a horse. But she was *sure* interested in holding it.

"What?" Tate asked.

"Nothing."

Seriously, what was she supposed to do here? She didn't want to insult Tate, but the minute she put her hand in his, it would become apparent that she was no closer to getting on the horse than she had been when she'd gotten out of bed that morning.

Vander materialized at her side, placing a mounting block at her feet then drifting away so they could all pretend the stool had been there the entire time and Tate's help would be of use.

Aida slipped her hand into Tate's. A floaty feeling came over her. Maybe his hand was all she needed, after all, because his touch rendered her weightless and free. His warm scent blocked out the smell of barn and his smile dimmed every other source of light. While she understood that she was getting on a horse, it was somewhat of a surprise to find herself actually in the saddle.

And now it was time to let go of his hand.

"Allez!" Suleiman called. The boys were already at the gate, ready to head out to the trails.

"You coming?" she asked Tate, her fingers still enveloped by his.

"I think you got the last available horse," he said.

She gave his hand a tug. Without thinking it through, she said, "Share with me."

Tate's face lit up, like she'd suggested they share a six-by-eight-foot box of gold coins. He stepped onto the mounting box then launched himself behind her on the horse. The animal turned its head to look at them with narrowed eyes, suggesting two humans were no big deal, but they could have given him a warning all the same.

Aida leaned forward to pat Rocky's neck but

froze when Tate slipped his arms around her waist. She closed her eyes briefly, settling into the solid warmth of Tate. Her heart stirred with a feeling it took her a moment to identify.

Longing.

She wanted this. A friend, a teammate, someone to laugh and strategize with, two strong arms around her waist that didn't want to be anywhere else.

"You okay?" Tate asked, his breath warm against her ear. Sunshine flooded her vision as the horse took long, purposeful strides out of the arena, following Suleiman and Antonio.

"Yep."

Just, you know, reevaluating my world view after 2.4 seconds in your arms.

Aida hadn't thought about dating since college. Most of the guys she'd dated were players on the men's team. Men who understood the demands on a college athlete and shared her love of the game but little else.

Aida had been so distraught when her soccer career ended that she couldn't remember breaking up with her boyfriend. It happened, but how had she felt in the moment? Was the breakup his idea or hers?

All she could remember was disappointment.

But Tate's magic was working on her. Helping him with the team and facing her past dissipated the pain. As she began to accept the loss of her dream, her heart seemed to wake up and admit it wanted more than soccer.

Specifically, it wanted six feet, three inches and a shock of dark brown hair.

Tate was still speaking; she could feel the rumble of his words in his chest against her back. He was saying something about this being his second time horseback riding, something about it being a good thing she was there to "steer the horse." She didn't answer. For the first time since senior year in college, she was happy even though her life had veered off the expected course. She was happy *because* of where she was.

Who would have thought that after all these years it was a loud, gregarious hipster from the city who'd lift her out of her funk?

She glanced over her shoulder at Tate. He raised one hand to brush a strand of her hair out of her face, tucking it behind her ear, still talking as though their activity required narration.

She wasn't going to act on this crush. She couldn't. Tate was charming to everyone. His concern for her may have her heart shouting "Olé!" but he was concerned about everyone: his students, his coworkers, her dog, Luci's hedgehogs. That was who he was. That care didn't translate into a relationship. She couldn't imagine he'd be in Pronghorn for more than a year or two. Eventually, he'd move on, back to one of the cities he was more comfortable in. A city where everyone jaywalked all day long and the police didn't even look sideways.

No, it was best not to get in too deep with Tate, or anyone. Her coaching partner had a way of making her feel strong and free, like anything was possible. It was the same way soccer had made her feel. She wasn't falling for that a second time.

While she'd make sure her future never included that type of heartbreak again, it was time to let go of the past.

She glanced ahead to where Suleiman and Antonio rode, racing each other across the expanse of prairie. Colter cantered out to meet them, his enthusiasm matching the kids'. Aida pulled up on the reins.

"We're stopping?" Tate asked.

Aida nodded. He readjusted his arms around her, like he didn't want this ride to end any more than she did. But to let go of her past disappointment, she needed to be honest about what happened in the first place. "Do you mind if we head back to the arena?"

The look on his face was a clear *no*, but he nodded.

"There's something I need to tell you. To talk to you about."

TATE WAS INTRIGUED. Aida wanted to talk, which was awesome. But she also wanted to stop horseback riding. Or horseback hugging, as he had begun to think about it.

Once they were near the arena, she slipped off the horse and Tate followed her lead.

"Is everything okay?" he asked.

"Yeah." She nodded then scanned the property as though confirming that everything was, in fact, okay.

"Thanks for coming today," he said. "The kids really wanted you here."

I wanted you here.

"No, it's good." Her gaze flitted to his as she took a few steps in the direction of the arena. "It's got me thinking."

Cautiously, he gave the reins a tug, and he and Rocky fell into step next to her.

The breeze pushed a few strands of hair across her cheek. She tucked them behind her ear as she said, "I wanted to play soccer professionally."

He nodded, letting the conversation flow or not flow, as she chose. She wound her arms around her middle and leaned forward, protecting herself.

"I was good enough. And, yeah, I know a lot of people think that, but I have statistics to back it up. I was as good, and in some cases better, than a lot of the women playing in the National Women's Soccer League." She kept her eyes straightforward, her voice steady, like she was giving a police report on a horrific crime she didn't want to let affect her.

"You were," he confirmed.

"I was told, and I believed, if I worked hard, I could realize my dreams."

He moved closer to her, sheltering her as they approached the arena.

Aida continued, her voice flat, "I set goals and I worked to achieve them. I encouraged and even coached my teammates in high school so we would be strong enough to take on real competition. I was systematic. I avoided injury. I set everything in place." She looked up at him, moisture rimming her eyes. "And then I failed. My senior year season in college came and went. I had conversations and callbacks and came so close. But I was never offered a contract." Her voice broke and she closed her eyes and swallowed hard as a tear slipped. "That's why I can't—"

Tate wrapped an arm around her shoulders. The horse walked steadily on the other side of them, alert to the emotion.

Aida swallowed hard, working to hold back the tears.

"I can only imagine how hard it's been," he finally said. "You know there are so many others right there with you? Our system puts a lot of athletes in this position."

"I know but—"

Tate rubbed her back, offering the only thing he could think of to make her feel better. "You want some statistics?"

She gave him a side-eye. *Right.*

Then again, he'd gathered this information in preparation for his own mental health as it related to sports and as an antidote to the pressure his parents had put on him. It might be helpful.

As they entered the empty arena, she glanced up at him, like even his sorry statistics might help.

"The vast majority of athletes don't continue to the next level," he said.

"I know but—"

"Less than two percent of all college athletes in

the US play professionally. That's a tiny percentage. It's not fair, and it hurts, but it is not your fault."

She shook her head. "But I can't let go. That *is* my fault. I care too much."

"Of course, you care. You go all-in. It's one of the things I admire about you."

She held his gaze.

"It hurts to care," she finally said.

"But it feels good, too, right?"

"Debatable."

The horse came to a stop at what could be a hitching post, Tate really wasn't sure. He was too focused on Aida to worry about it as he draped the reins around the...the something that looked like he was supposed to drape reins around.

"Aida, I'm sorry I pressured you into coaching. I never would have asked if I'd known."

"No, I'm glad you asked. I needed this."

"Really?" He was tempted to document the moment with a quick selfie with her.

"It's working. I feel better." She placed a hand on her heart. "I *feel*."

It took considerable restraint for Tate not to start doing Aida's victory dance. This really wasn't the moment.

"Everyone in this town has been treating me with kid gloves since I came home. You didn't know about my past, so you didn't know to tiptoe around me when it came to soccer."

Tate grinned. "I broke an unspoken Pronghorn rule?"

Her eyes flickered up to him. "You broke many Pronghorn rules, both unspoken and clearly posted."

He held her gaze. What kind of rules did the town have around kissing your co-coach?

Aida's eyes dropped briefly to his lips.

Did rules really matter anyway?

"Hey!" Mateo stuck his head into the arena. "What are you guys doing?"

Tate liked Mateo a lot. He counted the guy among his best friends. But *hello?*

"Talking?"

"Can you talk outside? With the students we're supposed to be chaperoning?"

"Yep." Aida took a step away from him. "Let's go."

"Don't you need to…?" Tate trailed off. What was he going to say?

Don't you need to open up more?

Spend more time with me in the arena?

Kiss me?

"What's your next game?" Mateo asked Aida as she headed for the door.

"Mountainside." Aida smiled. At *Mateo.* "It's like the big city around these parts."

"I didn't know there were big cities around here." Mateo and Aida headed into the sunshine, away from Tate.

This was unfair.

"Well, it's four hours away. 'Around these parts' is relative."

What was Mateo even doing, chatting her up about soccer games? If Aida's heart was opening, he was gonna be the one to sneak in there, not the math teacher. Tate looped the horse's reins once more around the post thing. The horse gazed at him, as though he were doing this so incorrectly it was funny.

Whatever.

Tate caught up to Aida outside the arena. Mateo finally got the hint and joined a game of cornhole, but it seemed like everyone wanted to talk to Aida. Her players were already waving her over to Colter's outdoor kitchen, vying for her attention. Tate needed to get in one last word. Or two.

"Thank you," he said. "It means a lot that you trusted me with this."

She studied the flagstones beneath her feet. "Thank you, Tate. I'm glad you landed in Pronghorn, even if it's just for a little while."

Tate frowned. He'd never indicated to anyone he was planning on leaving. Unless you counted the times when he grumbled under his breath while being handed a ticket.

He started to correct her, but Aida gave him a sly smile as she gestured to the joyful melee of kids. "It pains me to admit it, but you're doing a lot of good."

Tate slipped his hands in his pockets, grinning. "How much good was that again?"

"A lot," she admitted.

"Coach Aida!" Ilsa waved from where she and Mav were now arguing next to the buffet. "Have you had the barbecue?"

"Let me wash my hands and I'll come try it,"

Aida responded. She gave Tate a shy smile then slipped away, her soccer players commandeering her attention. She joined in their debate about which type of chips was best and tried the different types of barbecue that Colter had prepared.

Greg trotted over and sat expectantly next to Tate.

"Who needs his ears scratched?" Tate asked, kneeling. "Who's a good boy with ears?"

The dog didn't even balk at the ridiculous question, just enjoyed the ear rub.

Tate caught Aida watching him. He grinned back at her and asked the dog in a low voice, "Who's doing a lot of good in Pronghorn? Is it Tate?"

Greg answered with a dog kiss right on the nose and a cheerful bark.

"Good boy."

CHAPTER ELEVEN

"So this is Mountainside?" Tate asked, scanning the surroundings. He'd climbed into Colter's truck in the early hours of the morning, then dozed as they'd driven some interminable distance to game three. They were higher in elevation, and there were more trees here. As they'd passed through the town, Tate had noticed multiple businesses and even neighborhoods.

Now, as they stood with their team on the sidelines of a soccer field, it felt like they'd landed in a different world.

"A huge metropolis of two hundred people," Aida said.

"There are already three hundred people here to watch the game," Tate noted.

"Word gets out fast."

The crowd was large, the vibe decidedly different.

"Is it the result of the long drive or does it seem—?" Tate didn't want to vocalize what he was feeling.

"Yeah, it does." She squeezed his arm. "Mountainside takes itself pretty seriously."

He was taking her hand on his arm pretty seriously too. But then she was off, pumping up Cece for the game. Aida had been more relaxed since their conversation at Colter's ranch, more cheerful, often hanging out with the teachers at the hotel in her spare time. But he could tell Mountainside was making her tense.

Probably because their spectators were staring at the Pronghorn crowd with a little too much interest.

Tate twisted around from where he stood on the sidelines. Today's Moment and a small contingent from the commune stood among the ranchers and townsfolk of Pronghorn. Since most of the Pronghorn crowd now wore bright yellow and orange shirts and scarves, they didn't stick out as much as usual in their orange. But they did stick out. Tate became aware of people pointing at them, staring longer than necessary. He didn't fully understand the folks at Open Hearts, but he wasn't interested in anyone giving them a hard time.

Everything proceeded according to schedule, even if he sensed something was off. The teams finished their warmups and reassembled on the sidelines. The ref met briefly with the coaches. The team captains headed onto the field for the coin toss. But while Aida glared at the quarter, daring it to even think about landing with the tails side up, a clean Sprinter passenger van arrived at the field. A group of young people climbed out and lined up to watch the game.

All boys, all in khaki pants, boat shoes and navy

blue polo shirts. They looked like a convention of very young insurance agents on a river cruise.

"Who are those kids?" Tate asked.

Mason, who was at Tate's side, muttered, "Westlake Charter."

"Is that the school on a lake? Because I need an explanation for those shoes."

Mason kept his eyes on the team. "It's an all-boys boarding school. The school is public, but you have to pay to live in the dorms, and for the uniform. There are a lot of fees, so it winds up being expensive. I did the math."

Mason often *did the math*. It was his thing. But why would he calculate the cost of a boarding school? Unless—?

"Angie wasn't thinking of sending you there?" Tate was horrified.

"It was the only option if Pronghorn hadn't reopened."

Tate remembered that Mason hadn't been in a good space at the beginning of the school year. He'd been depressed, defiant and always getting into trouble. Online school hadn't been a good fit for him, and it was likely Angie had been grasping at straws to save her kid. That straw would have been almost impossible for her to afford, and he couldn't imagine Mason thriving away from his family. Or wearing boat shoes.

"I'm glad we reopened then. I'd hate for you to be anywhere they expected you to wear shoes with no socks."

"Me too."

"Let's go!" Aida yelled, having established a winning coin toss with the power of threatening thinking. She turned to Tate and Mason, pointing at the neatly dressed observers. "We meet Westlake Charter in a few weeks. They're here to see what we can do."

Her voice was meant to sound cheerful, but Aida clenched and unclenched her fists then wrapped her arms around her middle.

"You're tense," he observed.

Aida snorted.

"You're more tense than usual," he clarified. The whole situation was more tense than usual.

"I don't like that coach," she said, indicating the opposing coach with her chin.

"You haven't liked any of the opposing coaches," he reminded her. "Last week we were up against a tiny team coached by a nice middle-aged couple and you accused them of doping their players."

"They had energy drinks on the sidelines," she reminded him.

Those energy drinks hadn't done much good. Pronghorn had won nine to zero, and only because he'd forbidden anyone to score in the second half.

Today might be a little tougher, and he had a feeling that when they met Westlake Charter in a few weeks, it would be a lot tougher.

AIDA RAN DOWN the sidelines, cheering for Ilsa as she approached the goal. Behind her, the community roared with excitement.

Ilsa slipped around a massive defender then caught the goalie off guard with her left-footed kick, and scored.

"That's right!" Aida called, pointing at Ilsa.

"Olé! Olé! Olé!" Pete Sorel called out. The crowd responded with "Hup! Hup! Holland!" which was how they now responded to every goal, no matter what nationality the player. Then every Pronghorn fan, from the smallest child from the Open Hearts community, to Mrs. Moran, joined in Aida's victory dance.

Aida hadn't even realized she'd dusted off the dance until Tate had brought it up that first game. Now the whole town had picked up on it. It was a little disconcerting, but they were winning, so she wouldn't complain.

The ref blew his whistle. Aida looked up sharply to see the opposing team's coach on the field, arms crossed, talking to the ref. On the sidelines, she saw the coach from Westlake Charter watching the exchange closely.

The ref held his hands up, waved a yellow card and walked it over to Mav.

What?

Aida ran onto the field. The other coach, features set in resting grump face, met her at the midfield line.

The ref's sigh was audible.

"What was that for?" she asked.

"That kid's been insulting my players," the opposing coach said.

"He's the *goalie*," Aida reminded him.

Seriously. Those forwards aren't gonna insult themselves.

"It's against OSAA rules," the ref said.

Aida opened her mouth to suggest that no one had ever, in the history of soccer, followed that rule. But as a person who'd handed out a ticket for jaywalking in Pronghorn, she wasn't in a strong position to argue. She changed her tack.

"Mav? That's ridiculous." She waved a hand at him, like the most contrarian kid in Pronghorn had never picked a fight in his life. Then she called over her shoulder, "Mav, get over here. What's this guy talking about?"

"I don't know. Is a yellow card bad?"

She glared at him. He shrugged. Okay, maybe she hadn't gone over that particular piece of business, but who didn't know about a yellow card?

"He was baiting my player," the opposing coach snapped.

Aida craned her neck to peer around the large man. The Coyotes' least effective striker was looking uncomfortable on the sidelines. Goalies always talked smack to anyone close enough to listen, and vice versa. Was it even a soccer game without a little trash talk?

"What did you say?" Aida asked.

"Nothing." Mav raised his gangly arms in innocence. Tate joined the group, folding his arms and tilting his head to get the truth out of the kid. Mav sighed. "I just asked her who her favorite poet was."

Aida slowly closed her eyes. *Only Mav.*

"Then she said Shakespeare," Mav continued. "And I said Mary Oliver was better, and *she* got all upset." He gestured to the girl.

There was a smoldering feeling at the base of Aida's skull, which she was pretty sure indicated an actual fire catching and spreading through her brain. She couldn't believe Mav was discussing poetry during a game, but she was even more furious that a group of full-grown adults was standing on the field making an issue of it.

"Did you swear at her?"

"No."

"Did you insult her playing ability?"

"No." Mav looked down at his feet. "I did say some bad things about Shakespeare."

Aida turned to the ref. "Why are we here?"

"I just don't buy the hype," Mav added.

Aida stepped between him and the ref before a literary brawl could break out. "I want you to take that yellow card back, then let's finish out this game."

The opposing coach was bright red by now.

"No," he roared. "He was baiting her."

"There is no precedent for a yellow card being handed out for discussion of literature." She gave the ref a hard look. "Take the card back, and let's resume."

"That hippie kid is upsetting my players." The coach's eyes were dark with fury. "You try to keep that commune a secret and pretend they're not up to something, but I know they are." He pointed at

Mav, mustache trembling like whiskers on a musk-rat. "He's *weird.*"

The word seemed to catch on the wind, carried to the Pronghorn spectators. The crowd silenced. All the color drained from Mav's face.

"What did you say?" Aida asked.

"I said he's w—"

"You *do not* use that word." She took a step into his personal space. "We have some people in our community who live a little differently, but they are good, law-abiding citizens. Mav here is a big fan of Mary Oliver, and that's not a crime. If your play-ers aren't tough enough to discuss poetry during a game, that's on you. And their English teacher."

Tate dropped a hand on her shoulder. In that light, strong touch, she could feel that this had gone on long enough; she'd said her piece and they should get back to the game.

Aida ignored the message.

"We're winning, and I get that makes you mad. I'd be mad, too, if my team were losing one to nine, and I'd even wonder if that one goal was due to the generosity of the other team's goalie. But making up a foul and then insulting our community—"

The coach took another step toward Aida, as though he could invade her personal space when she'd already invaded his.

Not how this works, buddy.

"Your team is cheating," he said.

"No, my team is winning."

"I'm saying *you're* cheating by stacking your

team with all these soccer players from all over the world. This whole thing's a little fishy." He gestured to the team, who now stood in a large clump, watching.

Not unlike a school of fish.

But, of course, it was fishy. Anything involving Loretta was stock-pond-level fishy. Still, they were winning the game because they were better than the other team.

Aida turned on the ref. "You gonna call an end to this? He's insulting our players, and stalling."

The opposing coach waved a hand at the Pronghorns. "Where did all these kids come from?"

"Seriously, we need to have that conversation?" Aida asked. "Who was your health teacher?"

Okay, maybe she'd gone too far. The man was practically purple. He pointed to the team again. "You recruited international students just so you could win."

"I assure you, we—" Tate gestured between himself and Aida "—did not recruit them."

"You recruited them," the other coach said, pointing at Aida now. "I know all about you. You used to be some big-shot soccer player and now you think you can break the rules in order to have a winning team. Well, it's not gonna happen. Not in my town. You can relive your glory days on someone else's turf."

Aida felt as though she'd been ripped from her body. She understood she was standing on the field, fighting with an opposing coach, while three hundred people watched. But it felt like she was floating over herself, locked in humiliation, fear and regret.

Tate's hand on her shoulder had turned into a protective arm, drawing her closer, away from the argument. Tate's voice, firm but fair, took over the conversation. He laid out facts about not wanting to coach in the first place and recruiting Aida after the team had been assembled.

None of it assuaged the anger coming off the opposing coach.

None of it quelled the humiliation beating through her.

And on the sidelines, the boys from Westlake Charter watched. Behind them, their coach, a man in his midforties with mirrored aviator sunglasses, followed the interaction with interest.

The coach of the Coyotes continued down his trail of small-town soccer conspiracy theories. Accusing Mav of trying to convert students to the Open Hearts philosophy. Accusing Pronghorn of selective recruiting. Accusing Aida of doing anything to relive her days as a player, even though she had failed to make the NWSL.

And all the while, Aida hung over the field, suspended by her humiliation.

"Let's play." Tate's voice brought her back to the moment. He appealed to the kids from both sides. "Who wants to play some soccer?"

Whoops and cheers came from the Pronghorn crew and some of the kids from Mountainside as the players reassembled on the pitch.

"We're here to have fun, get a little exercise," Tate reminded both Aida and the opposing coach. "Mav, you've been warned. No more poetry on the field."

Slowly, the opposing coach returned to the side-lines. Aida was shaking so hard, it was difficult to walk. Tate's arm latched securely around her shoulders, guiding her back to the sidelines.

The sidelines were the only place she belonged anymore. Outside the game. She'd thought she was beginning to heal, to work through the past. But one mean-spirited coach was enough to send her straight back into her funk. And no matter how misguided the opposing coach was, he was right about one thing: Aida would do anything to relive her days on the field.

It was late, dark and cold by the time Colter dropped Tate and the other teachers at the hotel. Tate had wanted to ride home with Aida, but she'd taken off before they'd even finished shaking hands with the opposing team. She'd made some excuse about needing to get Flora and Mrs. Moran home early. As though there was any such thing as *early* when your soccer game requires an eight-hour round trip.

Aida didn't want to be anywhere near him. That was clear.

The teachers yawned and stretched as they climbed out of the vehicle, heading up to their rooms without so much as a snack. It had been a day.

Tate closed his bedroom door then checked his

phone again. He'd texted Aida twice. No response. Lack of internet, or interest. Or both.

Tate pulled off his sweatshirt and dropped it on the settee. All the teacher's rooms had a small sitting area with windows overlooking the school. Tate's sitting area had become more of a sweatshirt collection center.

Dwap. Dwap.

Tate looked sharply out the window, then shook his head. He was so tired, he was having auditory hallucinations of kids kicking a soccer ball.

Dwap.

Or auditory hallucinations of one person kicking the ball really hard.

Tate opened his window. It got so inconceivably dark at night when there was a cloud cover. He let his eyes adjust. *Dwap.* He turned toward the sound and could barely make out the shadowy outline of a woman weaving across the soccer field. A soft cry of frustration sounded from the pitch as she pulled her leg back then slammed the ball into the net.

Tate grabbed a sweatshirt and ran. His blood pounded through his veins as he hurtled down the stairs, across the street. He stopped abruptly when he saw her.

Aida flew down the field, the ball in a tight dribble before her. She cut left, as though around an imaginary opponent. Thirty feet from the goal, she drew her right foot back. With another cry, she launched the ball with extreme force then wiped her face as she watched it hit the goal box so hard Tate was concerned it might rip the net. She moved forward to retrieve the ball then backed up and kicked again. A cry of effort and angst split the air. She launched the ball once more, this goal straining the netting as though she intended to destroy it.

Then she covered her face with her hands and sank to her knees, her sobs echoing into the dark expanse of the valley beyond.

Tate knew Aida. She wanted to be alone, to mourn.

But he knew himself, too, and he couldn't walk away.

"Aida?" He ran to her side. She seemed disconcerted at the sound of her own name. "Aida." He knelt before her, gently touched her wrists and encouraged her to lower her hands from her face. She cried out again, but rather than push him away or snap at him, she let him wrap her in a hug. She sobbed on his shoulder, her chest shaking as she drew in enough air to cry.

Tate ran a hand over her hair. He readjusted his arms around her shaking frame, giving her all the care he could.

Aida pulled in a shaking breath then another. She swallowed hard but didn't let go of him.

"I'm sorry," she finally said.

"Do not be sorry." He lowered his head to look directly into her eyes. "There is nothing to be sorry about."

She pressed her lips together, a fresh round of tears flushing her eyes. "I miss it so much."

"Of course you do."

Aida sat back on her heels, still taking in deep breaths.

"I don't know how to stop wanting to play." Her voice cracked.

Tate realized he was crying too. He didn't understand what it was to be on the verge of a dream and to have that dream ripped away. But he knew loss, and grief. He knew Aida.

Tonight, in the dark and cold, he could offer little more than a shoulder to cry on.

But it was possible that, for now, this was all she needed.

CHAPTER TWELVE

"I'LL SEE YOU all over there!" Tate said as he rinsed his plate in the sink.

His coworkers looked up, still lingering over breakfast at one of the large, steel-topped tables in the industrial kitchen.

"You eat that toast fast enough?" Luci called after him.

Hopefully. He didn't want to miss Aida's arrival at work. But he didn't want to be there too early either. He needed to casually walk out of the hotel just as she arrived at her office and remember not to jaywalk.

In the weeks since the Mountainside game, since he'd been able to offer Aida support on the soccer field late that night, she'd begun to open up. She'd shared more about her past, and let him in on details of her work and life in Pronghorn. As they'd become closer, he'd found every excuse he could to invite her over to the hotel. His friends had welcomed her into their circle. He'd even heard Luci tell Willa she couldn't imagine their group without Aida.

Seeing Aida had become his favorite part of every

day. If he could see her more than once a day, even better. That meant getting breakfast over with in time to run into her on her way into the office.

Willa's concerned voice followed him out of the kitchen; some reminder about one slice of toast not having enough calories to get him through more than ten minutes of teaching. Luci's voice rose over hers, suggesting the word *hangry* had been invented with him in mind. Tate kept walking.

He stepped into the chill morning air of the courtyard. The temperature had dropped significantly in Pronghorn over the last few weeks. The mornings were cool, with a bite that didn't wear off until afternoon. In another month or two, it might snow. He could only imagine how beautiful this place was going to be in winter.

All of it made him want to settle in. Invest in this place, this community, put down roots in an old farmhouse and create the supportive, loving family he'd always dreamed of.

Tate stopped walking in the middle of the courtyard.

Was it the weather, or the landscape, or Aida, that made him feel this way?

He was getting ahead of himself.

He wasn't even going to ask Aida out on a date until after the league playoffs. A farmhouse full of kids, under the care of a very patient German shepherd, was a long way off.

The sound of a slamming car door hit his ears. Tate trotted out into the street.

Aida glanced over, like she'd been expecting him to emerge from the courtyard the moment she arrived. Not an unreasonable expectation since he'd been able to time it right for the last four days in a row. A shy smile lit her face and she waved.

Okay, maybe he'd ask her out after game five. Just past midseason.

"You ready for a big practice today?" she asked, grooving her shoulders like she did in her victory dance.

Who was he kidding? He was going to ask her out right now, at 7:00 a.m. on a Thursday.

Tate strode across the street, stepping over Connie the cat as he did so. Blatant jaywalkery.

Aida didn't seem to notice.

So, clearly, this was love. Or she was running out of tickets.

Tate put his hands in his pockets and allowed Aida to draw him to her like a beautiful, capable, magnet.

"Yeah." He stopped right in front of her. Her eyes connected with his, a faint blush rising to her cheeks. How was it she was so pretty in a brown sheriff's uniform and a no-nonsense ponytail?

Greg gave a muted whine, reminding Tate that he was there, too, and he also looked good in brown.

Tate dropped down on one knee and gave Greg an appreciative ear rub. "Who's a good boy this morning?"

"The same guy who was a good boy yesterday

morning." Aida said to the dog, "Don't let him question your worth."

Tate laughed. Greg leaned his chin over Tate's shoulder and soaked up the love.

"Practice might go a little over," Aida said. "We've got Westlake Charter coming up and I want to teach some new passing lanes. The Helmsmen are going to be better defenders, and we need to surprise them with combinations they didn't see at Mountainside. I've got a new drill. Then we need to go over the game plan for Saturday."

Tate repressed a smile. Practice had "gone a little over" for the last four days straight. He had a feeling it would go on all night if Aida was in charge.

And he wouldn't mind a bit.

Fortunately, the players' parents had no qualms about getting vocal when things ran too late, making for a natural end to the proceedings.

"And then, I was wondering…" She paused. "There's a Pronghorn tradition I thought we might want to revive. When I was in school, we used to have an actual pronghorn horn. Like an antler. At the end of every game, it was awarded to the best player."

"That's cool." Tate rose from where he'd been communing with Greg. "Where is it now?"

"I still have it."

Tate laughed. Aida didn't seem to think it was funny.

"After each game, you and I talk it out, and choose the most valuable player, the one who did the most to secure the win. Then on Monday, at practice, we award the pronghorn."

The concept was solid. There was only one problem Aida hadn't seemed to consider. "Wouldn't we wind up giving the pronghorn to Suleiman all the time?"

Aida shrugged. "If he's the best player."

"He scores an average of five goals per game, and the only reason it's not more is because we ask him to stop," Tate reminded her.

"Which is what made me think of the pronghorn."

"We can't give the award for 'most valuable' to the same kid over and over."

"Why not?"

Tate blew out a breath. "There are a lot of ways to be valuable to a team, and scoring the most goals is only one."

Aida gave him a side-eye and spoke slowly and clearly, like he was six. "I know that."

"And Suleiman could easily score the most goals without working nearly as hard as, say, Cece."

"What, you want to give a pronghorn to a different kid every time?"

"Ideally, yes. Sometimes, it takes more grit for a couple of these kids to step on the field than it does for Suleiman to score three times in a row."

"But the award is for the MVP."

"Okay, but how do we define MVP?"

She threw her arms out. "By the person who gets us closest to winning!"

Tate chuckled at her intensity. "You can get a little obsessed with winning."

Her face fell. Greg reacted quickly, pressing himself against her leg and sending Tate a warning growl.

"I know."

"I'm sorry, I didn't mean—"

"You did mean it. It's true." She had the same expression she got right before handing him a ticket. "I'm 'a little obsessed' with winning." She turned away, heading for the office door. "I told you that before we even got started."

"There's nothing wrong with—"

"The MVP award is a terrible idea, I get it. I shouldn't have suggested it."

"Aida, wait." Tate ran to catch up with her then stepped in front of her so she couldn't unlock the front door to her office.

She sighed and tried to reach around him. Tate had played enough basketball to be frustratingly large in front of an opponent without coming off as threatening. "Move," she snapped.

"I'm sorry. I didn't mean it like that."

"You meant what you said. I'm obsessed with winning. This isn't front-page news to anyone."

"It's okay to like winning." He tried to coax her smile back with one of his own. "I love winning. It's one of my favorite things."

"Safe to say I don't have the same relationship with competition that other people do."

Aida tried to step past him and Tate moved again.

"I will literally go around to the back door!" she snapped.

"Please don't be mad at me," he blurted out.

Her expression softened, less annoyed, more concerned.

"I'm not mad. I'm—" She shook her head and glanced back at the soccer field. "I'm worried."

"What are you worried about?" Tate asked quietly.

"This. Everything. Me. Don't you think it's all gotten a little out of control?"

Tate tilted his head to the side, inviting more information.

"Like, people in this town are acting like the kids on the team are heroes," she said. "And I just follow along and bring up the pronghorn award." Her voice was soft, as though this was a terrible thing to do to a kid.

"There's nothing wrong with adults celebrating young people for determination and teamwork."

She shook her head, like he wasn't getting it—which he wasn't.

"Did you see that drone at the last game? Someone's filming us so they can rewatch the game. Who rewatches a Single A, coed, high-school soccer game?"

"Parents. Grandparents."

"It's the kids, and folks are treating Greg more like a mascot than an officer of the law."

Greg's expression suggested he didn't have a problem with off-duty adulation.

"And then there's...you know, us." She gestured between them.

Tate's heart constricted. Was there a problem with "us"? Because he was real interested in "us." That was pretty much the most interesting thing to him right now.

"Like, everyone treats us as though we're the greatest thing Pronghorn has ever seen."

"How is that an issue?" Tate asked.

"I don't want..." Her voice trailed off.

Tate struggled to wrap a few neurons around her concern.

She gestured to the end of the street. "When was the last time we actually paid for a meal at The Restaurant?"

"What's wrong with free food at The Restaurant?"

Aida's gaze connected with his. Tate raised his brows.

Yeah, where do you even start with that one?

"The whole situation feels out of control."

"It is out of our control. How others act has never been in our control, and I, for one, am excited the reaction is positive. Given the possibilities, I'd say this is the best possible outcome."

Aida's eyes flickered across the soccer pitch.

Instinctively, he reached out and took her hand. She didn't pull away, but kept her eyes on the field as she wove her fingers through his. Her hands were soft, an unexpected contrast to her tough demeanor. It struck him that the silvery blue tones of a row of diamonds set in a simple platinum band would look beautiful on her hand.

"What is it?" he asked.

WHAT IS IT?

She felt alive. The town was coming alive.

It all felt a little too familiar.

Except for whatever this was she was feeling for Tate. It wasn't familiar at all, but wild and unpredictable.

This sweet, loud man that she couldn't wait to see every morning, every afternoon. This city boy who would probably move to another big city the first chance he got. He was bringing everything back to life.

She'd managed to limp along after her failed soccer career, hiding in a profession that required her to keep others at a distance. What if she fell for Tate and it didn't work out? That heartbreak wasn't something she could ever recover from.

She wanted to put the brakes on all of this, but she wasn't in the driver's seat. Everything, the town's reaction to the winning team, her reaction to coaching, her reaction to Tate…it was all just happening.

"Maybe we should dial it back a little?"

Tate's expression fell.

Unqualified appreciation of his skills was something he craved. He'd grown up in a home where, no matter how hard he worked, he was never good enough. He worked in a profession where he could do everything right and still get called out by any taxpayer, or tax evader, at any time.

For the first time, he had an entire community celebrating him.

She just didn't know if she could handle this a second time.

The sound of an engine approaching caught her attention. She knew everyone's distinct vehicle sounds. The warm rumble of Colter's truck, the insistent putter of Raquel's Subaru, the clean purr of Loretta's yellow Bug, the soft hiss of the Lyfcycles the folks from Open Hearts rode in from the commune.

This was Pete's truck. Aside from being on the school board, and aggressively supporting organized sports, Pete drove the school bus route in his big, white truck. He made what amounted to a two-hour drive, twice a day, to make sure four kids were able to get to school.

She turned at the sound to see him reflectively swerve around Connie. A flash of color in his truck bed caught her eye. Green, red and yellow flapping in the wind, alongside an American flag.

"Is that—?" Tate couldn't seem to come up with the word for what they had to be seeing.

The truck came to an abrupt stop just past Tate and Aida. They barely registered the students piling out of the extended cab, because the bumper of the truck held several more mysteries.

"And those are—" Aida pointed.

Tate shrugged. "I guess so?"

Pete waved out the driver's-side window. "Olé! Olé! Olé!"

"Hup! Hup! Holland!" Tate and Aida returned the greeting reflexively.

"You like my new flag?" Pete asked, pointing with his thumb to the back of the cab. "Senegal!"

"It's amazing," Aida said. She was quite literally amazed.

"I had to settle for bumper stickers for the rest of the kids because I only had two flagpoles." The back of his truck was covered with flag bumper stickers repping everywhere from Brazil to Romania to South Korea. "I figure, as we have more exchange students in the future, I'll keep adding to the bumper. You can't have too many flags on a truck!"

"That's...true," Tate said.

"You know what I did?" Pete leaned his elbow out the window, the official posture of an older man giving advice. "I ordered 'em off this site called Amazon. They shipped straight to Lakeview. Two days later, I make a quick, three-hour drive, and I've got my flags." He shook his head and chuckled. "That site has everything."

"Does it now?" Aida asked.

"Flags, oil filters...you name it."

"This is awesome," Tate said. "Thank you for being so supportive of the kids."

"You hear Westlake Charter decided to take a forfeit?" Pete chuckled.

"Wait, what?" Aida asked. "Since when?"

"I just got a call from Ed Gonzales, who heard

it from his cousin, whose ex-wife has a nephew on the team. Word is there's a regatta that weekend that half the team committed to and they can't let their boats down."

"No one misses a soccer game for a high school regatta," Aida said. "That's not a thing."

"Then I guess they're just looking for an excuse. Their coach musta realized they couldn't win against our team and didn't want a ten-point loss on his record." Pete chuckled. "See you at practice." He gave the two a wave and roared away.

Tate and Aida stared after the truck as it rumbled down the street, the American and Senegalese flags flapping together as the truck turned the corner and headed out of town.

"*Uau,*" Aida said under her breath.

"Yeah. *Uau.*"

The chatter of teenagers bubbled from the school behind them. Down the street, Mac's new Ice Cream sign stood out against the weathered wood of the old store. Angie kicked open The Restaurant's front door and put out the sandwich board. This morning it displayed not two but three breakfast options.

Fried eggs, wheat toast and sausage.

Scrambled eggs, white toast and bacon.

Miso soup with tofu and rice.

Angie straightened and put her hands on her hips. "What?"

"Nothing," they both said.

Angie disappeared back inside, grumbling about putting what she wanted on her own menu.

There would be no dialing anything back. As it had in her own days as a soccer star, the sport was bringing the town together. For better or for worse, she was at the center of the town's hopes, again. She couldn't control other people's reactions. She just needed to learn how to handle hers better than she had in the past.

Tate put his hands in his pockets and tilted his head. "Maybe I should have given soccer a little more credit a long time ago."

Aida bumped Tate with her shoulder. He had his own complicated history with the game. "This soccer experience is a little more fun than your last one, though, isn't it?"

Tate's smile broke out, well past flirtatious at this point, mirroring whatever was going on with her own emotions. "Significantly more fun."

"Ten minutes!" Vander's voice intoned from inside the school. "School starts in ten minutes."

Aida pulled in a deep breath. "You're right about the pronghorn. Or rather, you have a different idea than I did originally, and I think we should go with yours."

"The pronghorn was your idea," he said. "You brought it back from your own experience, and I don't want to commandeer it."

"No, you're right. There are a lot of ways to be of value to the team. But can we change the wording?"

"How so?"

"Like, rather than being MVP, let's call it something else."

"Like what?"

"I don't know. Something that an actual prong-horn antelope would do."

"Nibble sagebrush? Take over a field before practice?"

Aida gazed in the direction of Hart Mountain. "You know what pronghorn do? They show up. Let's choose the player who shows up in some significant way."

"I love it," Tate said, gazing at her.

"It feels right." She nodded, smiling back at him. "And I hate to say it, but you know who really showed up last week—"

"Suleiman. I get it."

"Just for the first week—" Aida's words sped up "—then we'll choose someone else, I one-hundred-percent promise."

"I'm glad we're reviving your tradition."

She took a deep breath. "It's time. I'm ready to pass it on."

All around them, kids were heading into the school. Tate backed away one step, still looking at Aida. Greg tilted his head, wondering where his scritches were in all of this.

She raised her hand and waved at him, despite the fact that he was only three feet away.

"See you after school."

"Yeah." He stood still.

Tate's all-school PE class was the first class of the day. He probably needed to get in and get ready. But he stood still, smiling.

She was doing the same.

"School starts in five minutes," Vander called, adding on, "Seriously, Coach Tate, get to work."

Startled, he turned toward the school, took one step and then spun back around. He seemed to momentarily wrestle with something before blurting, "Do you want to go out? With me?"

Aida's full-body reaction of, "Yes!" must have come out verbally as well, because a huge, adorable grin broke out on Tate's face.

"Really?" he asked.

Aida nodded, her body taking over the conversation before her brain was able to weigh in. "Like, on a date?"

"Very much like a date," he confirmed.

"Okay. In Pronghorn?"

"That's all we've got, so…yeah." His bright smile made a date in Pronghorn seem like an evening in Paris.

Aida could feel a blush running up her cheeks. She'd made an effort to dial things back, but her heart couldn't figure out which way to turn the knob.

She was all-in now, whether she wanted to be or not.

CHAPTER THIRTEEN

Tate Ryman could plan a good date. He was an imperfect human, sure, but coordinating activity and managing transitions for a fun, romantic evening was his specialty. In the past, when he'd been interested in a woman, he'd enjoyed pulling out all the stops.

And he'd never been interested in anyone like he was in Aida.

In half an hour, he would arrive at Aida's house to pick her up for what he was pretty sure was the best evening out the town had seen in half a century. Were there inherent challenges in planning the perfect date in Pronghorn, Oregon? Absolutely. Did they have to be on the road at 6:00 a.m. for an away game the next day? Unfortunately, yes. But with Aida as inspiration, he was up for it.

If they were in the city, Tate would take her out for drinks then to dinner. From there, they'd hit a couple of clubs and, with someone like Aida, he'd end the evening with a romantic, moonlight walk in a park.

Because this was Pronghorn, a few modifications had to be made.

It had been hard not to tell his friends, but what other option was there? He didn't need the interference and advice of four other people. Fortunately, most of the others had plans for tonight. Luci was meeting Sylvie and the Pronghorn student design team to create more merch for the soccer fans. Willa had a date with Colter. Vander was working at Jameson Ranch most Saturdays. Mateo might be around, but Tate could slip past him.

It would be fine. His coworkers would never even notice.

Tate checked his watch. Four thirty-three. He was picking Aida up at five.

He gave his outfit another once-over. The dark blue button-down and slim-fitting slacks were fashion forward for Pronghorn. *Too much?* No. Not too much for Aida. And since this was a first date that he could, conceivably, wind up describing on his fiftieth wedding anniversary, he wanted to look good.

Or, he would look good if his hair would just lay flat for once. Tate fussed with the unruly black strands. Whatever. It was going to stand straight up after thirty seconds on the ATV anyway.

Tate trotted down the grand staircase, glancing around to make sure the coast was clear before slipping out to the empty courtyard.

Tate sped around the side of the building to the dilapidated shed that housed the two vehicles provided for the teachers: one camo-painted ATV and one snowmobile. Not the smoothest fleet a guy could hope for, but it would get him where he needed to go.

Aida's front door.

Tate fired up the finicky ATV, steered clear of the sidewalks and took the back roads out to Aida's place. During his time in Pronghorn, he'd learned that the state-constructed roads and highways were just one way of getting around, and not nearly the most efficient. A network of trails, back roads and shortcuts across pastures was used by the native Pronghornians as they rode horses, off-road vehicles and even the strange Segway/bicycle things from Open Hearts.

Aida's farmhouse came into view. The time-weathered siding and wraparound porch were inviting, beautiful in their simplicity.

Tate's heart started doing its rhumba-in-a-mosh-pit routine as he parked around back, like Flora had instructed him the first time he'd visited. The warm, autumn-scented wind blew steadily. Tate swallowed then circled the house to the front porch. The land seemed to expand in all directions, a vast and elegant setting for the lone house, as though everything in the world led to Aida.

Tate walked up the steps, rehearsing what he planned to say.

Hey! Great to see you! Possibly a quick kiss on the cheek, nothing too romantic, more of a casual greeting. Then he'd lean past Aida and wave at Flora. *Nice to see you, Mrs. Weston.* If she invited him in, he would be polite, charming, quick.

This was going to go great. Better than great. Aida was his friend and co-coach. They had a ton to talk about, and this date was planned to within an inch of its life.

He knocked.

There was a quick shuffle of footsteps then Aida opened the door slowly. The hesitancy seemed to ask if they were really doing this. Tate opened his mouth to greet her and tried to smile to help her feel less nervous than he was.

He didn't manage to do anything.

Aida was wearing a dress.

It was white, sleeveless, with an eyelet pattern of flowers. His eyes traveled down the dress, which ended at her knee, showing off her strong calves and the bruise she'd gotten at soccer practice when Mav accidentally kicked her shin. On her feet was a pair of cute high-top sneakers. Her hair was in sort of an updo, swept off her face but falling down her back.

Some combination of "You look beautiful" and "Hello" and *"Uau!"* got all garbled up in his mouth. But Tate was pretty sure he said something because she smiled. And that made *him* less nervous.

"Hi." Her one word told him everything he needed to hear. *I like you. I'm happy you're here. I'm nervous too.*

Heat rose to his face. He leaned forward, the vanilla scent of her shampoo drawing him in, and brushed a kiss across her cheek. Nothing about the move felt casual.

"Hi," he responded once he caught his breath.

Then Greg nosed his way in between them.

Oh. Greg?

Okay. Tate loved Greg. He was an amazing, good dog. But Tate hadn't realized the pup would be joining them on the date.

Greg gave Tate a long look, reminding him that he and Aida were a package deal, and a pretty good package at that. Tate dropped to one knee and gave him a few scritches of acknowledgment.

A quick visit with Flora later and the two humans and one furry friend loaded up on the ATV and headed across the fields. It was impressive how well that dog managed himself on the vehicle.

Tate parked in front of the hotel, as everywhere he planned to take Aida was in a two-block radius. He hopped off the machine and offered Aida a hand. Greg headed down the street, toward the sandwich board warning the town of this evening's offerings.

"Are we heading to The Restaurant?"

"For starters," he said.

"This is the type of date with starters?"

"Yep. We'll have drinks at The Restaurant, then I made you dinner back at the hotel. Then dancing."

"Dancing?" She crossed her arms, suspicious of how and where dancing could happen in Pronghorn.

"Yep. I'm glad you wore the right shoes." She blushed again. This was awesome. "Then we'll go for a stroll in the closest thing Pronghorn has to a park."

Aida furrowed her brow. "And that would be the soccer field?"

"It's that or the empty lot on the other side of The Restaurant."

"Yeah, technically that's private property."

"No-go on the lot then?"

"We'd be trespassing." She glanced up at him, mischief in her eyes. "Drinks, dinner, dancing, a stroll. That's a lot of activities."

"It's a date," he pointed out. Had he planned too much? Was he just hurling fun at her and hoping some of it stuck?

She smiled and tapped her shoulder against his. "This is great. I'm excited. I was worried I might be overdressed. Now I realize I could have brought several costume changes."

Tate laughed. "You look perfect. Beautiful."

Aida flushed, tucking a strand of hair behind her ear.

"And it looks like your bruise is getting better." He pointed to her shin.

"It is! But, wow, Mav's foot packs a punch. We need to harness that on the field."

The scent of mediocre food wafted from The Restaurant. Greg parked himself in front of the outdoor water bowl, sniffing it like a connoisseur. They continued to brainstorm ideas to help Mav utilize his kick as Tate opened the door, but were cut off by Angie blocking the entrance.

"You two are sitting outside." She put her hands on her hips and gestured with her chin.

"Okay. Where do you want us?" Tate asked.

"Right up front." Angie pointed to a table that was actually on the sidewalk. "You're good for business. Why are you wearing a dress?" she asked Aida.

"I…um…"

"Never mind. Sit. I'll get your meals." Angie headed for the kitchen, but Tate tapped her arm.

"We just want drinks."

Angie stopped and slowly turned on them, eyes narrowed. One might have thought he'd told her they were there to borrow some bone marrow.

"Why?"

"We're thirsty," Tate tried.

She finally took in Tate's outfit then glanced back at Aida's dress and heaved a sigh. "Is this some kind of big-city date where you go out for 'drinks'?" she asked, using air quotes.

Tate didn't need to answer. Angie was already shaking her head, like a worse poser couldn't be found in the biggest city on earth.

"In my day, if a guy liked someone, he'd take her driving on dirt roads."

Tate tried to imagine spending his precious time with Aida bumping over a pasture in the ATV. "How is that a date?"

"It's romantic," Angie said.

"Sounds dusty," Tate replied, holding out a chair for Aida.

"No wonder you're single." Angie shook her head. "A person who can't stand a little dust doesn't deserve to have a girlfriend."

Angie stormed back into the building. Tate ran his hands through his hair then remembered he was hoping it didn't stick straight up this particular evening.

He sat down across the table from Aida. Did she want to go driving on a dirt road?

Before he could ask, a figure blocked the sun. Angie thunked a can of PBR in front of them, along with two glasses of ice.

"I've only got one beer left, so you have to share."

"Thank you, Angie."

"Besides, this'll be quicker. Since you have *so much else to do* this evening."

"That's thoughtful," Aida said with no sarcasm and an impressive display of self-regulation.

Angie harrumphed and headed into The Restaurant.

Now the date could begin.

Aida grinned as she picked up her glass of ice and rattled it. "I'd like my beer on the rocks."

Tate laughed. "I'd offer you a choice but—"

"This is The Restaurant," she finished.

Her gaze connected with his as Tate filled her glass.

"Hey!" Mateo seemed to materialize out of nowhere. "You guys having dinner here?"

Tate started, nearly pouring the beer all over Aida's wrist. "No! No, just grabbing half a beer."

"Cool." Mateo pulled a chair up to the table. "I'll go get a Coke and join you."

Before Tate could protest, his friend was already heading inside.

"I'm sorry," Tate said. "I'll ask him to leave."

"No, it's okay." Aida's eyes were bright with mischief. "We still have, like, twelve more activities left."

Tate ran his hands through his hair. "Too much?"

"No, not at all." Her eye caught his and he wondered if she, too, felt like all the time in the world would never be too much. "And I definitely don't feel like you used your lesson-planning skills to create this date."

Tate laughed. "Would you prefer a long, dusty drive on a bumpy road?"

Aida laughed, leaning her head back. So beautiful.

"*No.* Plus, I'd be tempted to troll for traffic violators. Why would I pick that over dancing? Which, I'm still not sure how you're going to pull off in Pronghorn."

"I have a plan," Tate said. "Although I should warn you. I'm not the best dancer in the world."

"You're not?" She tilted her head to one side. "Oh." Aida nodded slowly, then placed her hands on the table like she was about to leave. "I don't date anyone but the best dancers."

Tate laughed. "What if I were in the top twenty? In Pronghorn anyway."

She resituated herself in her chair and shrugged dramatically. "Ooookay."

Mateo came out of the door with a Coke in one hand. "Angie told me one of you could share your ice. That all right?"

"Of course." Tate lifted his glass.

Mateo sat down, turned his friendly smile on Aida then Tate. "What are you two up to?"

As they finished their shared beer, Tate racked his brain on how to ditch Mateo for the next stop on the date. But by the time they got to the hotel, Mateo turned out to be the least of their worries.

Tate led Aida into the dining room, which he'd tidied up for the occasion, only to find Willa and Colter. And the meal he'd prepared for Aida.

"Hey!" Willa waved at them. "I thought I'd go ahead and get dinner on the table, since you cooked."

"Tate, you cooked for everyone?" Aida asked, giving him a side-eye. "How thoughtful."

"I cooked dinner for—"

Tate was on the verge of setting everyone straight, but Aida ran a finger along the inside of his wrist.

It's okay.

Her light touch made everything okay, perfect even. And in Willa's defense, he had made a lot of food.

During the first, wild week of teaching in Pronghorn, the teachers learned that, among other things, they were responsible for preparing lunch for the students. As the health teacher, Tate had taken on this duty. He'd rallied the USDA supplies and donations from local farmers into appetizing meals for the kids. As time went on, parent and student volunteers took over the bulk of the lunch prep duties, but Tate still enjoyed planning the meals.

The trick, he'd learned, was to provide options.

To this end, his volunteers set up taco bars, sandwich bars, noodle bars.

All the bars, actually.

It worked. Kids enjoyed making choices. They'd grab a plate or bowl and move through the line of protein options, chopped vegetables and sauces, creating something relatively healthy that they actually ate.

Tonight he'd outdone himself.

"Is this a tapas bar?" Mateo asked.

"I think we can call it a tapas-inspired bar," Tate said. "I didn't find a lot of authentic Spanish ingredients in Lakeview, but the concept is the same."

Aida drifted along the banquet table, examining his creation. Rounds of bread he'd baked that morning topped with local goat cheese and fresh tomatoes. Individual chopped salads served in the hotel's teacups. Home-smoked venison sausage from Pete. Small plates of melon wrapped with thin slices of artisan ham. Cece's mom had caught a trout in the Blitzen River and offered it to the teachers. That afternoon, Tate had steamed small pieces of it, then paired the fish with pickled onion and wild dill.

The dishes went on and on. Aida finally reached the selection of fresh fruit he'd been able to come up with, most of which came from an overloaded pear tree he'd found outside Lakeview. She turned to him from the end of the banquet table, her eyes shining. "You made all of this?"

He ran his hands through his hair. "Guilty."

Her lips twisted in a smile as she mimed pulling out her ticket book.

Was *guilty* the right word? He certainly never would have accepted the title after any of the tickets she'd given him. But guilty of liking her so much, he'd prepared enough food for the entire population of Southeastern Oregon? Sure. He could cop to that.

"Oh, wait." Willa studied Aida and then Tate, as though just noticing their clothing, finally picking up on the chemistry. She pointed her thumb toward the door. "Tate, would you like us to—"

"No," he said, loud enough that a month ago Aida might have made an issue of it. "Stay. There's so much food."

Willa gave him a deadpan expression.

Okay, obviously.

Aida picked up a plate and handed it to Willa, who took it as her invitation to the meal. "Thank you. It's always so fun when you're here, Aida."

The words had a visible effect on Aida. It struck him that although she was a Pronghorn native, she'd been lonely here, nursing her heartache in chosen isolation.

"I've…I've really enjoyed getting to know all of you," she said.

"You're the perfect addition to our group." Willa said. "We need someone to help keep Tate in line."

Dinner was as noisy and boisterous as always. The small plates had everyone moving back and forth between the table and the buffet, trying different dishes, discussing their favorites. It was an active meal, which suited an active woman like Aida. He loved watching her laugh with his friends—their friends—and join in the banter.

And, between the five of them, they pretty much polished off the whole spread, save a few leftovers they held back for Vander and Luci. So maybe he hadn't gone completely overboard.

"Cleanup," Willa announced, standing.

"I call dishes," Mateo said.

"Hey, I'm gonna opt Aida out of cleanup." Tate stood and placed himself between Aida and the kitchen. The evening may have been hijacked thus far, but Aida's memories of their first date were *not* going to include dish soap.

"Of course." Mateo smiled at Aida in a way that still didn't make Tate completely comfortable. "And Tate cooked, so he's off duty." Mateo looked down at Greg. "You want to help?"

Greg gave Aida a low whine, likely asking about the leftover sausage. She nodded.

Perfect.

As the others headed to the kitchen, Tate slipped his hand in Aida's. She curled her fingers around his.

Everything was starting to feel a whole lot more like a date.

Tate led Aida into the ballroom. Early evening light shone through the skylight ring. About half of the bulbs in the wall sconces had burned out, unintentionally lending the space a romantic softness.

Aida was so pretty in the gentle light. Her palm

slid against his as she readjusted her hand, and that was all he needed to count this night as a success.

But he still had a lot more to go and they were getting to the good part.

Tate pulled in a deep breath. This next move was a little risky, but he needed to put himself out there. He turned to Aida and took her other hand in his.

"I majored in physical education in college."

"Is that a confession?"

He laughed. "No, an explanation. I took classes in nearly every sport imaginable. Tennis, volleyball, field hockey, ice hockey, baseball, swimming."

"That sounds like the making of a four-point GPA for you."

He shrugged. "Close to it. I also took ballroom dancing."

He waited a moment to see how this news landed. A lot of girls he'd dated found his dancing swoonworthy, but Aida might find the skill suspicious.

"Like waltzing and stuff?"

Yeah, she was a little suspicious.

"I can waltz, rumba, swing—"

"No." She laughed, shaking her head. "No one our age knows how to dance like that."

Tate took a step back and then another. He dropped her hands and cued up the playlist he'd made on his phone. The first notes of "Tuxedo Junction" by the Glenn Miller Orchestra filled the room. Aida looked around her, as though the music was a physical presence.

"You're serious."

He reached out a hand to her, his feet already picking up the beat. Aida didn't move.

"I thought you said you weren't the best dancer."

"I never placed in a competition."

She rolled her eyes. "What if I don't know how to dance like this?"

Tate grinned at her. "Part of learning to dance is learning to lead. I can guide you. Take my hand."

Aida held his gaze, a slow smile spreading across her face as the music seemed to catch in her feet as well.

"Trust me," he said.

TRUST TATE?

Yeah, it wasn't Tate Aida had trouble trusting. It was her own voracious heart she didn't think was up for this. The last time she'd let herself love anything, it was soccer; an all-encompassing obsession that she would never fully heal from.

But she was already falling for him, like everyone else who had the pleasure of his company. This feeling growing inside her felt like the music: big and full of dreams. Irresistible.

She slipped her hand into his. Tate gazed at her fingers then into her eyes as he pulled her closer. He wrapped an arm around her waist and took a gentle step toward her. Instinctively, she knew to move back, to follow the music. He drew her arms out, bringing their bodies closer to one another, then stepped back again and spun her under his arm. Aida laughed and he twirled her again. Dancing with Tate was freedom and safety, every perfect and frightening moment all at the same time.

"Is that Glen Miller?" A voice cut through the music. "Who's playing Glen Miller?"

Aida stopped, which made her dizzy, as though she'd stepped off a boat onto dry land.

Luci popped her head into the ballroom. "I love this song!"

Tate took a deep breath in through his nose, then exhaled.

"Why are you playing swing music?" Luci asked.

Aida liked and respected Luci, but *how was that not obvious?*

Tate, who'd done a remarkable job of not getting annoyed all evening as his friends crashed their date, tilted his head to one side and fixed Luci with a pointed stare.

"Because we're dancing."

"Without me?" she asked. "I love swing dancing."

Tate let out a groan. At that moment, Greg came trotting into the room, because if Luci was present, it was possible she had her hedgehogs with her. Mateo followed, then Willa and Colter, because apparently no one had anything else to do this evening. Aida had to assume Vander would be arriving at any moment.

"You know how to swing dance?" Mateo asked Luci.

"Yeeeeah. You don't graduate from the Breasely-Wentmore School for Girls without learning how to dance. How else are those debutantes gonna rock their coming-out balls?"

"Did you rock yours?" Mateo asked.

"No. For the billionth time, I'm not a debutante. I'm an Oregonian. I was fortunate enough to have excellent high school and college educations. Why do you care if I know a few ballroom dances?"

"I don't *care*," Mateo blustered. "It's just interesting." He paused awkwardly before admitting, "I, too, was forced to learn ballroom dancing. I do a heckuva fox trot."

"Stop mocking me," Luci snapped.

"I'm not mocking you. It was a requirement at the St. Xavier Military Academy."

If it wasn't for cheerful, 1940s-era horns still blasting through Tate's speakers, you could have heard a pin, or Luci's jaw, drop.

The easygoing math teacher had gone to military school? That did not fit anyone's image of Mateo. And he didn't seem any more comfortable with the information than anyone else.

Willa swooped in, as she did. "That's amazing! Am I the only one around here who doesn't know how to dance? Who's teaching me?" She panned left until her eyes landed on Tate. "You are. You're far and away the most qualified."

Tate started to protest, but Aida relinquished her date to Willa. They were friends, after all. And she wasn't going to deny her new friend the opportunity to learn how to dance with Tate.

"Who can help me out then?" Aida asked.

"Thanks to Lieutenant Amanda Bates, I can." Mateo gave her hand a tug and twirled her under his arm. It was fun, if not the magical trip through the stratosphere dancing with Tate had been. Luci helped Colter get the hang of things, and it turned out he'd done enough country swing to catch on quickly. A few songs in and Aida felt confident with the moves, even without a degree in physical education, a fancy private school education, or the backing of the US armed forces. The music changed, dance partners switched up, and all the while Greg ran between the humans, dodging feet and doing his own version of dancing.

The music slowed. An abundance of strings replaced the horns, changing the mood.

Tate stepped in between Aida and Mateo. "Time to switch partners."

Aida felt a full-body blush coming on. What was it about this music? It was swelling, flowing and piling up in her chest. Did they make it this way on purpose? How had people kept from constantly falling in love on the dance floor in the first part of the century with this playing all the time?

He wrapped his right hand around hers then pulled her close to him. His warm, clean, Tate scent surrounded her as he literally swept her off her feet.

He leaned in close to her ear. "I wasn't going to let Mateo get away with waltzing with my girl."

The music, and whatever tidal-wave activity was happening in Aida's heart, expanded in three-quarter time.

Tate had put so much care and thought into this evening, like he did with everything. And this care and thought was for her. And, wow, was it working.

She was falling for him.

This loud, gregarious, jaywalking man. Always the center of everyone's attention.

The center of her attention.

The music stopped. Tate's arms remained firmly around her waist, their eyes locked. If there were three other teachers, one rancher and a dog in the room, she couldn't see anyone beyond Tate.

"What are you guys doing?" Vander, in jeans, work boots, Stetson and all the dust presently available in the Warner Valley, stood in the doorway.

"Dancing," Luci informed him. "Let me guess, you also know how to ballroom dance."

"No. Why would I know that?" Vander slapped his hands together, releasing a cloud of fine silt into the air. "Can someone teach me?"

Luci let go of what Aida now recognized as a pretty tight grip on Mateo and walked over to him. "Sure, I—"

"Hey," Tate interrupted them. "I think Aida and I are gonna head out. Feel free to keep my phone for the music, though." Tate placed a hand on the small of her back and the two started for the door.

"Where are you going?" Luci asked.

Tate and Aida shared a glance.

Where were they going? Anywhere they could be alone. That's where they were headed.

"It's so nice out," Aida said. "We thought we'd

take a walk and make sure the soccer field is in good shape."

"It's beautiful tonight," Vander said. "Pure Pronghorn. This place has the prettiest evenings."

"It really does," Aida agreed.

Vander glanced around the room then down at his clothes. "I'm not dressed for dancing. I'll go with you guys."

Tate widened his eyes at Aida.

"It's nice to have friends," she reminded him.

"Clueless friends," he muttered.

"Sylvie's over there with some kids from school," Colter said. "Shall we join them?" he asked Willa.

"Let me grab a sweater," Luci said. "Aida, do you need a sweater?"

Thus, Aida found herself on a date with the entire teaching staff of Pronghorn Public Day School, and her dog.

And that was a drop in the bucket of humanity that awaited them.

The smell of barbecue drifted from the field, along with excited voices and pleasant chatter. On the soccer pitch, several kids played a pickup game, while their parents and host families grilled on the sidelines. They greeted the teachers and Aida like they'd been expecting them, and cheerfully offered burgers or grilled zucchini sandwiches.

But Aida wasn't interested in a second dinner. She tracked the game.

"You want to play?" Tate asked.

She shrugged. Obviously, she wanted to play.

He slipped his hands in his pockets and looked down at her, concern lining his face. "Are you up for playing?"

The emotions she'd blocked for so long, held back against a wall of cement and steel and barbed wire, pushed at her defenses. Cracks in the wall had been developing from the moment she'd agreed to help with the team, streams of feeling making it through, eroding her resolve. Tate threatened to take a sledgehammer to that wall, bust it open and let the emotion—good, bad, painful and profound—come crashing over her.

Aida was just so tired of trying to hold it all back. And if she needed a swimming instructor to stay afloat in all these feelings, Tate was probably the best there was.

She looked up into his blue eyes and nodded.

"Yeah. Yes. I really want to. Let's play."

A huge, gratifying smile broke out across his face. Tate took a few steps onto the field. "Who's winning?" he asked.

Suleiman raised a fist in the air and his team let out hoots of pride.

"You guys get me then. Coach Aida, you can help out Ilsa and her crew."

Ilsa's team let out a holler of approval.

Aida jumped into the game.

She cut in front of Suleiman, stealing the ball and turning it, the muscle memory doing the work while she laughed at the angry French-language insults Suleiman good-naturedly threw at her. She raced to-

ward the goal. Cece was exactly where she was supposed to be, as always, but clearly uninterested in
pushing things any further. Aida made eye contact
then launched the ball at her most hesitant player.

Cece stopped the ball and took a moment to grin
at Aida. That was when Antonio swept in and stole
the ball. They were back where they'd started.

The game continued, a cheerful, competitive,
back-and-forth. Aida laughed so hard, her chest
hurt. The competition felt awesome. It was competition, after all. But this was joyful and free.

"Aida, I'm open!" Tate waved at her.

She laughed out loud at his attempt at subterfuge.
"You're not on my team."

He shrugged like it had been worth a try.

Aida passed the ball off to Ilsa, reducing her
speed and finally coming to a stop to watch events
unfold on the other side of the field. Tate, in his
slacks and button-down shirt, ran at full speed, trying to block Ilsa from scoring. He said something
that made Mav laugh and then the other kids as well.
The sun dipped below the rim of the Coyote Hills,
bathing the valley in gold and red.

Tate didn't manage to get ahead of the ball, and
even Mav was no match for Ilsa's left-footed dagger.
Tate stopped to catch his breath as Ilsa celebrated
her goal with Aida's victory dance.

Tate's chest rose and fell as he dragged in air, his
hair stuck up in the front. He offered Ilsa a high five,
congratulating her for scoring against him.

He was so handsome, so open and generous with his laughter, his good will, his praise.

He was charming.

And Aida had been completely charmed.

Families lined the field, watching the game. The other teachers chatted easily with parents and students. The town was coming alive again, and so was she.

This man lit something inside her that had been dormant for years. But, unlike soccer, that fickle, unforgiving game, he was steady, uncomplicated.

As though feeling her gaze, Tate turned to her. His bright smile broke out. Then he glanced down as a flush ran up his face, as though she sparked the same feelings in him.

This was what falling in love felt like.

It was even better than soccer.

"Coach Aida!" Cece cried, warning in her voice.

Aida managed to look away from Tate to see Suleiman speeding past her with the ball.

Not on her watch. That kid hadn't had decent competition since he'd arrived in this town. It was time to set things straight. Aida launched back into the game, still a competitor, for all she was falling in love. The game flowed on, a perfect match to round out an evening she would never forget.

The sun had fully set by the time the party broke up. Aida, buzzing from the evening, and Greg, as exhausted as she'd ever seen her pup, hopped onto the ATV with Tate. She placed her hands lightly on his sides but took every bump and twist in the road as an opportunity to hang on a little tighter as he drove her home. The moon lit the way, covering the land with a watery sheen, making a ten-minute ride pass in seconds.

They pulled up in the little yard behind the farmhouse. Tate cut the motor, stood and offered his hand. Greg hopped off and headed inside through his dog door, where he could be heard slurping water on the screened-in back porch.

"Thank you," she said, hoping the word conveyed her gratitude for him helping her off the ATV, an incomparable date and healing her wounded heart.

It's all in the inflection, right?

He lowered his head so he was looking directly into her eyes.

"You had fun?"

"I had a blast. That was like the EPCOT center of dates."

"I had fun too. And again—" he chuckled in disbelief "—I'm so sorry about—" He gestured in the direction of town, indicating his boisterous, noisy group of friends and the rest of Pronghorn that had joined in.

"That's how things go around here."

His thick eyelashes obscured his blue eyes for a moment. He still held her hand.

The October moon hung bright and enormous above them. A cool breeze stirred the prairie grasses and brought an earthy smell from the copse of aspen trees at the edge of the property. Under normal circumstances, she'd feel chilly, but some type of radiant heat came from Tate's fingers and ran through her entire system. Right now, she didn't think feeling cold was ever going to be a problem again.

"I didn't have too much planned?" he asked.

"You had way too much planned. That was, like, four dates' worth right there."

He laughed.

"But that's not illegal." She moved closer to him. "Or even a bad idea."

A kiss was also fully legal. Aida glanced at his lips. She wasn't sure how this went down. First kisses in the past had been more of an agreed-upon convention. They came at the end of the second date, or second hangout. They were fine. She couldn't remember how to instigate a kiss. Particularly with someone who was tall enough that it wasn't going to happen by chance.

"I had a wonderful time," she said. "I'm having a wonderful time."

"Maybe we can do it again sometime?"

"Yeah!" Aida pulled in a breath then said more calmly, "I'd love to."

Tate studied her hand, which he was still holding. He ran his thumb across her fingers. "Me too." Then he took a step back. "See you soon."

Most days she had way more control of her feet but, at present, she found herself taking a step forward to eradicate the unnecessary space between them.

Tate raised a hand and…waved. Yes, he was waving goodbye. "See you tomorrow, 6:00 a.m."

And somehow, to compound the banality of his gesture, she waved back. "See you."

Tate took a step backward toward the ATV then another.

Wait. *No.*

"Um." Aida's useless filler managed to stop him. He looked over at her.

"This was a date," she clarified.

He held her gaze and spoke sincerely. "Best date I've ever been on."

"So then—" Really, did she have to spell it out for him? But then this was Tate, the same guy who thought ATVs were driven on sidewalks. Good at so many things, but zero skills in picking up on local customs. "Kisses?"

Tate stared at her for a long moment as her suggestion hit his neural pathways. Then he reacted, fast.

Suddenly he was in front of her again, one hand on the side of her face, the other cradling the back of her head. His warm breath sheltered her as his heart beat so hard she could feel it.

Then there were kisses.

Sweet, warm, long kisses.

Tate kisses.

Those definitely went on to the list of things he was good at.

They stood in the moonlight, Aida on her toes, Tate's arms wrapped around her, officially making this the best date in her, or anyone's, history.

But they really were meeting the team at 6:00 a.m.

the next morning. Aida finally managed to pull in a deep breath. Tate got the next one.

"I should go home," he said. He still had a hand along her jaw, his blue eyes locked on hers. "Let you get some sleep."

Like that was gonna happen.

"You too. We have a big game tomorrow."

Aida leaned forward and grabbed one last kiss. He grinned at her.

"I'm going home," he said, making no movement to do such a thing.

"You are," she confirmed.

"But I'll see you soon."

"Not soon enough."

He stared at her for a long moment. "I really like you, Aida."

She nodded, unsure how to respond in kind, how to tell him that he'd managed to put an end to the cold snap that had frozen her heart for five long years.

"Hard same."

Tate's bright smile broke out. Then he turned and headed for the ATV, a city boy on the most country vehicle she could think of. He glanced at her as he started up the engine then seemed to laugh at himself as he finally drove away.

Aida watched the ATV bump over the fields, and hit the shortcut through the Johnston property, back to town.

She may have sighed like a lovesick soccer coach.

She felt good. She felt like she'd scored the winning goal in the World Cup.

She felt like dancing.

Aida pointed to the dust ball that represented Tate on an ATV and shimmied her shoulders as she took a step to one side. She jumped then shuffled to the other side, rolling her fists over one another and swaying her hips.

Aida let loose with her victory dance, alone in the moonlight, until Greg finally came trotting out to collect her.

CHAPTER FOURTEEN

OVER THE NEXT two weeks, Tate found a number of places where he could kiss Aida.

In the ballroom, as he taught her to dance with the music on very quietly so as not to alert the others about what they were up to.

In the aspen grove on her property when they went for long, fall walks.

In her office, once her shift was up. Trying to kiss her when she was on duty did *not* go over well. Lesson learned.

There were any number of private places he could steal a kiss.

The front of his classroom in the middle of health class wasn't an option. Not as she presented to his students on the dangers of distracted driving. Absolutely not.

But, man, was it tempting.

He leaned against the cinder-block wall, his arms folded over his chest in case any of his students noticed his heart was about to beat right out of his rib cage. Aida was in the middle of a particularly gruesome story about a teen driver, a cell phone, a faulty guardrail and the thirty-foot drop into a dry river-bed. Even during these horror stories about texting and driving, Aida was beautiful, smart and caring.

But they'd decided to keep the relationship quiet until the end of soccer season, and interrupting a class presentation to kiss her would likely tip their hand.

Not that anyone in Pronghorn was lacking the sensory perception to see they were falling in love. Angie had gone so far as to box up meals for *him* to take to Flora, should he happen to be headed out their way. His friends had to know, but gave him space to explore this on his own. He wasn't ready to talk about this complex, intense emotion growing within him. If anyone in town suggested they were spending too much time together, they could always claim it was about coaching. He was willing to stare into her pretty eyes and laugh with her, for the kids.

"It took two hours to pry the car open," Aida said. His students were hanging on her words with rapt attention. He was pretty sure he'd seen Mason wipe a tear away. "And, needless to say, she never played soccer again."

Aida let silence hang over the room. It was likely that he, and every one of these students, would never so much as think about checking their phones while driving after this story.

"Now, I want to talk to you about choosing your music before the car ride starts with a story about changing a Spotify playlist, a hairpin turn and an escaped guinea pig—"

"Well! Look what the dog dragged in!"

The class started, Aida's spell over the room shattered as Loretta, dressed in a yellow pantsuit, appeared in the doorway and mixed up a metaphor.

"I think you mean the cat," Tate said.

"Don't be ridiculous, that cat couldn't drag anything." She turned to Aida. "I'm glad you're here, I need to talk to you and Tate."

Tate checked his watch. "We'll be finished with class in fifteen minutes."

Loretta waved her hand dramatically. "In fifteen minutes, I have an all-school assembly."

Tate heard a groan from across the hall where Luci was teaching. Loretta's voice really did carry.

"Just a quick check-in before I assemble the students," Loretta chirped. "You two are planning on winning the playoffs, right?"

Aida glanced at Tate. You had to know her pretty well to catch the eye roll.

"That's the plan," Aida said dryly.

"Westlake Charter isn't going to give you any trouble?"

"We'll bring the trouble," Aida promised.

"Hup! Hup!" Ilsa confirmed.

"Good. Make sure you bring plenty." Loretta stepped into the hall, already speaking through her bullhorn. "All-school assembly starts in ten minutes! Meet in the gym for an all-school assembly."

The class grumbled as the impromptu "assembly" was taking up part of elective hour. Art with Mr. V, Luci's debate club, Mrs. Moran's advanced

Spanish, Tate's net games; elective hour was the most popular period of the day. When the teachers had created the schedule, they'd left these classes for last so school ended on a high note. This also took advantage of the students' brain chemistry as they had core classes in late morning and early afternoon when they would be most able to focus.

"Do we have to go?" Cece asked.

"Yes," Tate said. Loretta was annoying and unpredictable, but she was also a powerful member of the school board. And, as long as she had her bullhorn, they'd be listening to her no matter what room they were in.

Aida wrapped up her presentation. It was a testament to her powers of persuasion that the kids would rather stay and listen to highway-accident horror stories than head out for an assembly. It was also a testament to how frequently Loretta called random assemblies for no reason.

"That was fantastic," he said as the last student filed out of his room.

Aida followed the kids into the hall. "They're a great class."

"Most days," he said. "But you did great. I didn't have to redirect a single student."

She graced him with a soft chuckle. Tate noticed a tightness in her smile. "What is it?"

"What's what?"

He tilted his head and gave her a look to call her bluff. Aida sighed.

"Fine." She crossed her arms. "What did Loretta mean by all that?"

"What does Loretta ever mean? Half of what comes out of her mouth is nonsense."

"No, about winning. It's like she expects us to win the league playoffs."

Tate stopped walking. "Don't you expect us to win the league playoffs? I mean who else is gonna win?"

"Westlake forfeited their game against us. It was their only loss this season." Aida glanced over her shoulder, as though she could see a hundred and twenty miles to the southeast, through the Coyote Hills, and make out individual members of the Westlake Charter soccer team.

"Right. Because they knew they couldn't win."

"Or because they didn't want us to know how good they are."

"How good can they be?"

"I don't know," she snapped. "That's the point." Aida followed along with the flow of students into the gym.

"Aida," he said softly. She turned around, her face unreadable.

What was upsetting her?

If Pronghorn won the league playoffs, that was great. If they didn't, no big deal. These kids had had an incredible experience this season.

He'd had an incredible experience. They could have lost every game and he'd still look back on this as the best time of his life, falling for Aida.

"Why is she involved?" Aida asked, indicating the gym where Loretta was reminding the kids that if their parents were looking for a real estate agent, she had a Home for the Holidays promotion that wouldn't last long.

Like there was anyone in a four-hundred-mile radius that didn't know about Loretta.

"Because she's always involved," he reminded her. "If there's a bandwagon driving through town, she'll jump on board and take the reins. We're fine."

Aida nodded. "You're right. I'm sorry. She just makes me tense."

"Can you give her a ticket for that?"

Aida smiled. "Creating a public nuisance *is* a crime, but sadly there's no law against being one."

The rest of the student body and staff filed into the gym. Tate reached behind Aida's back and grabbed her hand.

"We're gonna be fine," he assured her as they followed the crowd into the gym.

"Good afternooooooooooon, Pronghorn Public Day School!" Loretta crowed over the bullhorn. The words hit the cinder-block walls and came bouncing back, slapping the crowd with an abundance of enthusiasm.

"How often does she do this?" Aida asked.

"Every couple of weeks. We're just glad she's positive about the school rather than trying to shut it down again."

"I have some very exciting news to share with you!" Loretta lowered the bullhorn, going for a dramatic pause she didn't quite have the self-restraint to play out. "I have invited some special guests for the league playoffs!"

Tate's coworkers turned to each other. Had she somehow gotten more exchange students? That didn't seem possible.

"Our little soccer team, or as some of you call it, 'the Feet Ball' team—"

Suleiman planted his face in his palm.

"—has done incredibly well this year. So, for the league playoffs I have invited representatives from—" she paused again, letting the imaginations of the students run wild over what exciting representatives she could possibly have mustered up "—the *Lakeview Weekly Gazette*, the *Klamath Falls Community Circular*, the *Southeastern Oregon Weekly* aaaaand—" She dragged out the word. The echo finished, leaving the gym silent. Then she leaned forward and bellowed into the bullhorn, "NBC Sports, Gol TV and ESPN2!"

Everyone stared at Loretta. Could it be true? Did their eclectic, ragtag team really warrant national news? Or better question, how had Loretta convinced these news outlets that they were news?

It *was* a strong human-interest story. International kids landing in the middle of nowhere, coming together with locals to form an undefeated team. Sheriff Aida Weston, former Pronghorn soccer star, leading them all to victory. Reasonably proficient health and PE teacher Tate Ryman hanging on to her coattails.

Loretta grinned back at the kids, as though she had one more secret. She raised the bullhorn again.

"Aaaaaaand I've contacted a number of college scouts. They know the area well, as they were here to recruit your coach Aida Weston back in her day. I'm sure they'll be offering college scholarships to the whole team when they see us defeat Westlake!"

The students erupted in cheers.

Tate shook his head and laughed. Only Loretta could convince major college scouts to make their way out to Pronghorn, just like she'd convinced the teachers, and the exchange students. He laughed so hard his chest hurt. *ESPN2?* It was too much.

He glanced down at Aida to share the joke. She wasn't laughing.

COLLEGE SCOUTS?

The news media was bad. But scouts?

Visceral memories overrode the noisy gymnasium. The wind in her face, the scent of fall, dry sagebrush, prairie grass. Connecting with the ball, her shoes laced tight, the whisper of soccer shorts across her thighs as she ran. Her game was intuitive and free, made more so by an audience. Scouts. Showing up her sophomore year. Returning like geese each fall, returning for her.

The whole town breathless to see how far she'd go, only to watch her wind up in the exact same place she'd started.

A failure.

Loretta continued to squawk into her bullhorn.

The buzz of kids rang in her head like a swarm of yellowjackets.

"Aida?" Tate's brow creased. He dipped his head so his lips were next to her ear. "Are you feeling okay?"

"What? Yeah. I'm fine." She gestured to Loretta. "Can you believe her?"

"I know." His gorgeous smile broke out. "This is awesome."

Aida followed his gaze to the bleachers. The thirty-nine students of Pronghorn Public Day School were elated. All six of their teachers had some skepticism, yet were still joining in the celebration.

No, only five of the teachers celebrated. Mrs. Moran had a steady eye on Aida. The older woman gave her a reassuring smile. It didn't do the trick. There was no reassurance.

Aida would know some of these scouts. Some would be people she'd played with, or against. Others might be the same ones who'd come to Pronghorn to make her promises when she still believed in a world where an athlete could set goals and accomplish them.

The noise increased. Tate was joyful, words tumbling out of his mouth that seemed too loud for her to comprehend.

She needed to find a way to react. Then find a way to get Loretta to retract the invitations. Because the scouts would come all this way only to realize there wasn't anything here for them. None of the Pronghorn kids were D1 material. It was unlikely any of the international students would choose to go to college in the US. This was a fool's errand, and she didn't want her players getting their hopes up.

"Can you believe this?" Tate hollered, eyes shining. "This is going to be amazing!"

She looked past her boyfriend to the bleachers. Antonio stood up and gestured for the others to join him. Loretta had her hands over her head, applauding for herself. Ilsa pointed to Loretta and shimmied her shoulders. The other kids joined in. The bleachers groaned as everyone jumped then shuffled, rolling their fists. The entire student population of Pronghorn Public Day School was dancing Aida's victory dance for what would only be a lesson in humiliation for everyone.

"Hey." Tate's lips were close to her ear. "That's when we can announce our relationship." His eyes shone, his smile lighting the world. "When we win. We'll go public with all the cameras and the world watching."

Aida finally connected the last of the dots. Tate wanted this. Her worst nightmare was his cause for celebration.

Meanwhile, she hadn't helped kids create a healthier relationship with the sport. She'd set kids up for disappointment, and Loretta was calling in the media to document the moment their dreams were crushed.

DON'T RUN.

Tate forced himself to slow down as he finished his last few teaching duties before meeting Aida out on the field. He worked at a small school, without a clerical staff, custodial staff or functioning administration. And while falling in love with the most amazing woman and having their success as a coaching team deemed worthy of national news felt amazing, the trash cans had to get checked by someone.

The first few wild weeks of the school year, the teachers had covered all the duties even as they'd figured out what they were. Over time, and with the help of Colter, they'd recruited parent volunteers and come up with a system for managing operations. But day to day, they each had a number of extra duties. Checking to make sure the students assigned to trash duty had followed through fell on his shoulders.

Tate race-walked through the entrance hall. Willa, as lead teacher, was the only one who spent much time in the office, and she didn't produce a lot of trash. The reading nook they'd constructed for students who needed a quiet spot during the day was trickier. Some days, it went unused. On others, there might be five kids lounging in beanbag chairs, quietly being together but giving themselves a break from social activity. He scanned the area.

Super tidy. Bless those introverts.

He sped past the aggressively yellow lockers, glancing up at Loretta's inspirational signage. What had seemed so cheesy when they'd first arrived now spoke directly to his soul as he fell more in love by the minute.

These are your good old days.

Finally.

Childhood was stressful. By high school, Tate had developed a double identity: the popular, athletic school leader that he put on like a hazmat suit when he arrived each morning to protect the sensitive, empathetic kid inside. Even then, he'd known he would be a teacher. For the fifty minutes kids spent in his classes, they would feel valued for who they were and be given the tools and encouragement they needed to grow.

And here he was. Doing exactly what he'd planned, and in love with Aida Weston.

This weekend, the news media would arrive. His dad would turn on the NBC Sports and there Tate would be, on television, with a brilliant woman by his side. They'd be interviewed about their success. Dad would play the clip for Mom. Friends would send it to his siblings. Everyone would finally realize that the path he'd chosen mattered. They'd see that he was successful, that he was right.

Tate had never chased fame. He'd specifically chosen a life that didn't bring glory. But it sure was nice to get some recognition all the same.

Tate headed out of the entrance hall, ready to allow himself to run out to practice, to Aida. But a small wooden door, propped open, caught his attention.

"Mrs. Moran?" he asked, poking his head in her office. "Shouldn't you be at the pinochle club?"

The octogenarian Spanish teacher was about half

as tall as he was. Sometimes it was hard to tell when she was sitting down. She smiled at him.

"Mateo has it covered. I needed to speak to you after getting soccer practice started."

Tate frowned. Sometimes he wondered about her cognitive abilities. Most days she seemed as sharp as anyone around Pronghorn. Sharper, actually. But she didn't start soccer practice. Plus, she used an old janitorial closet as her office and spent way more time in there than she strictly needed to.

"Aida got practice started," he reminded her. Aida always got practice started. A couple of times they'd had to remind her that she couldn't expect the kids to show up before the school day was officially over. Then they'd have to remind the players that elective hour, as fun as they tried to make it, was still part of the school day.

"Aida went home, dear."

Tate sat down on an overturned bucket. "Home? Is she okay?"

If she wasn't feeling well, that might have be why she hadn't seemed enthusiastic about Loretta's news. He should have taken more time to focus on her instead of celebrating by passing out fist bumps and high fives to his students.

Mrs. Moran patted his hand. "You understand what soccer was to her, don't you?"

"I know what it *is* to her."

"You've been such a blessing for her, and for the town." Mrs. Moran smiled. "You're a good man."

Tate warmed at her words. "I'm grateful I landed in Pronghorn."

"But Aida still has a way to go. Healing from a disappointment like hers takes time. She's not ready for Loretta's media circus."

"I'm sure she's fine with it," Tate said. The speed of his response sounded suspicious, even to him.

"What was it about her reaction that gave you that idea?"

Tate breathed in deeply. Aida had to be okay with it, didn't she? The kids were so excited. And Aida *was* having a fantastic time coaching. She was having fun. *They* were having fun. Aida came alive when she coached.

"It would be best if Aida didn't have the added pressure of the news media and college scouts coming to the playoff game," Mrs. Moran said. "You need to ask Loretta to rescind the offer."

Tate's blood went cold, running like winter rain through his veins. *No.* The kids needed this positive acknowledgment of their hard work. He needed the media here, so his family could finally understand what he was doing with his life. And how perfect was it that the redeeming sport turned out to be soccer?

"I know Loretta can be hard to reel in when she's got an idea in her head," Mrs. Moran maintained, "but there might be a few ways around this."

"I don't want a way around this," Tate said. "I can't wait for the world to see what we've done."

Mrs. Moran gave him a patient look. But it was

also impatient. It seemed to say, *You'll figure this out eventually, and I will sit here until you do. But why don't you just come around and get it?*

Tate didn't want to be rude. He took Mrs. Moran's hand, her cool, weathered fingers shaking slightly as they curled around his. He meant to offer her comfort as he rejected her input, but instead found himself receiving *her* good wishes.

"It's going to be okay. You need to remember she's still working through her disappointment."

Tate opened his mouth to argue, to tell Mrs. Moran that Aida was already over her disappointment, that they were falling in love. But Mrs. Moran gave him a steady nod, one that had quieted classrooms full of students for over five decades.

"You go run your practice now," she said. "And think about what I've said."

CHAPTER FIFTEEN

AIDA LEANED AGAINST her weathered porch railing, watching for the cloud of dust signifying the approach of an ATV. It was only a matter of time. She wrapped her arms tighter around her middle, holding herself together. The cradle of rimrock lining the Warner Valley that had always felt protective now seemed to hem her in. But it didn't matter how far she ran. Failure would be waiting; here, on the other side of Hart Mountain, beyond the Coyote Hills.

She was a failure.

And somehow, Loretta and Tate and everyone else thought it was just grand to have the news media and college scouts come out here to confirm that fact.

Rising dust appeared over the property line, advancing steadily on her.

Her stomach dropped further. It was one thing to imagine this conversation with Tate. It was another to have it.

She should have been clear with him from day one. She should have said no.

This was all so *Tate*. She'd had no intention of ever getting involved with soccer again, then this loud, handsome man had charmed her straight back into the game. Now she was involved with setting kids up for disappointment, just like she'd been.

The motor cut and Tate called out a greeting. Then she was walking down the steps, walking into his arms. He pulled her close, cradling her head to his chest, wrapping her in his clean, warm scent.

She readjusted her cheek against his sweatshirt, as though she could get closer to his heart for this one moment. Because once they had this conversation, he wasn't going to let her anywhere near his heart again.

He pulled back, keeping both hands on her arms. "What's wrong?"

Aida mentally donned her sheriff's uniform. *Be firm and clear.*

"We can't have these scouts come. We need to cancel the whole thing. Loretta doesn't understand how harmful this could be."

He nodded, not acquiescing to her request, rather expecting her words. "Is this about your past?" His fingers massaged her arms.

A faint tap came from the house. Greg would be on the sofa, watching them through the window, concerned.

Tate persisted, "Because while I can only imagine how hard it is, this isn't about you. It's about the kids."

Aida stepped out of his grasp, as though losing contact would lessen the insult. But his condescending words were already burrowing into her skin.

She knew Tate; he meant to cajole, not hurt. "That's who I'm concerned about. The kids."

He chuckled, an unconvincing noise. "They seem pretty stoked, so I don't think you need to worry. I'm concerned about *you*. I know this probably brings up a lot of issues—"

"Tate, listen to me. College scouts will only get their hopes up."

He grinned, his eyes dancing, flirting with her. "What's wrong with high hopes?"

Aida's vision blurred, the mountains and rimrock closing in on her as she tried to patch her thoughts into something Tate could understand.

"Aida, this is a good thing." His voice was kind but tinged with impatience. "The kids are excited."

Right. She'd been excited when the scouts came for her too. She knew every wild dream of professional soccer stardom running through their minds. She knew what was waiting on the other side.

Aida turned to face Tate, his bright blue eyes coming into sharp focus as she forced the words out. "You don't know what it's like to have everyone pin their hopes and dreams on you and then fail."

His expression folded, hurt clouding his eyes as though she'd intentionally hit a nerve. He tilted his head to one side, giving a wry nod of acknowledgment.

"Yeah. Good memory. No one pinned their hopes on me because no one thought I would succeed in the first place."

"Tate—"

"No, you're right, I don't understand what you're feeling." The flirtation was gone as his gaze connected with hers. "But I do know how excited our players are, and I'm not taking this opportunity away from them."

"No D1 college scout would sign one of our players." Aida gestured in the direction of town. He had to know the truth, didn't he? "They're not special."

He pulled his head back as though really seeing her for the first time. "How can you say that? Look what our kids have done. They've overcome fear, and disappointment. They've stretched themselves, whether by moving across the world or putting themselves out there in front of their community. This team, this season, is extraordinary. There will never be anything else like it."

"One amazing season doesn't prepare a player for a top college program."

"Are you suggesting that Suleiman won't move up to the next level?"

"Of course he will, but he's heading home to Senegal. Antonio and Ilsa will return to their countries. And none of the Pronghorn kids have the skills to play at a D1 program—"

Tate spoke over her. "Half the kids on the team aren't even upperclassmen. They have two more seasons to improve. And given what they've accomplished this year, I'd say the odds of them getting significantly better over time are pretty good."

Aida's chest tightened. She didn't want one of these wonderful, goofy, smart kids to have the life knocked out of them like she had. She looked up at

Tate, willing him to understand what disappointment on this level felt like.

"Why do you want to get their hopes up?"

His expression was baffled, annoyed even. "Why do you think we have a responsibility to manage their hopes? People get disappointed in this life. They get over it. I'm not going to take away an opportunity from my students because it might not work out."

He wasn't listening to her. He wouldn't stop until he'd charmed her into accepting what he wanted.

"Aida—" He placed a hand on her arm, lowering his head to look into her eyes. His voice was gentle, like she was the one being unreasonable. "This is going to be okay."

Aida shook his hand off and marched up onto the porch. Greg pawed at the front window.

"Why can't you acknowledge you've done something great?" Tate shouted, finally getting frustrated. "I mean, sure, it's unlikely any of these kids will play at a D1 school, and that wouldn't be my first choice for them anyway. But what about a DIII school? What about community college?"

Could he even hear himself? "Then what? Community college doesn't set someone up to play professionally."

"*Then what?* Then they graduate, they get jobs, have lives and play city league, like a normal person."

THE COLOR DRAINED from Aida's face as he realized what he'd said. "I didn't mean that you're not normal. Please—"

"But I'm not, am I?" She drew the back of her hand across her cheek, scattering tears as they began to fall. "I'm stuck in failure. I can't get over the career I lost, and that's on me. But I am *not* going to set these kids up for the same type of disappointment. Loretta arranged this on a whim, for her own glory. We can shut it down."

"Why would we shut it down?" Tate ran his hands through his hair. "The scouts won't come if they don't think it's worth their time. They are choosing to accept what I have to assume is one of thousands of requests to watch a game. The media doesn't have to show up either. They've heard about our team, coming together, having fun and achieving what high school sports are supposed to achieve— teamwork and athleticism. We represent a healthy attitude toward high school sports. Ilsa can get a sound bite about the glory of Dutch soccer. Mav can promote more Mary Oliver awareness. Why wouldn't you want that?"

Aida gave him a glimmer of a smile through her tears. He took a step closer to her and continued, "I get this is hard for you and, believe me, I want you to feel okay about it. But this isn't about you, it's about the kids."

Aida blinked hard and nodded, like he was confirming some kind of secret fear. She pulled in a deep breath then raised her head and held his gaze. "No, Tate, it's about you. You want the cameras and the accolades."

Her words hit, tearing holes in his confidence.

Was it so wrong to want public recognition for all they'd done? Or were teachers just supposed to cough up their hearts for the job, day after day, and then wave away any acknowledgment?

Was it too much to ask that his parents be confronted with his achievements? To see that others valued his work, even if they didn't?

Anger flared through him, masking his uncertainty. "What's so bad about showing the world what we've done?"

"Because they're going to document my failure."

Tate finally made the connection he should have made so long ago. "Wow. Okay." He swallowed, trying to wrap his thoughts around this revelation. "So, you, doing the job that I've worked for, and built my life around, is *failure*?"

"No, Tate—"

"Because that's what you're saying."

"Tate, you don't know how this feels." She gestured to her chest, as though she somehow had exclusive rights to all disappointment.

"You're right. I don't. You were a great player. That skill paid for your college education." She started to argue but he spoke over her. "What is out-of-state tuition at UCLA, plus room and board? Maybe a quarter of a million dollars you're not stuck paying interest on because of your hard work and dedication to the game."

"Everyone believed I'd go professional—"

"You are not alone," he snapped. "Fewer than two percent of college athletes go pro, and my guess is in women's soccer it's significantly less. It's not about you or your talent or your dedication. It's about the numbers. You didn't move forward in the game, along with hundreds of thousands of other college athletes. That's what happens."

She blinked. Her voice was low and on the verge of tears. "You have no idea—"

"I don't. But what I really don't understand is why you can't get over it."

She let her arms drop, a hopelessness he'd never seen in her before washed across her face. "Well, I can't get over it. I don't handle disappointment well." She let out a sharp breath and pushed away another wash of tears. "I can't do this, Tate. I can't continue this relationship."

Her voice seemed to hover on the dry prairie like heat waves radiating from her. The words were wrong. She couldn't mean it. She didn't. Tate opened his mouth to contradict her, but only managed to say, "Aida, I'm falling in love with you."

She closed her eyes. Like she didn't want to hear it. Panic rose inside him.

"Aida, don't. We—" He swallowed hard, scrambling for the evidence that would stop her. "We love being together. One argument can't be enough to derail us."

"It's just going to happen eventually."

"You want to break up because we might break up? Aida, that's completely unreasonable."

"It's pragmatic. I don't want to get any more attached to you than I already am."

"I should have seen this coming." Tate shook his head. "The same woman who gave me a ticket for walking across the street is now trying to convince me to break up because we're falling in love."

"What if you got hurt?" Aida said as though his accidental death was only a matter of time. "I can't stand the idea of worrying for the rest of my life that you're going to get hit by a car, or roll that ATV, or walk off a cliff when you're not paying attention."

"And I don't worry about you? I worry every time you're on patrol, so, five days a week. Then you come back, and you join me at soccer practice, and I'm grateful all over again that you exist in the world."

He held her gaze, longing to pull her into his arms but not trusting that she wanted to be there anymore.

"What if you move away?" She swallowed hard. This conversation was difficult for her, but if she wanted his help breaking up with him, she was out of luck. "Your contract is only for a year and you're an amazing teacher."

Tate moved closer to Aida. "Is that what you're worried about?"

"Among other things." She shoved her hands in her pockets. "What if you get bored of this town, or our relationship, or…me?"

Tate took a deep breath and tried to speak softly. "I'm not going to get bored of us. Being with you is the least boring experience of my life."

"You say that now."

"Yeah. I do say it now. Aida, you are—" He

couldn't figure out how to express what she was to him; there were no words to describe the all-encompassing emotions she sparked. "You are everything."

She looked away as her eyes rimmed with tears. "That's what I can't be. *Everything*. This feeling is getting out of control."

"That's what love is, emotion beyond our control. I wouldn't have it any other way." He reached a hand out tentatively, brushing his fingertips over her cheek. "I've never felt like this. I've never known anyone who makes me feel like you do."

She leaned into his touch for just a moment before pulling back. "I *have* felt this way before, and it didn't end well."

Tate blinked. She'd never mentioned being in love with anyone else. Was there some guy who broke her heart or—?

No. No, this wasn't about an ex. She wasn't comparing him to another man.

"When did I become soccer?" He shook his head, the insult settling, festering in his chest as the truth hit him. "Is that all I am to you? A hobby?" An incredulous laugh hurt his throat. Aida started to backtrack, but he spoke over her. "I'd like to think I have more to offer than an after-school activity."

"Soccer was more to me than an after-school activity."

"But I'm not?"

She crossed her arms tightly around her middle and fixed her eyes in the direction of Hart Mountain.

"You're not good enough."
"You need to work a lot harder."
"You might as well just quit."

Every perfect moment with Aida in the last month, every smile, every kiss. It meant the same to her. He was just an addition to her soccer experience, an inevitable disappointment.

He'd been fully himself with Aida, and she was rejecting him. He was being marched off the field again, no second chances. *"You're not good enough."*

Tate took long, fast steps toward the ATV. He needed to leave before he lost the shred of composure he was hanging onto.

"Tate—"

"You talk to the kids about digging deep, hanging in. But you don't have resilience for the things that truly matter. You'd prefer to be numb rather than live? You go for it. Good luck with that, Aida."

He headed for the ATV, barely able to see it as he tried to hold his tears at bay. Aida called out to him, but he'd heard enough. He knew how this conversation ended.

Tate started the ignition, vaguely aware of Greg barking inside the house. He didn't look back as he pulled out of the yard. The pain in his chest expanded as he drove away, filling the empty space that had been created when Aida took his heart.

CHAPTER SIXTEEN

TATE LEANED BACK in the antique chair but he couldn't get comfortable. Were all olden-days people that much smaller than he was? Or did they just prefer to sit on tiny rock-hard chairs?

He forced his eyes off the piece of notebook paper trembling in his hand, glancing around his room. The community had put so much care into fixing up the old hotel. When the teachers first moved in, Tate had taken the fresh paint and polished furniture for granted. Over time, he'd learned that Angie and her kids had been responsible for the rigorous cleaning. Colter and Sylvie had painted the rooms and replaced the bedding. The five suites for the new teachers were pristine. Other rooms in the old hotel were faded; bulbs in the lamps burned out, windowpanes with broken seals letting in the air that had steadily been dropping in temperature.

Just the way he felt at this point.

Making it through the last two school days and soccer practices had been grueling. It took everything he had to smile and pretend like his heart hadn't sustained injuries worthy of a texting-and-driving story.

It took everything he had not to jump on the ATV and run to Aida to see if she was okay.

Tate readjusted his limbs in the chair, unable to stop himself from reading the letter again. Seeing her handwriting was somehow worth the pain of her words.

Hi Tate,

I don't know how to start this letter. I'm sorry. I'm sorry for hurting you, for agreeing to help with soccer in the first place when I knew I couldn't handle it. I'm sorry for the jaywalking ticket. It was absurd.

I'm sorry for being so drawn to you that I couldn't look away.

Everyone is drawn to you. I see your students light up when you interact with them. I see the way this town turns to you. I'm no different than anyone else, dazzled. You're too charming.

You said I didn't have the resilience to get over my disappointment. That I have resilience for everything except what mattered most to me. I hate those words, hate that you know that about me, and that it's true. I haven't recovered.

You're going to leave Pronghorn someday. You'll finish this year then head out into the world and change it. You'll question the way this country treats our young athletes and ev-

eryone will listen. They won't have a choice.
You really are so loud.

What I wanted to say in this letter is that I
wish I were a better person. If I were like you,
I could have faith in us. And faith in myself to
withstand it if we failed.

But I'm not, and I don't.

I know myself. I fall hard. I feel deeply. I
don't get over disappointment.

I miss you. I miss the kids. I'd give you some
excuse to tell them, but there's nothing to say.
I quit the team. That's shameful, and I am
ashamed of myself. You probably can't stand
me and I don't blame you.

But no matter what you think of me, you are
the best man I know.

Love, Aida

A heavy tear hit the *A* in her name. Tate pulled a
sweatshirt off the settee and blotted the tear so the
ink wouldn't run. Why had he said those things to
her? He'd been horrible, putting his petty desire
for fifteen minutes in the spotlight above her real
need to move forward through a significant disappointment. He'd traded her friendship and trust
for a moment of self-righteous reproach. Tate let a
fresh wave of tears fall. Then he started the letter
over again at the top.

A heavy knock sounded at his door.

Tate swallowed hard. "Gimme a minute."

"That's what you said two hours ago," Mateo reminded him.

Tate ran his hands through his hair.

Another bang on the door.

"This is an intervention." It was Luci's voice this time.

Tate could hear Mateo saying, "I don't think we should use that word."

"No, that's the right word," Vander chimed in. "That's exactly what this is."

A soft tap on the door came next. "Tate?" Willa's patient voice floated in. "I'm asking you to open your door."

Tate groaned. He could ignore Luci and felt like Vander and Mateo understood what he was going through well enough to let him blow them off. But he, like everyone else on earth, could not say no to a direct and reasonable request from Willa Marshall.

He sighed then stood and walked to the door.

He opened it to find his friends crowded in the hallway.

"Finally!" Luci said, stepping in to give him a hug. Vander's hand landed on his shoulder.

A fresh wave of tears started up and Tate ran his hands over his face. He shook his head, barely able to speak as pain washed through him. "I'm not taking this well."

"You're going to take it better once you've had something to eat," Willa said. Somehow, her arms wound around him, and this kind, determined phalanx of his friends ushered him into the hall, down the stairs.

It *was* good to get out of his room, out of the stale air and self-reproach.

Tate allowed his friends to corral him into the dining room, the momentary feeling of "better" slipping away as he passed the entrance to the ballroom.

Luci led him to a seat. Mateo set a plate in front of him.

Tate didn't want to eat, but the savory fragrance caught his attention. His plate was loaded with homemade mac and cheese topped with barbecued beef. What genius came up with this combination?

Tate gave a dry laugh. "What's this?"

"Heartbreak food," Mateo told him. "This is my go-to for a breakup."

Luci tried a bite then another. "This is amazing."

"I know."

"Like, almost worth getting dumped for." She savored another bite before realizing her mistake. "Sorry, Tate."

He grimaced then shoveled in a forkful. Then another. His heart was still a messy pulp at the bottom of his rib cage, but this meal made him feel like he could make it through the night, and possibly sleep this time.

His friends were right. Food helped, and it brought him to the point where he could admit that's what he needed.

Tate set down his fork. "I need help—" Willa had an arm around his shoulder before he could even finish the sentence. "I can't—" he gestured toward the school "—I can't coach on my own."

He couldn't do anything. Cross the street. Finish out the school year.

"Of course," Willa said. "We're here for you."

"Whatever you need, man," Mateo said.

But Vander shook his head. "You need support, not help." He loaded a forkful of mac and cheese into his mouth.

"What?" Tate wasn't in a space to critique anyone's friendship skills, but Vander's words felt a little harsh.

Vander swallowed. "You need support. But you're totally capable of finishing out the season on your own."

Tate shook his head. "The only reason we've had any success is because of Aida."

His friends exchanged confused glances.

"Oh, that's not true," Luci said.

"You did great," Vander said. "I know this sucks. You're in pain, and Aida is too. But none of this could have happened without you."

"I didn't do anything besides, like, get the permission slips signed."

"You stepped up in the first place," Luci reminded him. "Imagine if you'd refused to coach soccer. Think about how horrible this experience would have been for the exchange students who came to play."

"You stepped up and encouraged several kids from Pronghorn to join," Mateo said. "Cece, Mav and Mason are going to remember this season as transformative."

Willa nodded. "You got the community to rally around the exchange students and provide fun activities other than soccer."

"Then you enlisted the help of the most capable person in town," Vander continued. "A woman who was not terribly welcoming of you in the first place. You realized she had the skills you were lacking, and got her to commit to helping. Tate, that shows incredible capability and sacrifice for the kids."

Luci let out a frustrated snort. "And that example made me realize how mad I am at Aida right now."

Tate placed a hand on Luci's arm. "No, don't be."

"Don't be? I'm gonna be as mad as I want. See if I share my hedgehogs with her again."

"You don't understand what she's going through," Tate reminded her.

"I know what you're going through."

Tate shook his head. "Aida isolated herself in her work. We're the first friends she's had in a long time. She doesn't want anything to do with me, but she's going to need you. And your hedgehogs."

Luci kicked at the table leg. "I don't wanna do the right thing."

"But you will," Willa reminded her.

"I will." Luci heaved a sigh. "Maybe I'll steam my sweaters to get in the right frame of mind."

"Aida believed in you," Vander continued to Tate. "She got you to see yourself the way everyone else does. She's not here, but that doesn't make you any less capable. If you want to do something for Aida, start trusting yourself. Everyone else knows you've got this."

Tate ran his hands through his hair. All this time, he thought he needed public recognition, something to wash away the hurt of having parents he was never good enough for and siblings he could never live up to. He'd wanted to turn their beliefs upside down, and have them realize his way of approaching athletics for kids was right all along.

But his parents were never interested in what was good for their own kids, let alone anyone else's kids. They were interested in their own egos.

Tate didn't crave recognition. He wanted a supportive family who appreciated him through his success and failure. A family who believed in him.

He'd found that, right here at this table. These were the rowdy, caring siblings he'd always wanted. Mrs. Moran was a wise grandmother. Angie was a grumpy aunt who would do anything for her nieces and nephews.

And Loretta was that one family member who always showed up unannounced and stirred up the drama.

Tate had everything he needed in Pronghorn. He still wanted Aida, wanted her to be a part of this found family. He wanted her to return to coaching because she'd seemed so happy on the field. But she had pain to overcome. To win her back, he was going to have to let her walk away.

That meant dealing with the media and coaching the playoff game on his own.

CHAPTER SEVENTEEN

"SOME PEOPLE JUMP out of airplanes to feel what we're feeling right now," Tate said as he and Cece followed the rest of the team out onto the soccer pitch.

Cece gave him a dry look. "*Some people* need to get a hobby."

While some people did, indeed, jump out of airplanes or engage in less anxiety-provoking activities, it seemed like everyone else had driven to Pronghorn for the playoff soccer game. The tiny town was packed. The field was ringed with spectators and media vans. Student entrepreneurs offered everything from Pronghorn merchandise to sideline ice-cream delivery service. Nearly every team they'd defeated that season was there, along with all their fans too. Then there were the camera-toting, microphone-wielding members of the news media, hovering like buzzards.

Everyone was here, except for Aida. Tate hated that she was missing this. Yes, he was still distraught that she'd ended their relationship and left the team. But while he was hurt, his overwhelming feeling was that she was the type of person who enjoyed the rush of jumping out the back of a plane or coaching a high-stakes soccer game. She should be here.

"Our job today, and every day, is to show up and do our best. That's it."

Cece nodded and held up three fingers. Tate gave her a high three and she jogged out on the field to warm up with the others.

Tate kept his back to the fans, pretending to be absorbed in watching his players. He could do this. The team was excellent; he was adequate. Westlake Charter might be better than the other teams they played, but the Pronghorns would rally. Eventually, he would rally. It was all going to be okay.

Maybe.

"Coach Tate?" Mason materialized at his side. "Where's Suleiman?"

Tate scanned his players warming up on the field. Then he scanned a second time, in case he'd somehow overlooked a six-foot-tall West African student with a penchant for drawing attention to himself.

Then he scanned his players for a third time, because he couldn't seem to place an opinionated Dutch midfielder either. He glanced down at Mason in shock just as the kid said, "I don't see Antonio."

Every fear response arrived on the spot: fight, flight, freeze, pray the ground would open up and swallow him. Cold sweat, blood crashing through his veins, his breakfast trying to make an escape out the way it came.

Tate had taught his students about the brain chemistry responsible for human reactions to fear, so that they could more effectively manage those reactions. But no understanding of the amygdala and cortisol production could help Tate once the realization settled.

They were about to start the playoff game against an unknown opponent, missing one coach and three star players.

And the media crews from at least ten different outlets from local to national were there to capture every minute of the horror.

THE SWOOSH OF sponge against the gritty cleanser in the bottom of the kitchen sink was abnormally loud. Or the world it filled was abnormally quiet, one of the two. The big house was empty. Flora had gone to the game. Greg wanted to be at the game and wasn't speaking to Aida in protest. Even the usual creaking of old wood and gentle conversation of nature had ceased, as though the birds and the wind had also headed into Pronghorn to catch the big game.

Aida was alone. Just like she'd set herself up to be.

It was all starting to feel a little silly at this point.

She didn't like the way coaching this team had thrust her into the soccer spotlight again. But she was probably more conspicuous in her absence than she would be standing in the middle of the field arguing with a ref. It was hard to fabricate an excuse using her ailing grandma when said grandma was at the game, probably yelling her lungs out at this very moment.

Aida threw the sponge in the sink. Tate had been there for her as she'd worked through her complex relationship with soccer, every step of the way. And she responded by ghosting him just when he needed her the most.

This was ridiculous. She was being ridiculous.

Greg lifted his head from the back of the sofa, where he'd been staring out the window in the direction of Pronghorn, to confirm her suspicions.

She was ridiculous.

But to show up now, late? To face the same college scouts who had once come for her? Have a camera thrust in her face for an interview where they would remind the world she was once a major player?

No way.

Aida rinsed out the sink. As she turned off the flow from the faucet, silence fell through the house once more. She cast around for something else to clean. When was the last time she'd organized the canned goods?

Greg's paws scrambled against the wood floors, his collar shook and he went so far as to vocalize some excitement.

What, was there one lone squirrel that hadn't gone to the game?

Then Aida heard it. The steady rumble of a poorly maintained ATV.

Oh, no.

Aida launched herself out onto the front porch, furious. It was one thing for her to miss a game. But if her absence had inspired Tate to come out here, leaving the team to forfeit while he comforted her, she would never forgive herself. She'd be mad at Tate, too, no doubt. But putting others above winning was on point for his personality.

The cloud of dust came closer. Aida tried to make sense of what she saw.

Tate was larger, wider, bafflingly louder as he spoke to himself.

The vehicle neared the house.

Oh, no, no, no, no.

It was the teachers' ATV, but there were no teachers on it.

An international contingent of soccer players pulled up and clambered off the machine into her yard.

"What are you three doing?" Aida ran down the stairs, simultaneously wanting to hug them and yell at them. Was that what parenting felt like? "It's not safe to have more than two people on an ATV. Does Coach Tate know where you are?"

"We've come for our coach," Suleiman said, crossing his arms and widening his stance.

"You guys need to get straight back to the game," Aida admonished them. "It's fifteen minutes until kickoff. You're going to be late."

"Whose fault is that?" Ilsa asked.

"Yours," Aida said. Would Tate think that was

rude? If something was the fault of a teenager, you could tell them that, right?

Antonio shook his head. "We're not playing without you there."

Aida let out a sharp annoyed breath. She pointed in the direction of town. None of them so much as moved. She tried barking a direct order. "You guys get back to the field, immediately."

"Not without our coach," Suleiman said. "If you don't like us because we're annoying, that's fine. But we're not playing this game without you."

Where was that coming from? "I like you. Teenagers in general, ugh. But *our* team and *our* fans are great."

"Fine," Antonio said. "If you think we can't win—"

She scoffed. "Of course you can win. Those guys wear boat shoes, on purpose."

"Then why did you leave?" Ilsa cried, the frustration all her players had to feel finally spilling out.

Aida closed her eyes. It was one thing for her to wallow in her own pain. She couldn't stand these kids thinking they were the problem.

"I just can't—" Aida flailed her arms. Was she really going to express her disappointment to three international students who'd found themselves in the middle of sagebrush-and-cattle Oregon and still rallied to make the most of the year? It all felt so immature. "I haven't come to terms with the end of my soccer career," she admitted. "I thought I was going to go pro. Everyone thought I was going pro and then I…failed. It's petty. I know. But this whole circus Loretta has brought to town is bringing it all back up."

The kids stared at her. Then Ilsa shook her head. "I'm sorry. You were really good, right?"

"I was."

"That sucks," Antonio said sincerely. Like he got it.

"Yeah. It's been hard."

Ilsa took a step toward her then reached out a hand to pat her shoulder in sympathy.

"I am sorry you couldn't keep playing," Suleiman said. "But you are good at this. You are the best coach I've ever had."

Aida shook her head, but Suleiman continued, "You catch every detail in our playing. You are patient enough to make sure we do everything correctly, but not so patient that I'm not afraid to let you down. You help everyone. You don't pick favorites."

Aida was surprised to find moisture gathering in her eyes. "Everyone is my favorite," she admitted.

"You prepare us for everything that can happen during a game, in practice. I'm never nervous on the field because I know I can handle anything that comes up," Ilsa said.

"And you're funny when you're mad," Antonio added, like that was the ultimate coaching perk.

Aida let the words sink in. Her days as a player had always been limited. Even if she had made it to the next level, her body would have worn down eventually. What was it Tate had said? The average professional soccer career lasted less than eight years.

The heartbreak had always been waiting for her. She would have had to come to terms with the end of her career eventually. Everyone did.

But working with kids?

If Mrs. Moran was any indication, there was no expiration date on that.

And loving Tate felt like something that was going to take more than one lifetime to explore.

Greg interrupted her thoughts, vocalizing his concern. He was right; it was getting late.

"We need to get to the game."

Suleiman gestured to the ATV. The four of them riding on this contraption was dangerous. And so illegal.

But, also, the fastest way to get there.

"Pile on kids," Aida said, launching herself at the vehicle, "I'm driving."

SMELL THE SOUP, cool the soup.

Tate breathed in deeply. The scent of sagebrush and dry grasses mingling with popcorn from the old machine Angie had managed to get working.

"My team is happy to wait for another—" the coach of Westlake Charter checked his Apple Watch "—three minutes."

How generous.

"Thanks, man," Tate said with a smile he hoped might buy him three more minutes after that.

"Then we'll call it a forfeit," the coach said.

If Aida were here, she'd be in this guy's face right now. Tate looked past him to the sidelines where the Westlake Charter Helmsmen stood patiently on the sidelines. They'd clearly been coached to be all business, but Tate caught the glimmer of a smirk on one boy's face and a self-satisfied glint in another's eyes.

They were loving every minute of this.

Panic roiled through him, leaving a sheen of cold sweat in its wake. He was about to fail, dramatically and publicly.

It was exactly the way he'd felt on the soccer field when he was nine years old.

His father's voice arrived on the persistent wind.

"You're not good enough."

"You need to work a lot harder."

"You might as well just quit."

Tate checked his watch. Three minutes narrowing quickly to two. Where were those kids? And, more importantly, were they okay? Tate could believe they'd gotten themselves in trouble; they were teenagers, after all. His imagination could come up with a hundred scenarios, none of them calming his fears.

But there was only one logical explanation. They'd gone to get Aida and she'd refused to come back.

The Pronghorn Pronghorns *could* forfeit. It wasn't his fault his star players were AWOL. No one would blame him. It was Loretta who had somehow convinced every sports news syndicate in the country to cover the game. He'd done his best to convince

Aida to stay. He'd done his best every step of the way, and it wasn't working out as anyone had hoped.

He could walk off the field. Be done with this.

But he wasn't nine anymore.

This might not be the moment of glory he'd imagined when Loretta had made her announcement. But he wouldn't ruin the day for the kids who had showed up. Their star players were phenomenal, but the others weren't bad.

And he could do this alone. He didn't want to, but he could.

The one gift he could give right now was to dig deep and bring his best to this game.

Tate ran his hands through his hair, giving the ref and the opposing coach the biggest smile he could muster. "We're not going to forfeit. Give me a second to switch up the game plan and we'll meet you on the field in two minutes."

Tate turned back to the sidelines. The entire community of Pronghorn, every student from the school, almost every member of the Open Hearts Intentional Community, watched him intently.

Along with representatives from the *Lakeview Weekly Gazette*, the *Klamath Falls Community Circular*, the *Southeastern Oregon Weekly*, NBC Sports, Gol TV, ESPN2 and four major college programs.

Tate waved at the crowd, signaling this was all going to be okay. Cameras flashed, documenting his fake confidence. Tate gestured for his team to circle up. The kids were long past asking where their teammates were. Cell service, never strong in the area to begin with, hadn't been on their side to track anyone down yet.

"We're going to be a player down on the field," Tate said. "That means that no one gets a break today. You'll all play for the full hour."

Cece swallowed, tracking the cameras trained on them. Mav shook out his arms and stretched.

"We're going to rotate into the forward positions. Today, I'm gonna ask you all to roll with whatever I tell you. If I say move into striker, it's because I believe you are the best choice in that moment, so please don't question me, or your abilities."

The players nodded solemnly.

"We're missing three players—"

"And Coach Aida," Mason reminded him.

Tate nodded, allowed himself to feel the pain of her absence and accept it. "We're missing some pretty important people, but their absence does not alter what you're able to bring to the game today. We're Pronghorn."

The kids gathered in and placed their hands together in the center of the circle.

"And what do Pronghorns do?" Tate asked.

"Show up!" the team yelled.

Their voices were a spark, igniting a flame of cheers rising from their spectators. Tate glanced up, confused. He'd given a pretty good rallying speech, but it hadn't been *that* good.

The cheers rose to a crescendo, joy and excitement wild on the spectators' faces. Out of the corner of his eye, he caught a flash of color. Pete was waving his Senegalese flag and yelling happily in the direction of the field. Tate turned around.

A camo-painted ATV rolled down the center of the soccer pitch, loaded with his star players, a proud dog, and the most beautiful coach he could imagine.

The crowd roared. Tate was speechless.

Aida parked the ATV on the sidelines and ran to him.

And there she was, just like he'd dreamed and wished she would be; standing in front of him, taking his hands, weaving her fingers through his.

"Tate, I'm so sorry."

He shook his head, still unable to speak. *He* was sorry, he shouldn't have pushed her to do this, he should have recognized and honored her vulnerability.

"I missed you," she whispered.

Missed didn't begin to describe what the absence of Aida felt like. If a large chunk of his heart wandered off, *miss* wasn't the word he'd have chosen to describe the pain.

Tate leaned forward, placing his cheek against hers. He cradled her forearms, gripping her elbows and pulling her closer.

Emotion rose in his throat as he tried to speak.

Aida's breath brushed his skin. "I'm so, so sorry, Tate."

He shook his head, trying to communicate the intense feelings that didn't require any kind of apology from a woman who had overcome so much to be here with him.

The ref's whistle cut the air. Why was that guy blowing on a whistle?

Right. There was a world that existed beyond Aida. They were about to coach a soccer game, and the whole country was watching. Across the field, the implacable Westlake Charter coach now looked like a malfunctioning pressure cooker, trying to keep it together while steam poured out at any weak seam.

A spark lit Aida's eye. "You ready?"

Tate nodded. "Let's do it."

CHAPTER EIGHTEEN

AIDA LET EVERY FEELING, hope and fear surrounding soccer flow. It was as though once she'd decided to care, all the pent-up love for this sport, her community, and its loudest, least law-abiding citizen came rushing out.

And, for once, the outcome of a game was not a foregone conclusion.

The Helmsmen played like a machine. They were consistent, emotionless and relentless. Because Westlake Charter was a boarding school, there were kids from all over eastern Oregon, and some from as far as Boise, Idaho. They were good.

A stream of frustration, mostly in French, came spewing out of Suleiman. A defender had stolen the ball from him and was now passing it down the field. The Pronghorns were shocked. Aida was the only person who'd ever been able to pick a ball off him.

Cece was so confused by the move, she threw herself in the middle of a pass and turned the ball. Then she was further confused by her own success. She glanced at the sidelines, as though to confirm with Aida that she was doing the right thing. Aida held up a confirming high three and Cece kept running the ball down the field.

The crowd and Cece's teammates were ecstatic. She got the ball to Ilsa, but the Helmsmen's defense seemed aware of, and ready for, Ilsa's left foot. They moved in, and the shots coming off her left, which surprised other teams, were summarily blocked.

It was as though Westlake Charter had studied every game they'd played and were ready for them.

Aida glanced across the field where the Helmsmen's coach had his arms crossed, watching the game behind his mirrored sunglasses.

That was exactly what they'd done. They'd studied the Pronghorns relentlessly, probably filming their games, and had a solution to every trick Pronghorn had up its sleeve. They would have taken hours and hours of study and practice to beat one team.

And even to Aida, who loved winning, it seemed a little weird.

Suleiman managed to score twice out of sheer frustration, like his anger put a special spin on the ball to maneuver it past their goalie. Each time he scored, the opposing coach pulled the goalie out of the box and gave him a stern talking-to, one hand on the kid's shoulder, face serious. As though, in allowing Suleiman to score, he'd let down all the sockless, boat-shoe-wearing graduates of Westlake Charter.

Aida was aware of Tate tracking these conversations, could feel how much he wanted to tell the coach to back off.

At the other end of the pitch, the Helmsmen seemed immune to Mav's antics. He blocked balls with his trademark combination of flailing limbs and literary references, but he wasn't completely successful. As the Pronghorns got rattled, the defenders lost confidence, leaving more for Mav to deal with.

But as his favorite poet Mary Oliver noted, he had one wild and precious life. Right now, he seemed to want to dedicate that life to stopping soccer balls.

By halftime, the Westlake Charter Helmsmen were up four to two.

If the Pronghorn crowd was nervous, they weren't showing it. They yelled their "Olés!" and their "Hups!" and danced Aida's victory dance as one unified fan base. This seemed to annoy the opposing fans as much as Suleiman's goals.

Aida studied the Pronghorn fans more carefully. Ranchers, commune members and most of the teams they'd beaten that season were all dancing together and wearing homemade merch created by Pronghorn students. That was worth something.

No, it was worth *everything*. This team had brought their community together, and that was far more important than winning.

"How are they doing this?" Antonio demanded as they circled up. "They know my every move."

"They knew about my left-footed kick before we even got started." Ilsa scowled. "It's supposed to be a surprise attack."

"They did know," Aida said. "They've been planning for us since our first win. My guess is their coach created and rehearsed a strategy solely to beat us."

The group grew silent. Mason glanced over his shoulder at the Helmsmen then back at their crew. "Does anyone else find that a little creepy?"

"People can get real weird when it comes to high school athletics," Tate said.

Aida squeezed his hand.

"They've been tracking us," Aida said. "Probably filming our games. You guys remember that drone we've seen?"

Antonio's face screwed up in horror. Ilsa let out a string of words in Dutch and Aida got the sense they shouldn't be translated in a school setting.

"They know what to expect and have prepared for it. I don't want to bring up old business—" She glanced at Tate, biting her bottom lip. "Do you all remember that really horrible drill Coach Tate had you doing on the first day?"

The team groaned.

Aida placed a hand on Tate's arm in apology. Also, to have her hand on his arm. "It was complicated, but once you got the hang of it, you knew what to expect. That's what's happening here. They know all our tricks."

"That's awkward," Cece said. "It's like, this is small-town soccer and those guys spent the entire season trying to win one game?"

"It is awkward. And I'm sorry," Aida said. "I know we all wanted to win the league championship."

"We can still win," Tate said.

"Of course." Aida nodded, so the kids could see she still believed in their abilities. And while she absolutely did, and wanted to win, it was all going to be okay if they didn't. It really would. "It would have been nice to have one of our regular nine-point leads when the press and college scouts are here."

"No, the competition is good," Suleiman said. "They get to see us play a real game."

"And when we come from behind and win, it's going to be that much better of a story," Cece said.

Aida sputtered out a laugh. "How are you all so wise?"

"It's what Coach Tate told us," Ilsa said. "We show up."

Tate closed his eyes briefly at Ilsa's repetition of his words. This was why a person coached. Ilsa and the others would take these words with them into life. When things got hard, or were frightening, even when there was the possibility of failure, these kids would show up and give their best.

Aida smiled at Tate, but he was staring across the field. Something flickered through his mind. He looked at Ilsa then the rest of the team. "I know how we're going to win."

TATE SCANNED HIS motley team. "If they know what to expect, that means we have to mix it up."

"Like, use different strategies?" Ilsa asked.

"No." Tate shook his head. "Play different positions."

The team balked. You'd have thought he'd suggested they all swap lungs for the next quarter.

Tate spoke over the group. "At the start of the game, I asked all the players who were here *on time* to roll with whatever I asked. If Coach Aida and I move you into a new position, it's because we think your skills, in that position, will lead to a win."

"He's right. This is our best chance. It signals that we're on to them, and that it doesn't matter where we are on the field, we have the confidence to win," Aida said. She glanced around the circle. "Suleiman, you're in goal."

"What?" he and Mav roared, outraged.

"Mav, you're playing forward. That means you may have to argue with yourself."

He nodded seriously. "I can do that."

Tate grinned at Aida as they continued to negotiate new positions for everyone.

"What about me?" Ilsa asked.

"You remember that right foot we've been talking about?" Aida asked.

"No." Ilsa shook her head. "The left foot is my thing. I spent a long time developing that kick."

"You're gonna give something new a try."

Ilsa knit her brow and muttered another stream of probably inappropriate Dutch, but took a cautious swing with her right foot.

The ref blew his whistle. Out on the field, Westlake Charter had their starters in. A murmur of surprise rippled through the crowd as the Pronghorns took up their new positions. The opposing coach stared, whipped off his sunglasses and stared some more.

Then he jerked his head over and glared at Tate and Aida.

"Is it me, or is he trying to smite us with that look?" Tate asked.

"I think he is. Do you feel anything? Any part of you going up in flames yet?"

"Not yet." Tate grinned back at the man and waved, prompting a return of the sunglasses.

"This is a brilliant idea," she said.

Tate gazed down at her. "I felt inspired."

The whistle tweeted again and the second half began.

Things were...okay. The boys from Westlake Charter were thrown off their game by the switch, but not any more so than the Pronghorns. Suleiman was adept and focused in the goal, but Aida could feel how hard it was for him to stay in, or at least near, the box.

Mav got a penalty for an inadvertent handball that he quickly turned into a yellow card for arguing.

Aida pulled him out for a rest.

Ilsa had a breakaway run in her squirrel-like manner, and even if someone knows what a squirrel is going to do there's no stopping one. She passed the ball to Antonio, who was doing the world's worst job at staying in position. But it was easy to let that go when he scored.

Twenty minutes left on the clock and the Pronghorns only needed two more goals to win.

Suleiman was clearly bored out of his mind playing goalie, since the befuddled Helmsmen hadn't made many attempts to score as they'd adjusted to the new reality. He also missed the stardom of his regular position.

Tate almost laughed when Suleiman sighed as he stopped a goal. He lifted the ball for an overhead throw, aimed at Antonio. Then he paused and scanned the field. At the far end, Cece stood, uncertain in her new position as forward. As his nearer teammates called to him and the Helmsmen shuffled in hope of reclaiming the ball, Suleiman made eye contact with Cece. She placed a defender between herself and the goal, then nodded.

Meanwhile, the majority of the Westlake Charter Helmsmen had honed in on Antonio. Suleiman faked an overhead throw then dropped the ball. A powerful, perfectly aimed kick launched it two-thirds of the way down the field. Cece tracked the ball, stopped it with her chest then turned to the goal.

The lone defender headed straight for her. Out of habit, he blocked her left side, because that was what he'd been doing with Ilsa for the first half of the game. But Cece cut right, keeping a tight dribble on the ball. The Helmsmen's coach screamed at the kid to cover her right. The defender seemed to remember that the world had been turned upside down, and moved to defend her right side. The goalie moved to prepare for a right-footed kick. The boys were doing exactly what they'd been coached to do.

What they couldn't have known was that Cece was a southpaw.

Cece's face screwed up with concentration as she launched the ball with her left foot, a beautiful cut into the upper corner of the net.

The crowd, already on its feet, leapt off the ground in celebration, shaking the Warner Basin as they landed. The team swarmed Cece. Suleiman was hollering in all three of the languages he spoke as he rushed the field, arms spread wide, to congratulate her. Hugs, adulation and high threes ricocheted through the group.

The Pronghorns, with twelve minutes left to go, had tied the game.

Aida threw herself into Tate's arms. He lifted her into the air and spun her around, then settled her in a hug.

"Can you believe that girl?" Aida asked. She turned to the field and screamed again, "High three! High three!!!"

Cece held up three fingers to Aida, her smile so wide and bright, it seemed to dim the sun. Then she, and Aida, and the rest of the team, joined the crowd in the Pronghorn victory dance.

The ref tweeted his whistle, suggesting there needed to be less dancing more soccer.

Tate settled an arm around Aida. "Cece has come a *long* way."

"You helped her get here." She poked him in the chest. "You're magic."

Tate shook his head. "*We* helped her get here."

A flush ran up Aida's neck.

"We're good at this," she said.

"Because it matters. When something matters to you, you figure out how to do it well."

A brush of fur against his leg and a polite yap reminded Tate there was another coach who wanted to celebrate.

"And you," he said, kneeling down before the dog. "Who is the best four-legged coach? Who is the fuzziest?"

"Stop with the questions!" Aida demanded.

The ref blew his whistle and the team reassembled on the pitch.

It was only then that they noticed the Helmsmen's coach had whipped off those sunglasses once more and was heading straight for the ref. The crowd silenced as they watched him stalk across the field.

"I want this game called for cheating," he yelled.

The crowd murmured in surprise. The Pronghorns looked confused. Even the implacable ref furrowed his brow.

Tate and Aida ran onto the field.

"Did I break a rule?" Cece asked.

"No," Ilsa said. "You did nothing."

Cece shrugged her shoulders in quick succession, not containing a grin as she muttered, "Nothin' except score."

The coach of the Helmsmen glared at Cece. Tate

picked up speed to protect her from that laser glare, but he was gratified to watch Cece cross her arms and glare right back.

Another skill she'd picked up from Aida.

"Hey, what's going on?" Tate asked, smiling at the ref and the opposing coach.

"Get off the field," the Helmsmen's coach barked at his team. "This game is over. The Pronghorns will forfeit and admit to recruiting and unsportsmanlike conduct."

The Helmsmen did as they were told, jogging off the field and reassembling in a perfect row on the sidelines. Tate had played on enough competitive sports teams to recognize their compliance wasn't a result of respect for their coach but fear.

"We're not forfeiting," Tate said. "We've been over this with the league; we're good to play."

"That kid—" the Westlake coach pointed at Suleiman "—you recruited him from Senegal."

"I've about had it with the recruiting," Aida said. "I can assure you, no one from Pronghorn traveled to Senegal, or anywhere else, to recruit players."

"I would not have come," Suleiman offered. Aida shot him a warning look, and he raised his hands in self-defense. "I like it now. But I wouldn't have chosen to come here."

"Why doesn't anyone think I was recruited?" Ilsa asked. "I score almost as much as he does."

"Why would I believe anything you say?" the other coach yelled at Aida. "Pronghorn is a bunch of liars and freaks, everyone knows that."

"Sir," Aida interjected, "you're creating a public nuisance. I'm gonna need you to step off the field."

He was doing a lot more than creating a public nuisance. He'd embarrassed his players, caught them up in *his* unsportsmanlike behavior. But this coach was one grown adult who should know better.

"Let's just play," Tate said.

"I want this game called. Say you forfeit."

Aida swallowed hard. She wound her fingers through Tate's as though drawing on his strength. Then she said, "If the ref thinks we've done something wrong, the game will be forfeit. But we've still got twelve minutes on the clock and a really great crowd. You guys drove a long way to get here. We should let the kids play."

"There are no grounds for a forfeit," the ref said.

"I'm not going to let you humiliate my team," the coach barked.

The ref, completely baffled by this point, said, "I think you've already taken care of that, sir."

Tate backed away, turning to the team from Westlake. "You guys want to play? Let's finish this out, have some fun."

The kids looked at one another, unsure.

Suleiman ran to stand next to Tate, waving the boys in with his arm. "Yes, let's play. You are better competition than any of the other teams."

Tate gave him the look. Most of the other teams were here right now.

"They gave a nice try, though," Suleiman amended, waving at the other teams. Then he refocused on the boys from Westlake Charter. "Come. *Venez*. Let's play football."

The other Pronghorn players joined in, encouraging the boys to return to the field. The crowd on both sides of the pitch echoed the invitation. The Helmsmen's goalie was the first to break the line. He took one tentative step onto the field then ran to the goal box. His bravery pulled the rest of the team out with him.

"Can we go back to our positions?" Suleiman asked.

"Go for it," Aida said. "Let's have some fun."

"Can I use my left foot?" Ilsa asked.

"I'm just gonna block it," a Helmsmen defender said.

"Challenge accepted," Ilsa snapped. "Let's go! Hup! Hup! Holland!"

The ref blew his whistle. Tate and Aida ran back to the sidelines, leaving the Westlake coach on the field as the two teams launched into spirited play around him.

Tate glanced back at Aida to make sure she was okay with this. The opposing coach would protest the game, and they might not get credit for a victory if they won—which wasn't a sure thing because Westlake was legitimately prepared for them.

Aida smiled at him then pointed to the players with both index fingers, shimmied her shoulders and took a step to one side. The fans picked up the dance and, like the wave, it spread to all the spectators. The whole crowd jumped then shuffled to the left, rolling their fists over one another, and swayed their hips.

Because a group of kids having fun playing soccer in Middle-of-Nowhere, Oregon, was an absolute victory.

AIDA HAD NOT expected to be partying on the streets of Pronghorn when she'd woken up that morning. The tense soccer game had morphed into a joyful scrimmage, after which players and spectators had flooded the tiny business district, heading to Angie's, lining up for ice cream or just celebrating in the middle of the street.

Jay-celebrating, as it were. But Aida wasn't in the mood to hand out tickets, and she didn't have nearly enough tickets even if she had been.

She just wanted to enjoy the joyful party raging through the tiny town, even though the Pronghorns hadn't won their final game of the season.

They'd tied.

At the end of a normal playoff game, a shootout would be employed to determine a winner. But this game had been so far from normal, even Pete would have been hesitant to make the drive to get there. When the ref had blown the final whistle, the team captains had met on the field and negotiated a settlement. They'd chosen to go on record with a tie, then to meet for an unofficial, postseason scrimmage in a few weeks. Hopefully, the Helmsmen could find a new coach by then.

And Aida wasn't even fazed by the lack of a win.

Their players had done their absolute best in every aspect.

She was, however, fazed by the cameras being shoved in her face and glossy sports commentators demanding interviews. Inasmuch as she had the loudest, most charming boyfriend on record, she could leave that job in his capable hands and lungs. He had it covered.

Or he would have, if Loretta wasn't trying to commandeer all the media attention.

"Aida! Aida Weston!" A woman with short, spiky hair was waving to her through the crowd. She wore a UCLA sweatshirt.

It took Aida a moment before she remembered Katelyn McNary. She was a bit older, but she wore the same optimistic smile as when she'd recruited Aida, and her hair was a more vibrant shade of blue.

"That was amazing!" Katelyn said, holding her arms out for a hug.

Aida had never been one for gratuitous hugging, but she *was* in a pretty good mood.

"Nice to see you," Aida said, surprised to find it was true. It was nice to see her.

"I always knew you were going to do something incredible with your life."

Aida tilted her head to one side, probably looking a lot like Greg. Didn't Katelyn know Aida's soccer career had ended at graduation?

"You were a great player, of course," Katelyn continued, "but your real gift was bringing a team together and allowing the fans to be part of the journey. When I saw you for the first time on the field, you were only sixteen. Watching the way you encouraged others and rallied the team, even as you played so fiercely, I knew you were something special; someone who inspires others to love this game as much as you do. And, of course, you've always been a fan favorite. Even now."

"Th-thank you."

"Thank *you*. This has been a pleasure. I'm so happy you landed here."

"Me too," Aida said softly. "I've become happy here."

Katelyn pulled her in for a second hug. Okay, two was the limit. Fortunately, Katelyn scanned the crowd and asked, "Now, is it worth my time talking to number seven, or is she planning on college in the Netherlands?"

"I think she'd be open to a conversation," Aida said. She waved Ilsa over, introduced her, then drifted away. Ilsa, and the rest of these players, would have their own journeys. She didn't want one moment of heartbreak for any of them, but it was a part of life, a mirror to the joy they felt now, ultimately creating the satisfaction of living with passion. You had to show up.

Flora and Mrs. Moran sat together on the sidelines. Those two had been showing up for decades, and had been there for her since she was born. Aida waved, letting them know it was all okay. She was okay.

Mrs. Moran patted Flora's hand, as though Aida's

okayness had been the subject of more than one conversation. Flora said something and the two of them laughed, beautiful in their age-old connection.

Aida wanted this, too: friendships that lasted through decades and disasters. She wanted her people, the ones who would always hold a spot on the sidelines. To have those friends, she needed to be that friend. Hopefully, Luci and Willa could lean on her someday.

She glanced up to see Tate watching her as he gave another interview, which he could do since he was like a foot taller than everyone else. He gestured her over. Suddenly, Tate's idea of announcing their relationship in front of the whole world seemed like a very good idea. She wasn't a failed soccer player. She was a former player, capable sheriff, successful coach and Tate Ryman's girlfriend.

That was totally newsworthy.

Any hesitation she'd had about the world seeing her for who she was evaporated. Aida ran to Tate and launched herself into his arms. Cameras flashed and reporters circled around them, plying them both with personal questions she finally felt ready to answer.

"How'd we meet?" Tate repeated the interviewer's question at three times the volume. "She tried to give me a ticket for asking for a substitution at the local restaurant."

The interviewer chuckled then turned to Aida. "I understand you were quite the soccer star back in the day. How's it feel to return to the pitch as a coach?"

Aida looked straight into the camera. "It wasn't a natural fit for me at first. I had a little trouble letting go of my own career. But I have this really patient co-coach who helped me redirect my love of the sport into coaching. I can honestly say this was the best soccer game of my life."

Tate glanced down at her, surprised.

She grinned up at him. The cameras were still trained on them, and she didn't really care. "There's only one thing that could make it perfect—" Tate's gorgeous smile broke out as she finished with "—kisses."

His arms circled her waist and Tate lifted her off her feet, his lips meeting hers in a kiss that was even better than winning a soccer game. If there was video rolling, their entire team and the town of Pronghorn watching, that was the type of attention she could get used to.

EPILOGUE

THE HAIRS ON Aida's arm stood up. Something was amiss. She turned slowly in her chair, surveying the town through her office windows.

The back door was ajar, letting in the last warm evening air they were likely to have for a while. As they moved into November, dark, cozy evenings had returned, made cozier by the addition of Tate in her life. But it was only four o'clock. There was an hour of daylight left, and something was wrong.

Or different.

Aida finished the rotation in her chair with a view of the street out the front window of her office.

Tate Ryman was jaywalking.

He caught her eye and raised his eyebrows, daring her to come out.

It wasn't the first time he'd blatantly broken a law to get her attention. She held his gaze and shook her head. There was paperwork to finish, and he knew it.

Aida refocused on her desk and picked up a pen.

A loud pop sounded.

She glanced up again to see that Tate still loitering in the middle of the street, now holding an open bottle of champagne that was making a mess everywhere.

She gestured to the champagne, indicating that one did not drink alcohol on the streets of Pronghorn. Tate held eye contact and lifted the bottle to his lips.

His actions were now illegal and uncouth.

He was trying to get her away from her desk, and she was *not* having it.

Tate whistled. Greg, the traitor, stood and headed to the back door.

"You are not going out there," she told her dog.

Tate whistled again. Greg gave her an apologetic look before slipping outside.

Tate was now jay-standing, drinking champagne and snuggling a police dog without permission from the handler—the triple crown of lawlessness.

Aida slammed her pen down and stalked through the door.

Tate wanted a ticket, she'd give him a ticket. And maybe a kiss too.

As Aida walked out into the street, the town seemed too quiet. Obviously, it was never exactly bustling in Pronghorn, but this felt different. Tate, making a spectacle of himself, would normally draw a lot of attention, meaning she could add creating a public nuisance to his list of crimes, but no one was out. The hairs on her arm quivered again.

What was going on here?

"Tate, I have actual work to do. And even though

you *think* you're above the law because you're the sheriff's boyfriend—"

Aida stopped.

The sheriff's boyfriend dropped to one knee in the middle of the street.

The hairs on her arm started doing something akin to her victory dance.

"Aida Weston, I am in love with you. From the first day I saw you, I was captivated. You are so funny, so beautiful and determined." He gave Greg's ears a scratch. "Your coworker is such a good boy. I wanted to get to know you. And sometimes, yes, I would argue about the tickets you gave me just to keep talking to you."

"And to get out of paying the fine."

"That too." He grinned at her then took her hand in his. "Aida, you are the home I have always been searching for. Please, let me be that home for you."

At this cue, Greg stepped forward, raising his head so Aida could see the ribbon tied around his neck, from which dangled a small box.

Her hands began to shake. Aida looked into Tate's blue eyes, bright and full of love. *Magic.*

His fingers brushed hers as he helped her untie the box, and he opened it, exposing a platinum band with a row of sparkling diamonds.

Greg gave an encouraging yelp and wagged his tail.

"Aida, will you be my wife?"

"Yes!" Aida placed her hands on Tate's jaw and drew him into a kiss. "Yes," she said again, softer so she wouldn't lose her voice while saying it a thousand times over.

Tate stood and pulled her into a hug, but Aida's body wouldn't keep still. She hopped and shimmied her shoulders.

A lifetime with Tate?

"Yes!" she couldn't keep from yelling again, this time her voice cracked with emotion.

As though on cue, the street filled with noise.

Their players, the rest of the students, all the teachers and a good half of the town came pouring out of the old brick buildings on main. People came from the restaurant, the store, the hotel and even the post office, cheering.

Tate whooped loudly. "She said yes!"

Angie snorted. "Of course she said yes. I called it."

"*I* called it," Pete said.

"We knew from the beginning," Cece said.

"They did not know," Suleiman clarified. "But we knew."

Tate looped an arm around Aida's shoulders and led her to where his coworkers were waiting to congratulate them.

Luci picked up Aida's hand and examined the ring. "Do you like it? I helped pick it out."

"It's perfect." Aida leaned in and hugged Luci then Willa. On purpose, because she wanted to hug them. Engagement to an amazing, smart, thoughtful man was the perfect occasion for gratuitous hugging.

And Willa and Luci were her friends.

"Congratulations," Mateo said. Vander tipped his hat to her. "You're gonna be real happy together."

Tate wrapped his arm more tightly around Aida. "We already are."

"Another wedding!" Loretta managed to appear right in the center of their tight knot. How did she even do that? "We should talk venues before all the good ones in Pronghorn are gone."

"*All* the venues in Pronghorn?" Tate asked. "Does she mean Angie's place and the high school gym?"

"This soccer season has been such a success!" Loretta continued as though Tate and Aida's love and commitment were on a par with high school activities. "I'm thinking next steps. We need to do something even bigger. Like a holiday musical!"

"We don't have a music program," Willa reminded her.

Loretta waved her hand dismissively. "We didn't have a soccer program, or even a school a few months ago. You kids need to learn from me. If you wanna make a milkshake, you gotta rattle the cow."

"Pretty sure that's not how it works," Luci muttered.

But Loretta didn't pay her any attention. She was already stalking off, presumably to go set up a music program. Or come up with a grand plan for one and then let the teachers work it out.

"For the record," Vander said quietly, "we do *not* have the resources for a music program."

"Really?" Aida asked. "From what I've seen so

far, you all can pull off anything she throws your way."

"Shhhh!" The teachers all shot her whatever hard stare, side-eye, stern expression they used to make kids stop talking.

Aida held her hands up. "Sorry. I'm just calling it like I see it."

"With Loretta, there's no telling what she'll do next," Luci reminded her.

There was no telling what Loretta or the world would throw at any of them. But life was as unpredictable as soccer. The best any of them could do was show up. And showing up with Tate Ryman by her side, Aida felt prepared for anything.

Greg gave a polite bark and Tate knelt beside him for scritches. "Who's ready to be the best dog in a wedding? Who's gonna look handsome in a tuxedo?"

Aida rolled her eyes but joined in on the scritches. Greg leaned into her attention then gave Tate a dog kiss on the nose, wagging his tail in joy.

Tate's gaze connected with hers. "I'm so grateful the love of my life turned out to be you."

Heat rushed to her face as she gave him the most romantic reply she could think of: "Hard same."

Tate laughed. His guffaw rang out over the sagebrush and prairie grass. The sun dipped below the Coyote Hills, flooding Warner Valley with pink and gold.

Before they'd met, the two of them had been good people, maybe a little broken, trying their best in an unpredictable world. Together, they shared strength and comfort. She didn't have to be focused and fast and agile and tenacious all the time, it was okay to take a few minutes on the sidelines to watch her partner shine. With Tate, she had someone to scheme with, someone to pass to, someone to celebrate the wins and mourn the losses with.

She had the best teammate imaginable, and she was ready to get back in the game.

* * * * *

Don't miss the next book in Anna Grace's
The Teacher Project miniseries,
coming December 2024 from
Harlequin Heartwarming